"I am not a witch!"
Gilliane crossed herself.

"I've heard you whisper no chant, no spell at all, but I swear I'm ensorcelled," Jamie said as he stepped closer. A hint of a smile creased his lips. "Be not afraid of me," he whispered, forcing himself still.

So completely had he captured her attention that a cry escaped her when he touched her. She had not known he had moved so close. He spoke of being ensorcelled by a witch, but surely he had lied, and was the devil himself to beguile her to silence and stillness and into forgetting her danger.

She jerked from the hand he placed on her arm. "Touch me not."

"I canna help myself." The mocking smile returned to his lips. "But don't be denying that you feel it, too."

She readied the lie, but could not speak it....

**This is what the reviewers said about
Fire and Sword, the first title in
Theresa's ongoing saga of the Scottish
Clan Gunn that continues with
*Silk and Steel!***

"Spellbinding…"—*Romantic Times Magazine*

"Beautiful…5★★★★★"—*Affaire de Coeur*

"…a banquet for the heart."—*Booklovers*

"…solid GOLD 5★ writing."—*Heartland Critiques*

Silk and Steel
Harlequin Historical #536—November 2000

Silk And Steel

THERESA MICHAELS

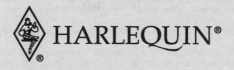

HARLEQUIN®

TORONTO • NEW YORK • LONDON
AMSTERDAM • PARIS • SYDNEY • HAMBURG
STOCKHOLM • ATHENS • TOKYO • MILAN • MADRID
PRAGUE • WARSAW • BUDAPEST • AUCKLAND

ISBN 0-373-29136-1

SILK AND STEEL

Copyright © 2000 by Theresa DiBenedetto

This edition published by arrangement with Harlequin Books S.A.

® and TM are trademarks of the publisher. Trademarks indicated with ® are registered in the United States Patent and Trademark Office, the Canadian Trade Marks Office and in other countries.

Visit us at www.eHarlequin.com

Printed in U.S.A.

Please address questions and book requests to:
Harlequin Reader Service
U.S.: 3010 Walden Ave., P.O. Box 1325, Buffalo, NY 14269
Canadian: P.O. Box 609, Fort Erie, Ont. L2A 5X3

Chapter One

Scotland, 1384

The group was fifteen strong, men-at-arms, led by a knight, riding their foam-flecked horses without care across the newly tilled fields of Deer Abbey.

At the far edge of a field, two novices dropped their hoes, gathered the hems of their robes and fled to give warning to the abbey.

After a harsh winter, spring had arrived, and with it bands of roving men, most bent on thievery of one sort or another. Those who gave this thought placed blame on a weak king and greedy nobles, who allowed this state of affairs to go unchecked.

In a room bright with sunlight that formed patterns across the uneven flagstone floor, now swept clean of the foul winter rushes, the abbess, Lady Ailis, knelt at her prayer bench. There was much to give thanks for and much to trouble her this spring morning.

She took a deep breath of the clean, sweet scent borne on a breeze from the open window, thankful the winter's soot from the constantly burning fire had been washed from the stone walls, unadorned but for the large wooden cross above her.

She fingered her beads, giving a most blessed thanks for the safe return of the son born to her clan chief and nephew, Micheil, and his wife, Seana, her ward for many years. Her prayers were filled with gratitude for the end to the bloody feud that had carried fire and sword across her homelands and claimed the lives of her brother and her niece, among so many others. But now peace had come to her family, if not between them and their neighboring clans.

The sharp knock at her door brought a swift end to her morning prayers. Nor was the summons unexpected.

"Could they be reivers, Reverend Mother?"

"Nay, Sister Joan," Ailis answered as she hurried down the hall. "They will be the ones expected, those hunting for that poor child."

Ailis needed to say no more, for all had witnessed the arrival last eve of Lady Gilliane de Verrill, in a state of such terrified panic she could barely speak.

Ailis gave no thought to risk when she bade Lady Gilliane stay and feel safe. She knew the hunt would end at the abbey's gates. And she promised herself that it would end.

"Reverend Mother, is it true? They come for me?"

Ailis spared a brief glance for the young woman hurrying down the hall behind her. "Return to the chapel. All will be well." She added in a whisper to the nuns that accompanied her, "Keep her in the chapel. None must see her." In a normal voice she continued, "Are all my charges within the abbey?"

"Aye, just as you ordered," one of the nuns answered.

Ailis passed through the arched opening that led to the courtyard. She ordered those milling about, nuns and novices alike, to see to their chores within the abbey walls. Her voice, always soft, could make novices, nuns or even visitors of noble birth quake when she was delivering a reprimand. It could also comfort those tormented souls within her care.

Knowing that her charges were safe behind the thick stone walls, Ailis motioned those who had accompanied her to remain behind as she proceeded alone to the gates.

The wooden gates were nearly a foot thick, made from tree trunks joined with iron bands. Ailis slipped through the opening and ordered the gates to be held closed.

She was thankful that no ladies of noble birth had yet come for retreat, for the roads were deep, muddy ruts from the melting snows and early spring rains.

Ailis had been educated in a French convent, like so many others, for the English king, Edward, had died trying to subdue Scotland, and had left the legacy of implacable hatred of Scot for Englishman that allowed an alliance with France these seventy-five years past.

She had served her novitiate with Gilliane's aunt Jeanne, and the friendship begun then grew through the years with their continued correspondence. Jeanne was a nursing sister of some renown at the ancient Abbaye de Fontenay near Burgundy, too far away to be of help to her niece in this hour of need. Jeanne's brother, Philip, lay dying, and knowing of their friendship, had sent his only child fleeing for safety to the abbey.

Ailis's religious vows demanded that she give protection to those entrusted to her care, but she never forgot the fierce Highland blood of Clan Gunn that made warriors of her family. Even her choice to take her veil had required her to fight a battle, and with the aid of her brother, she had won.

Alone, and calm, she stood now, breathing deeply of

the salt tang of the North Sea, swept inland from the coast by the freshened wind. She could almost smell the delicate perfume of the primroses newly blooming beside the abbey's gates.

Her gaze drifted from the thatched roofs of the small village nearby to the party of horsemen. Beneath the thin soles of her leather shoes, she felt the vibrations of the pounding hooves as the riders approached.

She felt no fear. Her habit and office protected her from all harm, no matter how lawless Scottish lands had become.

From the group, a single knight came forward, his raised hand motioning them all to slow as he walked his horse to where she waited.

With a true Highlander's love of good horseflesh, Ailis noticed the horse before the man. Her family bred some of the finest warhorses to be found anywhere. This knight's stallion showed its hard use, for the animal hung its head with weariness. The urgency of the search, as well as the wealth of their lord, was imparted by the fine but weary mounts ridden by the men-at-arms.

They drew up before the abbey gates, arranging themselves in a rough semicircle. The heat of the animals' sweat-damp hides enclosed Ailis and made breathing difficult.

She took note of the pikes held by some of the men-at-arms, and the crossbows that hung from the saddles of others.

At last she looked to the knight at their center.

He wore no heavy armor. From his head he removed his helmet—an old style, she thought, a circular pot that sat flat on his head, with a nosepiece that dropped from the low forehead band. His surcoat of costly brown velvet, devoid of lavish embroidery or device, was mud-stained and covered most of his finely linked mail shirt.

His move to rest his hand on the hilt of his broadsword drew her glance to his gloves, which had plates of metal sewn on the backs to protect his hands.

Ailis quickly judged them all Normans from their dark, beard-stubbled faces, dark eyes and dark hair, and the fact that the men-at-arms wore mail shirts, although their surcoats were not of velvet but of heavy, serviceable wool dyed a variety of browns and greens one would find in a forest. It was not strange to see Normans this far north in Scotland, for many lords, knights and their retainers had come years ago with King David and had chosen to remain.

But there was a subtle menace about these men that warned her to tread lightly and yet strike boldly. Her deceased brother, Ingram, God rest his soul, had vowed that it was always better to attack than to defend.

"You have traveled far. There is a well before the stable around back if your men wish to drink. 'Tis obvious you have not come on pilgrimage to pray at our small abbey," she said in flawless Norman French.

"To hear the sweet sounds of my language spoken so well makes my journey seem like nothing. Do I have the pleasure of addressing a fellow countrywoman?"

"I am the abbess of Deer Abbey and Scot by birth and blood."

"A pity. 'Tis long since I've heard a civil tongue so far from home. But I am remiss. Allow me, good sister, to introduce myself. I am Sir Louis Marche, in service to Lord Guy de Orbrec. And yes, I and my men have traveled far. I come to escort Lord de Orbrec's bride to him."

Ailis swallowed her quick denial of Lady Gilliane's presence at the abbey. She studied the stocky knight's face, finding nothing pleasing about him. The scars were his badge as a fighter, but the heavy jowls and the small eyes boded ill. His voice, too, held a hardness at the last.

She shook her head, her veil fluttering about her shoulders.

"You err, good knight. The only brides within the abbey are those who have dedicated their lives to the Lord."

"Reverend Mother, do not insult me. I know you harbor the lady Gilliane de Verrill within these walls. She was observed entering these gates yesterday eve."

"And what if she was? You cannot think to violate the sanctuary of the abbey without putting your soul and the souls of these good men who follow you in grave peril."

"For men such as these and for myself, there is always coin to pay the priests for Mass and to light candles. We have ridden hard to reach the lady. Do not seek to delay us. My lord expects our return by tomorrow with his bride.

"You may not be aware that she was promised to him by her dying father. Alas, the poor man had barely set his seal upon the contract when he drew his last breath. But my lord is determined to see his dearest wish fulfilled."

Ailis bit her lower lip to stop her smile, but did not hesitate to answer him. "You make a grave mistake. The young woman you claim was seen entering the abbey came at the express wish of her father. She carried a letter written by his hand, commending her into my care."

Louis Marche nudged his horse closer until the nun had to step aside to avoid the animal. He glared down at her serene features. To his shame the lady Gilliane had slipped past the guards he had set on her father's manor house while the old man lay dying. No one could have foreseen that she would leave before her father drew his last breath, and so no one intruded. But she had escaped and left Louis to face the wrath of de Orbrec—rage that ended with two servants dead, one maimed beyond use and the threats of more punishments to come unless she was found and returned to him.

Pride more than threats made Louis determined that he would not fail at this task, just as he had not failed at any other set for him in the past ten years.

He would not allow a woman, even one dedicated to the church, to stand in his way.

"I give you warning, Reverend Mother. You should not make an enemy of my lord. Send the girl out to me."

"I know little about your lord, and more of my own. But hear me well. Even if he had the king's ear, it would matter not to me. I hold my office from the church. Now leave my abbey's lands."

"Try not my patience," Louis muttered. "Gilliane de Verrill!" he suddenly shouted. "You cannot deny your place. Come out to me or you will have more deaths—"

"Enough!" Ailis shook with anger. "She is under the protection of the church. You dare not violate that. Go back to your lord and tell him that the lady Gilliane de Verrill is beyond his reach."

"You defy my lord's orders?"

Ailis wanted to laugh and tell him that she defied the devil every day of her life, but his raised fist held her silent.

"I ask you again. Do you defy the order of Lord Guy de Orbrec?"

Ailis clenched the edges of the sideless surcoat of white wool that marked her office. The heavier wool of her brown robe beneath it did little to protect her from a sudden deep inner chill. Louis's throaty demand held an added menace-laden threat to his raised fist.

She took a shallow breath, released it and swallowed

several times to relieve the parched feeling of her mouth and throat. The closely packed bodies of horses, and men who had little acquaintance with bathing, made every breath difficult.

"Answer me!"

"Do not seek to threaten me so, Sir Marche," she stated with a calm that hid her growing fear. "You know that you lie. Gilliane never agreed to this marriage. Her father refused your lord's offer several times."

His sharp, piercing gaze seemed to pin her in place. Ailis was not about to back down. "Yea, I know of this. Whatsoever your lord claims to the contrary is a lie."

"Nay! 'Tis not so. There are witnesses to swear she is promised as his bride."

Goaded by the black temper that Ailis shared with her family, she stepped away from the gates and closer to Louis's horse. The animal shied, but Louis held him still.

"In the name of all the saints I hold dear, leave her be. Tell your lord that I have given Lady Gilliane the protection of the church and that of my clan. If she is harmed, my clan will hunt him and his minions into hell itself. Ask any Scot what happens when Clan Gunn takes the *crois taraidh* across the land."

"Your words hold no meaning for me and make for empty threats."

"Fire and sword, Sir Marche, and neither king nor Norman will stop them."

Louis lowered his mailed fist to rest on his powerfully muscled thigh. He saw that his grin infuriated the abbess. But he had to remember that he held his place not only for the strength of his sword arm, but because he could think for himself.

Ailis was furious. She longed to slap the grin from the

knight's face. The desire told her she would do penance for a week for this transgression to do violence.

She suddenly felt light-headed and realized that two of the men-at-arms had brought their horses close behind her. Nausea roiled in her stomach from the strong, fusty odor that came from them.

"Truly, I weary of this verbal battle, good sister. You make claim that your clan is most powerful. I can only hope that they are wealthy as well." Louis nodded.

Ailis sensed the nod was not for her. She screamed for the gates of the abbey to be barred before she was silenced. Rough woven cloth enveloped her, cutting off her breath, and strong hands held her still long enough for a fist to connect with her jaw.

Louis straightened in his saddle. "Send out the maid," he yelled, "or I take your abbess for ransom!" He had every expectation that Lady Gilliane de Verrill would come forth.

Minutes passed, and finally Louis motioned to two of his men to toss Ailis's limp body over one of the horses. He gave some thought to sending his men over the abbey walls, a pleasant moment's contemplation of dragging forth the reluctant bride. But he had carried no scaling ladders or ropes with him.

He had to dismiss it. He could feel the stares from the village they had passed, and was sure only his lack of violence against the abbey prevented them from attempting to attack his force.

The maid would have much to answer for once she was again within his lord's grasp. Just thinking of de Orbrec's rage over this day's mishaps was enough to send a shiver up Louis's spine.

But he had not survived those rages all these years to

be done in now. He would turn this to an advantage for his lord and perhaps earn himself a reward.

"Listen well!" he shouted at last, knowing there were many within the abbey's walls to hear him.

"Return Lady Gilliane de Verrill to her rightful lord and master or you will bring the king's vengeance down upon your abbey. I now hold your abbess. Her life rests within your hands. Your abbess made much of her powerful clan. Pray they are wealthy as well.

"Send to them for the ransom I demand in my lord de Orbrec's name. One hundred gold crowns for each day's delay." The awed murmurs of his men silenced Louis for a few moments. 'Twas an outrageous sum, and so named to force them to hurry the bride to where she belonged.

"Hear me!" Louis shouted again. "The maid and coin are to be delivered to Lord Guy de Orbrec or you will forfeit your abbess's life!"

Louis thought he heard a cry. He waited, sure now that Lady Gilliane would order the gates unbarred, and deliver herself into his hands.

But he waited in vain.

The gates were not opened. No one called out to him to wait. There was no response at all to his demand.

Now Louis felt goaded to issue harsher demands.

"A fortnight! That is all the time I will allow. Bring the ransom and maid to the keep at Castres."

His horse reared as he jerked the reins hard and raked the animal's sides with his spurs. His men parted for his wild stallion, and Louis led the way. In the moments of confusion, as outriders galloped ahead and other men fell in behind the knight, none heard the frantic cry for them to wait.

Chapter Two

"God have mercy! This is bad. Verra bad!" cried Sister Ceit.

The elderly nun's voice broke the absolute silence in the courtyard.

"Thieves! Blackguards! Scoundrels! We must have the king's law on them!"

"Hush now, Sister Beitris, come away with me. You will overexcite yourself and be laid low for days if you do not calm down."

Sister Beitris glared at the young novice attempting to lead her away. "Unhand me! And stop that blithering! Rogues running free o'er the land... I can feel my blood boiling! Poor Reverend Mother taken from our very gates. I shall be lucky if I dinna keel o'er dead this second. What's to do? What's to do?"

The question formed on almost every lip, with the younger novices muttering dire threats against those who had dared violate the sanctuary of the abbey.

Lady Gilliane closed her mind to the loud babble of voices behind her and tried to summon what little strength she had left.

She had struggled free of the two serving women who

had held her silent, but her cry had gone unheard or un-
heeded. She still grasped the bar across the gates, but had
not the strength to lift it alone, and none would help her.
It was too late now. Lady Ailis was gone, taken by that
madman's henchmen.

Gilliane pressed her forehead against the wood gate.
The thought of Ailis in de Orbrec's hands brought the
cold sweat of terror. The same terror that had sent her
fleeing her home at her father's insistence, to keep her
safe.

But while de Orbrec lived she would never be safe.

Cutting through the terror came grief. She knew her
father's suffering had ended. Guy de Orbrec would never
have sent his men after her unless her father was dead.
She bit her lower lip until it bled, to hold back the scream
of agony that welled inside her. Dear gentle Papa gone!
And she had not been there to see him laid to rest beside
her mother.

Another crime to lay at de Orbrec's feet.

She attempted to stand and leave the support of the
gates, but the weeks of nursing her father as the wasting
sickness took its toll of his strength had also stolen much
of her own.

Exhausting as the physical toll had been, the constant
fear of knowing that de Orbrec waited for her father's
death, like a carrion crow, had battered already bruised
faith in God's mercy and depleted her inner spirit. She
knew she had to rally her reserves and not give in to the
loneliness, not give way to grief and be stricken helpless.

The madman would win if she gave way.

She had run like a thief, against all her wishes, obeying
her father's order. He had been convinced that safety lay
in fleeing to the abbey and Lady Ailis.

Safety?

Gilliane pressed a fist against her lips to stop her cry. What she had sought, what her father most desired for her, was gone. Guy de Orbrec had snared the abbess in his filthy web.

Gilliane was struck anew by the pain of knowing her father was gone. She had not been there to give him the last kiss of peace. She had not heard him breathe his last breath, with her prayers to guide his soul to rest.

A low keening escaped her lips. Her knees weakened. She shivered violently despite the sun. Her heart beat sickeningly in her breast. With her father dead she was defenseless against de Orbrec. She had more to fear. This day's work of kidnapping the lady Ailis would bring a clan's wrath and that of the church down upon her.

Despair settled like a burden on her shoulders.

Stop this! she warned herself. Stop now! This way lies madness.

The pain and terror of being alone would subside.

She had to make it subside or the Norman lord would win. And at all costs, that must not happen.

If she could not bring order to her thoughts, far better to take her dagger to her breast and end her life.

The thought should have shocked her, even more that she would dare have it upon holy ground. But the months of fear had dulled the edges of reason.

Gilliane knew that even to think of taking one's life was the ultimate sin. The one sin that could not be confessed, forgiven and absolved.

Had she a measure of courage, she would have faced de Orbrec in his own foul lair with a long knife in hand to end his life.

Murder!

Aye, she told herself. It would be murder, but there

would be many tormented souls freed of his monstrous reign.

Gilliane lost track of time while she sagged against the gate. Moments or minutes, she was unsure how long she stood there.

From a deep inner core, she willed her immediate distress to abate. She prayed for needed strength.

There would be time enough later to deal with her grief.

She roused herself. Ailis was the one in danger. Gilliane could not forget that. Who knew what the Norman would do to her in one of his rages? He respected nothing but force greater than his own. The abbess could be slain, with none to know her fate. The scheming madman would think nothing of taking the ransom, slaying the clansmen who brought it and then claiming they had safely left his lands.

If only Ailis had truly believed everything Gilliane had told her. But it was too late now.

As Gilliane regained control of herself, her mind cleared.

Once more she was assaulted by the shouts and cries, wailing and weeping of some forty-odd women of all ages.

But she ached for comfort, which she desperately needed now. Her throat closed with fear. She pushed it back and stifled the wail rising in her breast. Helpless wailing would aid no one. She must act. A sob of pure terror escaped her. Not yet. Not yet.

She drew her tall, slender body up straight and buried all thoughts of escape. She had brought these troubles here, and it was up to her to solve them.

Gently nudging and pushing, she made her way through the crowd.

Two of the elderly nuns were being led toward the

chapel by several young novices. Others milled about, their voices softer now as they worried over what was to be done.

Gilliane searched for the young nun who had led her to the abbess when she'd arrived last eve. She did not see her. So intent was she on studying the faces turning toward her, she did not understand for a few minutes that accusations were being aimed at her.

Gilliane did not attempt to refute that it was her fault the Reverend Mother had been taken. That the copper shades of her long hair indicated she was the devil's spawn, however, brought a mutinous set to her lips. She held her silence, knowing the nuns were as frightened by what had happened as she was.

"Send her out," someone called. "Surely they will be watching the abbey. 'Tis not too late to rescue our Reverend Mother."

"Give them the Norman. Send her out!" yet more cried.

Gilliane felt a new fear well up. But with it came anger, and she could no longer be still.

"Have you all forgotten your vows, to treat me thus? None could be more sorrowful than I for what has befallen your abbess." Gilliane stopped herself from telling them what she knew and suspected of Guy de Orbrec. There was no point in frightening them more. "Please, turn your thoughts to helping me find her clan for the ransom. Not even your abbey could have such riches."

Gilliane studied the faces, some young and unlined, a few aged with deep wrinkles, still others most plain.

What struck her anew was the panic and fear in the gazes that met her own. She forgave them for crying out against her. She also understood that hysteria and despair were not far behind.

"Please, will no one help me save her?"

A lone, gentle voice of reason answered. "I will have word sent to our Reverend Mother's clan. I heard there are few who stand against them."

Sister Ellen stood near the pillars that supported the roof of the walk to the cloister garden. She was newly invested with her full nun's habit, now that she had taken her final vows. With a gliding grace she made her way to where Gilliane stood.

The nun smiled at her. "Fear you not. I know her nephews. They will soon have their aunt free."

Gilliane took her reassurances to heart. The two of them were of a height, she noted—tall for women of the time, both slender and of a similar young age.

"Come walk with me in the garden, though it is yet bare of growing things," the nun said. "We will speak of what needs to be done."

There was something in her gaze that brought instant trust from Gilliane, and she went with her without hesitation.

The paths, of broken stone, all led to the center of the garden, where a statue of Mother and Child rose high above the plantings. A few of the trees showed greening buds, but most were still bare.

"I wish to explain why I am determined that it is I who will accompany you," Sister Ellen began. "Two years ago I helped Seana nic MacKay, who is now wife to the clan Gunn's chief, to escape the abbey. She was held here due to a clan feud and feared death at the hands of her betrothed—the very Micheil who is now clan chief. I mention this to set your mind at ease. We will succeed in reaching them."

But far from easing Gilliane's mind, her words only

brought forth the fear of what the Gunns would do to her for causing them to lose a fortune to rescue their aunt.

"There is one thing more, my dear lady Gilliane. We are of an age, but I understand as few here do what it means to flee an unwanted marriage with a man one knows to be cruel. I was not fortunate to have a place to run to. My father was a small landholder and needed a strong overlord. God's mercy saved me years of heartache, for within a year my husband was killed in a drunken attempt to jump his horse.

"It was a cruel blow to lose the child I carried, but that, too, I have come to accept as God's will. I had a strong desire for convent life and the midwife's pronouncement that I would be unlikely to bear another child freed me to seek the path to peace that I desired.

"But this is not the path for every woman."

Gilliane sensed the question left unspoken, and she answered truthfully. "I never thought about taking the veil. If I must choose between that or de Orbrec, I will choose this life. But I had dreams of marriage and children."

Sister Ellen patted her arm. "Do not lose hope that all will be well. Now come. I have kept you from the others to allow them to find calm, or what passes for it."

They had no sooner left the garden when a short and very stout nun blocked their way.

"Sister Edeen," Ellen said, "we were about to discuss what is to be done."

"Word must be sent to the Gunns. Quickly, too," the elder Sister Edeen said. "They will be outraged by this day's work."

"Send word?" Gilliane ventured to ask.

"How else will they know what has happened to their aunt? The bishop must be told, too."

"You mistake my question, Sister Edeen. I will go myself to tell them. The fault is mine, and they must be told that. They must also be told the manner of madman who holds their aunt for ransom."

"Dear child. To make such a journey…" Sister Edeen protested.

"I must agree, Lady Gilliane," another nun interjected. "It is a long and dangerous journey. The Highlands are never truly at peace, and safe passage will not be easy to arrange."

"I must be the one to bring them word," Gilliane insisted. "They must hear from my lips why she put herself at risk for me. No trickery is too foul for this man. He knows not the meaning of honor."

"There is much danger in your plan to travel north," stated Sister Nairna in her sweet young voice.

"Perhaps there is a way," Sister Ellen said after listening to the others.

"My safety matters not," said Gilliane. "If I am gone, then in truth you can say I am not within these walls if his men should return. You all need to look to your own protection, too."

Sister Edeen patted Gilliane's shoulder. "You show great courage, child. We will send word to the neighboring landholders of what befell us. None would allow the abbey to be attacked." Her words were met with nods of agreement.

Courage? Gilliane hid her surprise. She did not feel courageous. She wished she could hide in the lovely guest room given over to her and never come out. But that would repay Lady Ailis's kindness to her with short coin.

Sister Ellen held up her hand for silence. "I am of the same mind as Lady Gilliane. She must be the one to go to the Gunns. Not only to tell them what happened, but for her own safety as well. Come with me, Lady Gilliane," she urged, taking hold of her hand. "It will be far safer for you to travel under the guise of a novice. And I will accompany you."

This last statement brought a flurry of protests.

"Nay, my good sisters, listen well. I am acquainted with Lady Seana, the clan chief's wife. I did her a great service and know she will remember it. She will also make us welcome, and if there are none to issue orders of what is to be done, she can. Lady Gilliane cannot go alone to Halberry Castle. It is far to the north."

Ellen paused, waited, but other than a few mutters of concern, heard no other protests.

"I believe it would be best to wait until the bells of compline have rung before we leave. The dark will be our friend if any of de Orbrec's men have been left behind to watch or follow all who leave the abbey."

"Then all of those who go forth with messages must leave at the same time," Gilliane proposed. "And they must go forth in pairs, to confuse any who watch."

"We are agreed then," Sister Edeen said. "Come now, Sisters, and you, too, Lady Gilliane. We will go to the chapel and pray for our Reverend Mother's safety and for your journey as well."

Gilliane declined, and was thankful that none faulted her for not joining them.

Alone in her room, she released the fear she had held aside. And she shook with it. She tried to pray, but memories of every whisper and rumor about Guy de Orbrec would not let her be. She wished to grieve for her father but could not get past the fear for herself.

Berating herself for such selfishness, she hoped God would forgive her.

From the beginning, when he'd settled on his estates, there had been rumors and whispers about de Orbrec's lechery and debauchery. His first wife's death passed unremarked, for women often died in childbed. But then the second young woman died after birthing a daughter. The darker tales began then, tales of black rites, but most of the landholders had dismissed them.

Not a year later, his third wife met a similar fate. It was then that de Orbrec began courting Gilliane's father for her hand in marriage. Gilliane knew her papa was not a worldly man, being too wrapped up in translating his scholarly works, but even he found the dark countenance of Lord de Orbrec disturbing.

Together they had realized why the offer had come to her.

Gilliane would not, could not, be his fourth broodmare. That de Orbrec was possessed of the devil, no one denied, and all knew of his obsession to have a son.

Restlessly pacing her room, Gilliane seized hold of the rough brown wool robe that someone had left for her. She closed her eyes, her thoughts once more on her father as he had been, strong enough to refuse de Orbrec's offer for her.

Then she wept—wept for her father's death and for herself. Never again would his kindly brown eyes rest upon her as she recountered her day's work to him in the evening. Never would his soft voice read to her tales of great heroes. Gilliane could read Latin and French, and write them as well, but she enjoyed the expression in her father's voice as he read a tale he had translated from Greek or Castilian or the rare Arabic book that had survived the destruction of great libraries during the many years of the Crusades.

Then her father had sickened. That was when she'd turned her thoughts to de Orbrec's offer of marriage. She had no great holdings to be considered a marriage prize.

They had a small manor house and rents from two adjoining farms. Her father's work earned him little coin, but their needs were simple and their wants sufficed.

But in talking this over with her father she finally understood what made her desirable.

With her father dead there was no one to stand for her. Each of the young women de Orbrec had married were either wards of lesser landholders or orphans on the verge of losing what they held. Marriage or the veil were the two choices women had. And Gilliane knew that no family descended from the great Norman barons who had come with King David to Scotland would give a wife into de Orbrec's keeping.

A soft knocking at the door broke into her painful thoughts. She called out that she needed a few minutes more, then hurried to change into the habit of a novice. She had some trouble wrapping her long braids and hiding them under the head cloth.

Once she had secured the sandals on her feet, she stood before the plain wood cross. Her prayers—for the safety of Ailis and the success of her own journey—were brief.

"What I need," she whispered as she hastily crossed herself, "is a hero straight from Father's tales. Not a courtly lover from one of the romances, but one who wields a sword to smite this monster from the earth."

Even if she found such a man, she had nothing to offer him to fight de Orbrec for her.

She glanced back at the refuge that had been hers for so short a time. She would reach Clan Gunn, but there was fear in doing so. She had heard stories about the wild Highland warriors, and wondered if they were true. She had never seen one.

But she would. Long before dawn broke the sky, she would meet one.

Chapter Three

"Inverness, Jamie. There's where you'll be finding the thieving Keiths that stole our furs for trade. I left three men to watch them."

"Aye, 'tis well done, Crisdean, to find them so fast."

Jamie Gunn reined in his stallion on the ill-kept track they had been following. It had brought them to the top of a broken ridge. Below, on the near side of a meandering river, lay a few houses of stone, a church, a priory and a huddle of roughly built huts. It was not much of a town when compared to those below the Highland line, but there were hiding places enough for their clan's enemies to lose themselves.

The sun had burned off the early morning mist and now reflected the coppery shades in Jamie's chestnut hair as he ran a careless hand through its shoulder length.

"'Tis a poor tanist our clan's chosen not to send more men to guard the carts."

"None could know they'd take such a notion, Jamie."

"Truth to tell, Crisdean, I didn't think they would be reiving now. A reiver earns more reward for his trouble after the harvest."

"Jamie, dinna fash yourself. 'Twas a hard winter for

all. An you're no' forgetting you had the vote of every man in the clan to be war leader. Even your brothers voted for you.''

A wide grin creased Jamie's mouth as he slanted a glance toward his boyhood friend and fellow clansman. His eldest brother, Micheil, had won the place of clan chief, and their younger brother, Davey, served the clan with his gift, or sometime curse, of second sight.

Jamie allowed his horse to stretch his neck to nibble a few blades of a new grass barely showing at the side of the track. He took Crisdean's teasing as it was meant, to lighten his anger with himself over the raid, for Jamie was secure in his place. He had won the coveted position of tanist five years ago with a show of arms that went unrivaled in the clan, and through his unusual uncanny good luck in outguessing his clan's enemies' plans of attack.

The unusually harsh winter had kept their homeland free of war after the ending of the bloody feud with the MacKays, but Jamie had known what was coming once warmer weather arrived: a renewal of the feud with the Keiths.

He wearied of it. But could not lay blame on one member of the clan for being out for Gunn blood or anything else they could lay their hands on. They had to avenge the accidental death of their chief's heir after he was captured by the Gunns. The boy's taking was in retaliation for his clan's betrayal.

A muddle that needed a clearer mind than his own to separate. Still, Jamie felt the loss of so young a life.

Peace was his brother Micheil's desire, and Jamie's as well, but they had little enough of it. War in all its forms was his to fight.

"Crisdean, find your men. I'll wait here for you."

Jamie did not watch him ride off. He stared at the

mountains in the distance and thought of folktales of what lurked beneath them. Kelpies and demons, which the crofters dreaded, or dens of outlaws and robbers, which the king left to the clans to hunt.

On the near slopes, sheep and cattle grazed, and in a hundred or so patches the earth was newly turned for spring plantings of rye and oats. From the river came the sound of fishermen singing as they spread their nets in the sun.

Jamie stole these moments of respite, drinking deep of the quiet to fill his soul, thinking deeper thoughts.

He wondered how many of the chieftains from a hundred glens and islands of the north and west understood how they brought tales of feuds and fear with them when they crossed south through passes that had never known a road, or waded through rivers that had never seen a bridge built to cross them. The line grew sharper each passing year—that unseen boundary slicing across the northernmost jut of Scotland. Some had begun calling it the Highland line, a line that divided language from language, Celtic custom from the half Roman, half English law, marking the separation between an older way of life from one more like that of changing Christendom adopted by southern Scots and the English.

He saw these things when he visited the fairs to sell the clan's horses, for breeding them was his love, and each year he found himself stared upon as if he came from some foreign land unknown to others of his race.

Jamie's gaze turned westward beyond the river to the flat heath and deserted meadows. He wondered if the whole of Scotland would ever have a king strong enough to bring peace to all his people.

It was a worthy goal to strive toward, but he doubted he would see the day.

A deep, abiding passion stirred inside him as he looked out over the land. He loved it, och, how much he loved it all. The fierce bite of winter's wind, the rich smell of the newly turned soil in the spring and the heat of the summer sun sparkling on cool, trickling burns making their own merry music over the stones.

The Highland fling, the sword dance, the grateful smiles of the crofters when he kept raiders from burning or stealing their crops. Even a well-matched sword fight brought him pleasure in his strength.

All these things were small joys, and there were more, but for him it was not enough. He hated cruelty, but life was such that he had to be cruel. He was proud of being a warrior, for he lived in a brutal world where a weaker man could not protect those he loved. And he knew who to thank for much of the lawlessness that pervaded his land in north Scotland—the king's justiciar and the greedy Albany who gives him orders.

Bah! His thoughts had turned to a sour place when he needed his wits about him to recover either the furs or the coin the Keiths had gotten for them.

He heard the soft fall of hooves coming up the sandy track before he was hailed by Crisdean and two others. Jamie turned in the saddle and smiled a welcome to Gabhan and Colin, who along with Crisdean were his closest friends, clansmen and most trusted warriors.

"'Tis well you come now, Jamie," Gabhan said, his blue eyes alight with the thought of facing his enemy. "There's Iain, Neil and Donald of the clan Keith swilling ale and bargaining away our furs."

"We'll soon put a stop to that," Colin stated.

"Aye, lads, we'll stop them, but go gently into the town, for I've no wish to have any of the garrison sent forth from Mar's Castle."

Jamie studied his men. Crisdean's tall height matched Jamie's own, but not his breadth of shoulder. Colin was a slender wraith with a slippery grace to any who faced him with sword or dirk. Gabhan, shortest of them all, was incredibly strong, and a terror with a two-handed claymore. Below waited the last of their group, Marcus, adequate with a sword, but lethal with a Welsh longbow.

"A formidable force, lads." Jamie smiled to see his orders had been followed. None wore clan badges. "Are we going to tarry or make merry, lads?"

"Merry, Jamie!" came their reply, and then Colin added, "I've a thirst of my own that wants quenching."

Somber faces looked to Colin, for all remembered the treacherous betrayal of the Keiths when their clan chief went to sue for peace between the Gunns and MacKays. Colin lost his eldest brother that day and had yet to avenge the death.

Jamie and Colin rode down along the river near the edge of town. The river showed blue beneath the sun on its way to the distant Loch Ness. Gabhan and Crisdean followed another track into the village. Colin led the way to where Marcus waited, and where, Jamie hoped, they would surprise the Keiths who had stolen their furs.

It was not the stealing alone that had to be revenged, but the recovery of the cargo of furs that came from the clan's northern holdings, where trade was carried on with those who ventured across the North Sea and beyond. This fur trade added riches to the Gunn coffers.

Carts filled the way, their owners' lusty shouts drawing attention to their wares. It was too early in the year for one of the many fairs to be held, and few crofters or even clans had many goods left from the winter to trade or sell. Fewer still had coin to buy.

Jamie and Colin were forced to dismount as the way

became crowded. They led their horses over the dirt tracks and ignored all who attempted to engage them about their fine mounts.

The faint aroma of baking bread wafted on a strengthening breeze and brought with it the stronger smell of fish and the odors of close-packed bodies.

Jamie could not turn up his nose, for he and his men had been trailing the Keiths across rivers and through forests for three days. Inwardly, he longed for the clean scents of the moors and the sea that his home, Halberry Castle, looked down upon.

Colin held up his hand for Jamie to pause. Jamie tightened his hold on the reins. He looked across the small square and saw that Marcus was signaling to them. Almost at the same moment, Jamie spied the arrival of Crisdean and Gabhan at the mouth of the alley to their immediate left.

Few of the villagers took note of the five men, for their attention was drawn to the loud voice rising in protest near a merchant's shop.

Jamie found Iain Keith and his kinsmen arguing over the furs a perfect distraction for him and his men to move closer. Jamie bent his knees a bit to shorten his height. He wanted their surprise to be complete. He handed over his reins to Colin and worked himself into the crowd that had gathered. A quick look showed that Crisdean and Gabhan were doing the same.

It took Jamie a bit longer than he liked to maneuver his way around to where the Keiths stood holding the packhorses loaded with furs. He kept his gaze moving to spy any danger from clansmen hidden in the crowd. But Iain, his tall form and fair head Jamie's beacon, never once looked around.

Jamie drew his dirk from his belt. There were too many

innocents around for him to use his sword. He had worried needlessly that he would be spotted. Close enough to reach out and touch the heavily muscled body of young Donald, Jamie understood that the Keiths had been celebrating before their sale was complete. They were drunk, as their loud, cursing voices told anyone who could hear them.

"Thieves! Outlaws! Reivers!"

The shouts came from various points within the crowd, but none had a doubt who the calls were for, and the Keiths turned like animals at bay, facing the crowd with swords drawn.

"Who dared?" demanded Iain. "I'll cut the lying tongue from his mouth."

"Aye!" Donald agreed. "Find them! Show them to me!"

"Sirs, good sirs, you claimed the right of these furs. You offered them for sale in good faith. And so I did accept your bargain. I willna buy them if they are stolen."

"Cease your prattle," Neil said to the merchant, whose rotund body shook with his desire to flee.

Again came the cries, but this time from other places within the crowd.

Seemingly of the same mind, the three Keiths took a step forward until they stood side by side, with their swords extended to hold back the crowd, but foolishly leaving none to protect their back.

Drunk they might be, but Jamie felt disgust for the men's training, to position themselves to such disadvantage.

Not that Jamie was about to foolishly complain over how easy they made taking one of them captive.

Jamie slipped up behind Iain, silently warning the merchant, who saw him, not to give him away. The flashing point of his dirk was enough for the man to understand what his fate would be.

Iain was his choice, for he was the largest of the three Keiths, and Jamie moved up behind him with the quiet stealth of a mountain cat. His soft boots made only a light scraping sound as he lunged to grab Iain and hold the dirk to his throat.

Iain's snarl of rage died aborning as Jamie pressed the point beneath his jaw and drew a spot of blood. "Tell them to lay down their swords and you do the same."

"Neil, Donald, set your swords down."

At the sound of their kinsman's choked voice, both men turned. Drunk or not, it took them a few moments to see Iain's danger. The clang of Iain's sword falling to the ground freed Neil and Donald to move.

The foolish Keiths, thinking Jamie alone, went toward him with their swords extended, obviously intent on cutting him down.

"Hold!" Jamie shouted, not so much to stop them as to let his own clansmen know where he stood, for he could no longer see them in the growing crowd.

Jamie grabbed Iain's wrist and brought it up behind the man's back at such an unnatural, twisted angle that Iain's arm would break if he dared move to free it.

"Drop your swords and your dirks or I'll cut his throat."

A small trickle of blood from Jamie's dirk ran down Iain's neck.

"And don't be forgetting the *sgian-dubhs* in your boots." He watched their hesitations. "Do it," he ordered with more promise than threat in his soft voice. "Don't think I'm alone here." All the golden glints in Jamie's eyes disappeared until the brown was so dark it appeared nearly black.

But what happened then surprised them all.

Several village men rushed to take hold of the pack-horses, to move them out of the way or to steal them, none knew, but Donald took it as a threat and spun around. He slashed his sword in a wide arc, forcing everyone back and away.

Neil took advantage of the distraction and advanced on Jamie.

Jamie could not release Iain.

Neil closed the short distance between them, then suddenly dropped to a crouch and swiped at Jamie's leg with his sword.

Drunk or not, Neil brought his blade within a hairsbreadth of slicing Jamie's calf.

"To me!" Jamie yelled. "To me!" He darted to one side, hemmed in by the press of villagers that threatened his grip on Iain.

Jamie would have slit the Keith's throat, but he had promised his clan chief to bring the fur thieves before him and the clan for justice. Much as it galled him, he had to protect Iain's life as well as his own.

His own clansmen would have much to answer for over their desertion. He had no time to figure out what had happened to them, dodging as he was the very deft wielding of Neil's blade.

And then there was other steel to meet the Keith's sword.

Marcus spat curses as he engaged Neil's attention and gave Jamie time to pull back. Time, too, for the Gunn clansmen to reach their tanist's side.

Jamie held his tongue as Gabhan took hold of Iain and tied his arms behind him. He stripped Iain of his dirk and *sgian-dubh,* the boot knife that most Highlanders carried.

Colin came forward, leading all the horses, including those belonging to the Keiths.

Crisdean, his face a red flush of rage as he took charge of Donald, grabbed the Keith's weapons and ordered him to mount. He tied Donald's feet beneath his horse's belly just as Gabhan did the same to Iain.

Jamie wanted to draw his sword and finish Neil himself, but he would not shame his young clansman, who was barely managing to hold his own against a far more expert swordsman. Jamie wiped the blood from his dirk on Iain's dark breeks.

"You'll pay for this, Jamie Gunn. Oh, how you'll pay."

"Iain, 'tis no' me that's tied like a sack of grain. There'll be payment, all right, but the Keiths will be the ones making it." He turned from his prisoner and motioned Crisdean to his side. "Finish Neil. I want to be gone from this place. I've no liking for the look of these villagers, and fear they'd set upon us for the furs alone."

Marcus took a cut to his sword arm seconds before Crisdean used the hilt of his sword to knock Neil down. It was not the most honest or gracious way of ending the engagement, but then he had been ordered to finish it, and not told how to accomplish that.

It was nearly two hours more before Jamie sat with his clansmen and heard of their difficulty in getting through the closely packed crowd.

"I vow, Jamie," Gabhan said, setting his mug of ale down hard on the scarred wooden table, "if you'd given us leave to use our blades, we'd have cleared paths quick enough."

"Aye," Colin agreed, glancing about the dimly lit inn. "The damn fools were all for touching our steeds, and I was of a mind to let the beasties loose among them."

''We accomplished what we came to do. But I worry about Marcus's arms,'' Jamie admitted. ''I know naught of these nuns at the priory. Not all are taught healing skills. If it weren't so late, I'd be for riding to my aunt's abbey. I know her to be skilled with wounds. My father praised her often enough. Greed for the rich furs, a dull winter—God alone knows what was in their minds.''

Jamie pushed aside his wooden cup. '''Tis a poor place to spend the night, but the storeroom's door is stout enough to hold the Keiths inside. We'll leave at first light. God willing, 'twill be a quiet night for us, lads,'' he added as the serving wenches came to their table with food.

Platters heaped with fried herrings; another of colcannon—cabbages, carrots, turnips and potatoes, first mashed, then stewed with butter; crowdie, a fresh cheese that had been oversalted, came along with coarse-grained bread that held the taste of must due to the long winter storage of the grain. Pitchers of heather ale accompanied the meal, which the men fell upon, for they'd eaten little but hard cheese and nearly tasteless bannocks for three days.

Marcus arrived before they were half-done, smiling despite his earlier fears that he would lose the use of his arm. He needed his right arm limber to use his longbow.

Jamie stood at once and made room for his clansman on the bench. ''Your arm?'' he asked softly.

''The cut's no' as deep as I feared, Jamie. Sister Mairi sewed me up and put some poultice made of moss and herbs on it. As you can see for yourself, the packing barely shows.''

There were toasts to his bravery, and to his first blooding, and Jamie sipped a little ale at each, but limited himself to a single glass of ale. He was growing uncomfortable in the warmth of the inn. Uncomfortable in a way that he could find no reason for, but it persisted.

Since he had an end seat on the bench, he stood and walked to the inn's door. He motioned his men to stay, and went outside. The night was cool and he thought of his soft, green wool cloak, the dye for which came from broom plants. He'd left it behind on the bench, but until he discovered the reason for his disquiet, he would not return inside.

Jamie walked around the back of the inn to the stable. He should have done this earlier to ensure that Killen, one of the Gunns' prize gray stallions, had not inflicted injury on the grooms. The horses were valued for their endurance and strong killing streak, but also for their determination that none but their masters should ride upon their proud backs. Not one gray was beyond wreaking terror on the smaller men who handled them.

But all was quiet within the small stable. Jamie took the lantern from its hook, lit it and walked along to see that the hay and grain ordered for their horses had been doled out to them. Both held the same musty smell of their bread, again due to the long winter storage.

Jamie paused in front of Killen's stall. The stallion stretched his long neck over the door and butted Jamie's shoulder with his head.

"Wanting a bit of attention, braw laddie?"

His question earned him a snort and Killen's show of affection, a gentle nibbling of Jamie's shirt. Jamie obliged his horse with a thorough scratching between his ears.

After a few minutes, he left the stables still feeling that vague disquiet he could not put a name to. He had just returned to his place at the table, where a fresh pitcher of ale was being poured around, when a ragged street urchin burst through the doors yelling for the Gunn clansmen.

"Here now, lower your voice, boy!" The innkeeper made to grab the filthy child, but the boy had spotted the table and the men around it.

"You!" he cried out. "Are you the man that was hurt? The sister said to fetch you, for a kinswoman is in need." The boy rushed forward, spilling his words so fast that none could make sense of what more he had to tell.

"Easy, lad, easy now," Jamie said, urging the boy to his side. He motioned to the innkeeper and the few others who rose to stay back.

"Now, tell me who sent you."

"Sister Mairi. From the priory."

"That's the one that cared for me arm, Jamie."

"And she told you to come fetch Gunn clansmen?"

"Aye. Another good sister came this eve, crying some foul deed. I saw her from my place by the gate. Her habit was all ripped."

"Something's happened to my aunt."

"Jamie, you can't be knowing that," Crisdean cautioned. "Don't be running off half—"

"I've been feeling uneasy and not knowing why. I'll go. You await word here. If this is some trickery—"

"Nay! I've told no lie. Sister Mairi sent me to find you. Will you come? The young one was in a terrible taking over the other one lost in Findhorn wood."

"Guard well those Keiths," Jamie snarled. "If this is some ruse of theirs to free their clansmen, I'll slay the lot. And if any dared harm my kinswoman, they'll pay in blood."

In a moment it was decided that Crisdean should follow Jamie to protect his back.

Chapter Four

"You'll crown folly with lunacy to ride out tonight," Crisdean declared to Jamie. "'Tis a wild tale the good sister Ellen told of your aunt and this missing bride."

"You didn't believe her?"

"Aye, Jamie, there's the rub. I do believe your aunt was taken and held for ransom. But think, man, that's all I'm asking you. There are three men tracking a lone woman, and the Findhorn wood is not an easy place to ride."

"Och, Crisdean, keep your old woman's worries to yourself. That tale of a witch is the stuff to make bairns behave and no more. I need to find her. Didn't you hear Sister Ellen say that the woman she dressed as a novice is the missing bride? I mean to have her. She's the ransom—or part of it—to free my aunt."

Jamie saddled Killen and led his horse from the stall.

Crisdean hurried to saddle the other horses while Jamie gave orders to his men.

"Colin, you're the best tracker among us. Go to Deer Abbey and find the trail the Normans took. Stay close to his keep. I'll depend upon you for information once we come." Jamie squeezed Colin's shoulder. "Take care. I'll not like having you taken."

"Dinna fash yourself, Jamie. I'll have a care."

"Go then, for yours is the longest ride." Jamie turned to Marcus and Gabhan. "'Tis for the two of you to get word to Micheil, but you'll have the added burden of bringing the Keiths before him. Stop at the priory and take Sister Ellen with you. Micheil will want to question her as well.

"Crisdean, rouse that merchant, and get a good price for our furs. We'll need the coin. Ride hard, lads, but you, too, have a care for yourselves."

"Jamie, hold. You canna ride off without me," Crisdean retorted. "Micheil would take a piece of me off slice by slice if anything happened to you. Wait until I've dealt with the merchant."

"Go with him now," Gabhan said. "Marcus can fetch the nun while I deal with the merchant. Aye, go with him," he repeated with a special look for Crisdean. They both knew Jamie's recklessness and where it could lead him.

"Are you agreed, Jamie?"

Jamie eyed first Crisdean, then Gabhan. He knew what they were about, knew what his brother, the clan chief, had charged them to do. For a moment or two hot resentment flared, then Jamie snuffed it out. He understood his brother and his fear. They had lost both parents, and within the year, their precious sister, to the bloody feud. A feud based on lies. His brother would not forget they'd almost lost their own lives, but he should not worry so. He had a wife and son of his own now. And Jamie was a man grown. And war leader besides. He could not stand to have his own trusted warriors coddle him like a babe out of swaddling.

"Jamie?" Gabhan murmured, becoming alarmed at the look in his tanist's eyes.

"Agreed," Jamie snapped. "Hurry then, Crisdean, if you intend to protect my back. I need this lass within our grasp." He said nothing of the feeling that had been growing within him—that the lass needed their aid, and needed it quickly.

"Daft is what you are to go scaring off in the dead of night." Crisdean said. "The nun said she lost sight of her near Findhorn wood. Where, I ask? South of it? North? Where the devil should we go looking?"

"Within the wood is where we look. That's the last she saw of her. An' I'm not daft, just eager. Tell me your blade is not quivering to meet one of the men who dared to touch a Gunn woman, never mind one of the cloth!"

Crisdean secured a bundle he had brought from the inn. "Aye, Jamie," he said, "I'm anxious, too. Just remember to keep one alive so we'll be knowing what this whoreson Norman lord thinks he's about."

But Crisdean said the last to Jamie's back, as he had already flung himself into the saddle and ridden off. Crisdean raced after him.

Thick clouds scudded across the new moon, hiding what little light penetrated Findhorn wood. Lady Gilliane had to struggle to retain her seat, for her mare was spent after her grueling ride.

Last night...Lord, she thought, was it only last eve when Sister Ellen and she had left the abbey?

She knew it was, but the intervening hours had seemed more like days once de Orbrec's men spied them and began the chase.

An owl hooted and sent a shiver down her spine, but the poor beastie she rode shied and whinnied. Gilliane crooned softly, holding the reins tight, the quivering of her horse a match for her own body. She had thought she knew the feel and taste of terror. How foolish to believe that. Running like a hare before the hounds had taught her a new meaning of fear.

The night was so black she could not see where to guide her mare. Added fear came from the crackle of dry twigs beneath the horse's hooves, which had to give away her direction. She wanted nothing more than to rest, but she had to find Sister Ellen.

None had foreseen that the knight Marche would leave behind most of his men-at-arms to watch and follow those who fled the abbey. Two pairs of sisters had left before them, and they had watched at the gates to see them followed.

Each pair by a single man.

What had alerted them and brought three to chase her and the nun on a wild, harrowing ride that forced them to separate, she did not know.

But the men were still searching for her.

There! Surely that was one of them closing in on her!

Gilliane did not wait to be sure. She bent low over her mare's lathered neck, praying she would not be ripped off by a low-hanging limb. As it was, she would go fast and the branches would snag the cloth of her habit, forcing her to stop and tear the cloth free. She had long ago lost the head veil.

An opening appeared to her right and she set her soft-shod heels to the mare's already heaving sides, begging the animal to find the strength to go on.

Only once did Gilliane look behind, and she was sure she saw a mounted man pick up her trail.

Gilliane knew the mare was failing. She heard its labored breathing, felt the flecks of foam flung back against her face.

"Please," she whispered. "Please, be strong. Just a little farther. Please…please…"

But no one heard her plea.

Three things happened at once: the clouds cleared the moon and reflected in some low-crawling predator's eyes, causing the horse to rear. Gilliane, despite her grip on the sweat-flecked horse, was unseated, and a man was heard shouting that he had found her.

Stunned for a few moments, Gilliane could do nothing about the horse that bolted, but she could scramble and hide within a thicket.

She pressed her fist between her teeth, biting hard to stop her teeth from chattering. She could not stop the trembling that took hold of her.

The light reflected on a sword blade, and the barely visible form of a man who slashed his way through the bushes. She closed her ears to his foul cursing when he could not find her. She curled up tight, her breathing shallow, fear forming a hard ball in her stomach.

"Alf! Alf, did you find her? I missed catching her horse, but she cannot go far on foot."

"Come help me search, Hugh. I swear I saw her fall close by."

Sweet Mother of Mercy, Gilliane prayed, draw the clouds to hide the moon again. Save me. Please save me.

"Where did Cob take himself off to?"

"Didn't you see him chase the other one, Alf? Ho, but it's a fool's errand we're all on. Can't see in the dark. Can't see what his lordship wants with this woman. There's plenty around that's willing."

To show his anger, Hugh poked his sword into a knot of thick pines and sliced off several branches, which brought more curses when he smelled the strong pine sap that stuck to his blade.

"Keep your voice low, man," Alf warned, hurrying to the other's side to see what had happened.

In a whisper, Hugh told him about the sap as he rubbed hard to get rid of it.

"You're wasting your time, Hugh. You need to scrape it off with your knife after dipping it into boiling water. We've none of that here. An' you'd best not let any other hear you complain about his lordship, no matter what he orders. You can't be wanting to die, can you?"

"No. I don't want to be spending the night looking in these woods for what I can't see, either. There's talk in that village we stopped at, you know. Talk of a witch woman that lives hereabout."

"There's always talk of some old hag." Under the cover of darkness Alf made the sign of the cross. His tone remained dismissive of any of Hugh's repeated superstitions.

But their talk had a benefit neither man could imagine; it helped Gilliane's terror to recede. They had moved away from where she had hidden and a glimmer of an idea came to her with their talk of a witch in the wood. The good Lord knew she likely appeared haglike with her torn robe and half her thigh-length hair ripped from its neat braided coil.

If she could make them think there was a witch...or that the wood was haunted...

She was not afraid to try so dangerous a scheme. With bated breath she waited for them to move off a little ways, and then she slowly uncurled her body and after a few moments managed to stand on shakey legs.

There came a crashing sound of some great beast running through the wood, and darkness came with it as the roiling movement of the clouds once again hid the moon.

Gilliane forced herself from the thicket. She heard the men running toward where she thought the sounds had come from, but could no longer see them.

She needed to escape them and find Sister Ellen.

She had run a short distance when she came upon an unexpected track, unexpected in the sense that it was wide and clear of brush. She hurried along, frequently glancing over her shoulder to see if the men followed her, but there was no one.

She walked faster, as fast as her aching body would allow. The way became harder as the land sloped upward, but the track remained wide and clear. She thought it might lead to a village or some crofter's hut where she could seek refuge.

Coming to the top, pausing to catch her breath, she realized she stood on the saddle of a small glen. Once more the moon shone its light to allow her to see. But Gilliane felt the eerie stillness that surrounded her.

No breeze rustled a leaf. No small night creatures crawled over the dried leaves and twigs and grasses of winter. No night bird took wing. There were no sounds at all.

The track dipped downward. Gilliane looked back once before she followed the only way open to her. She was frightened, but not with that same paralyzing terror that stopped her from rational thought.

The glen was small, and the way grew narrow and seemed somehow more shut-in as she descended. Granite cliffs peered down into the glen over the tops of birch trees.

The track twisted and at times seemed to disappear, and

the ground was littered with loose stones, making the way difficult.

Gilliane knew there was no place to run if Alf or Hugh showed themselves now. And she had come too far to think of turning back. Whatever lay ahead, she had to find the courage to face it.

Gilliane was not sure what called her attention to the left. She stepped closer and saw what might be a path through the trees. She looked up and saw that if she did follow this way, it led to the cliff.

Rubbing her arms against the night's chill, she stood undecided. It might not be a way out, after all, but it could be a good hiding place until morning's light.

Truly, she told herself, there was no choice. She could not go back to where she knew de Orbrec's men were searching for her.

She forced her way through the young saplings and came suddenly to a little grassy clearing. With the aid of the brightened moonlight, she saw that three slabs of stone appeared rounded like the sides of a cauldron. She was sure that, from above, the overhang of rock hid this place from sight. But this was not a natural place, not with its eerie quiet.

Gilliane stepped out into the clearing and thought it might once have been a quarry. Her mouth was dry, her breath shallow, but her heart beat so rapidly that she stood unable to move.

Her gaze followed the play of moonlight up the mossy granite wall and she barely stifled a cry. She crossed herself, whispering prayers and pleas for protection.

The curious carving was one she had seen before, on writings that her father had labored to transcribe: a serpent, chiseled in the Pictish fashion, doubled back upon itself.

But instead of fleeing, which all reason warned her to do, she stepped closer. Her gaze dropped to the ground to make sure the way was clear, and that was when she saw dwelling below the heathen symbol.

"Is anyone there?" she called softly. "I come here in peace. I am lost and seek only a night's rest."

Nothing stirred, and no voice came, in welcome or anger at being disturbed.

Gilliane hesitated. Almost against her will, she seemed to be carried forward. Closer now, she saw that the dwelling appeared to be part cave and part built with stones by human hands. In the wall of rough stones that enclosed the front was a doorway, screened with an untanned bull's hide.

It was the deepening cold that drove her forward. She called out again before her hand lifted the leather curtain. She stooped to enter and let the hide fall closed behind her.

Jamie, followed by Crisdean, crossed the Findhorn River, earning a thorough wetting for their hurry.

Crisdean held his tongue, for he sensed that something was driving Jamie to rush, and he had a healthy respect for Jamie's instincts.

Alert and on guard, they rode along until they found a path into the western edge of Findhorn wood.

Almost immediately the horses began fidgeting as their riders urged them to follow the path. The stallions had their ears pricked forward, their sudden tension communicating itself to their riders.

Jamie felt driven to go forward, but despite most of his clan thinking him at times too reckless for his own good, he did use caution. Right now, with every sense heightened, he started to draw his sword.

Ahead, just around a bend, a man's shouted demands rent the night.

"Stand! Stand till I catch ye or I'll slit your throat!"

"The lass," Jamie whispered. He barely spared a glance for Crisdean. He set his spurs to Killen's sides and raced down the path.

The trail widened, allowing the Gunn men to come together. Around the bend there, Jamie drew hard on his reins to bring Killen to a stop as Crisdean did to his horse, Mhor.

A man was half falling out of his saddle as he attempted to grab the loose, trailing reins of a badly frightened horse.

The riderless animal reared and whinnied, its forelegs pawing the air. The man tried to turn his own mount to make another try to get hold of the animal, and his horse was struck on the rump. He barely regained his seat as his horse backed and tried to rear.

It was the riderless horse's second attempt to strike the man with his pawing forelegs that brought to Jamie's attention the lady's sidesaddle on its back. He alerted Crisdean to this, and then ordered him to search the wood nearby.

A cry of pain drew Jamie's attention back to the man. The horse had struck his arm. And likely had broken it, Jamie thought, seeing the way the men cradled it against his body.

"Hold there!" Jamie shouted, drawing his sword. "Where is the woman who rode this horse?"

In the moonlight, the man appeared startled to see him there. His eyes widened, and he looked all about. His actions did not puzzle Jamie for long. The man was looking for help, which meant others were nearby.

"I asked you—"

"An' who might you be? I'm on my lord's business.

This mare belongs to him, as does the woman who stole her.''

Jamie believed in luck, but this...good luck indeed to find one of the very men he had come searching for.

''And who is your lord?'' he demanded with all the arrogance that belonged to the blood of Gunns.

''My master is Lord Guy de Orbrec. Be on your way now or you'll be answering to him for your interference.''

Crisdean rode up beside Jamie. ''Not a sign of her. And look at the mare. She's trembling and cut, too.''

''Fetch her for me. And if that whoreson moves, slay him.''

''Jamie,'' Crisdean cautioned, grabbing hold of his shoulder. ''We need information. He'll be no trouble with that arm.''

Jamie jerked free, his eyes never leaving the man-at-arms. He thought of what Sister Ellen had told him of how they had run like deer before the hounds, with never a moment to rest with the three men after them. He fought the raging need to put his hands on this man of de Orbrec, tempering that need with Crisdean's caution. He dare not call out loud for the woman to show herself, for there were two others still at large.

''How are you named?'' Jamie asked, his hand clenched on the hilt of his sword.

''Cob of Castres Keep,'' came the reluctant answer.

''Where are the others?'' Crisdean demanded before Jamie could.

''There's no one else.''

''The man's a liar, Crisdean. There are two more somewhere about.'' Jamie eyed the horse, then suddenly dismounted. He tossed his reins to Crisdean. ''Watch him.'' Then he walked toward the still-trembling mare.

''Easy lass, easy now. I'll no' be hurtin' you,'' he

crooned in a thick Scot's brogue that worked best with his horses.

The mare moved, sidling away from him. Jamie smiled and showed no annoyance at the time this would take. He kept on with his crooning, knowing that in the end the horse would come to him. The mare would sense, then know, much the way a woman did, that she had nothing to fear from him. It was no lie, this calm and trust that he projected, for he had never marked a horse or a woman. Gentleness and patience always rewarded him with what he wanted.

So when she stood for a few moments and allowed him a little closer, he made no grab for her dangling reins. He kept talking to her until finally she stood, sides heaving, ears pricked, but no longer attempting to move away from him.

''There's the pretty one, now,'' he murmured. Extending his hand toward her nose. ''Crisdean, what do the Gunns do with a man who lies?''

''Cut out his tongue,'' Crisdean replied promptly.

''The man's thrice a liar. He lied about his companions. He lied that the mare was stolen, for she belongs to the lady. And lastly,'' Jamie said, turning his head to look directly at Cob, his voice low and thick with promise of retribution, ''aye, last of all, he lied that the lady Gilliane de Verrill belonged to his master.''

''You can't! You can't be doing that to me! I said what was told me. I'm a simple man-at-arms. What's to me the doing of my betters? I follow my orders. Aye,'' he babbled, ''I lied about the others. Alf and Hugh are still searching. I took out after the other one. There were two women, you know. But I lost her and came upon the mare. I swear,'' he yelled as Crisdean walked his horse closer with his dirk in hand, "I swear I never saw the lady. The mare had no rider. Do you hear?"

Jamie motioned for Crisdean to stop. "We all hear, but do we believe?" he muttered in a soft voice, for the mare had allowed him to stroke her neck. He felt the welts coming up beneath her sweat-damp hide. Very carefully he examined the shallow cuts that indicated she had been hard ridden in the woods.

"Believe me! I'm not lying now. I wouldn't lie to you. Not with that blade coming for my tongue. Do you think me daft?"

"Crisdean, we have found a pretty songbird. Do you wrap it for my leisure, good sir, while I tend to finding this sweet lass's mistress."

"You'll not go riding off without me," Crisdean warned.

"Nay, rest easy. We'll go together."

Crisdean walked his horse forward until he stopped behind Cob's mount. "And this one? Do we let him keep his tongue?"

"For now," Jamie replied, keeping his voice soft so as not to startle the mare, who let him lead her forward to where Killen stood.

Cob attempted to bolt, but Crisdean blocked his way.

"That's another mark against you. Even my patience has a limit. Silence him for me, Crisdean."

Crisdean worked quickly to do Jamie's bidding. He cut strips from Cob's tunic and bound his injured arm to his chest, his good hand to the saddle, and tied his feet together beneath the horse's belly. Lastly, with a wide grin, he gagged the man, then took his weapons.

With a glance upward, Jamie remarked, "We'll lose

the moonlight soon. We'd best hurry if we're to find the lady.''

''Are you so sure we'll be doing that?''

''Aye, Crisdean. I swear it.''

Chapter Five

They had been riding for more than an hour on a winding trail that made it impossible at times for Jamie and Crisdean, as well as their prisoner, to keep each other in sight.

Jamie led the mare, hoping she would sense her mistress and whinny. He trusted his own instincts, and those of Killen, to warn him of the nearness of de Orbrec's men.

He was not sure what hand, if any, guided him from one path to another, each leading him, and those who followed, deeper and deeper into Findhorn wood. He had taken in the tales and superstitions rampant in the Highlands with his mother's milk, and knew there to be some truth behind each one.

And now he felt that some unseen force compelled him to ride as he should, and that he would find the woman he searched for.

It would be soon, he thought, for the night had grown quiet, with an almost eerie stillness that affected the horses as well as the men.

They were following the ridge of a saddle when the moonlight sprang free of the clouds and revealed the glen below. Unlike Gilliane, who had found the glen first, Jamie knew what the place was as soon as he saw the carving.

"Glen of the Snake," he whispered, recalling Crisdean's worry about the witch in the wood, which he had dismissed. If there was one, it was here she lived.

Jamie thought of his dead grandmother, who some had believed to be a witch. He had respect for her gifts, which in part had been passed down to Davey. If any could help him find the missing bride, the one who lived below could do it.

"Crisdean, stay here with the horses. I'll go down into the glen."

For once Crisdean offered no protest or warning. He, too, sensed the unseen forces at work here in the eerie quiet.

Jamie dismounted and removed his gilded spurs. His gaze cast about the wood before he hastily made his way down to the grassy clearing. His eyes narrowed as he drew close to the hide covering and smelled the thin wafting smoke of a fire within the stone dwelling.

He warily laid his hand on the hilt of his sword as his other hand reached for the leather.

Jamie pushed the covering aside and ducked below the lintel. Light came from the single candle and a small fire in the hearth. A woman knelt before the fire with her back toward him, but Jamie knew he had found the missing bride.

He stood and stared, hardly daring to breathe lest he disturb her. He was entranced by the play of soft light upon the glinting copper tangle of her hair, which she wore like a cloak. That most glorious color was the one physical trait he remembered Sister Ellen describing to him.

As though some unknown force had brought these two

together in this moment, Gilliane slowly turned and stared. A sudden, breathless hush filled the small dwelling as they gazed upon each other for the first time.

He was a man of flesh, tall and powerful, towering over her, yet for Gilliane, he was also a man from her secret dreams. A hero from a hundred tales of romance—the *Song of Roland,* the *Epic of the Cid, Deirdre*...all and yet none.

She stared, knowing that her life would be changed from this moment. She drew air fraught with tension as she rose to her full height. A moment's panic caught her, then just as quickly receded. This was not one of de Orbrec's men. His breeks, fine cream linen shirt, leather jerkin and sporran marked him a Highland warrior.

There was a quickening inside her as she gazed at his strong looking hand on the hilt of his sword. Gilliane found her voice then. "You will not need your weapon."

Jamie did not respond. His hand remained on the hilt of his sword, but not out of fear that he had walked into a trap.

He admired her courage, and her calm. Few women he knew would greet a stranger in the middle of the night without a sign of panic when their only avenue of escape was cut off.

But she did not move to flee or take up poker or broom for protection. She held his gaze with a directness he oft associated with men. The hushed stillness surrounding them, and her continued calm, held him motionless. He could still hear and feel the softness of her voice, like a caress against his flesh. He was entranced. He had to be. There was no other way for him to explain his reaction to her.

Jamie finally moved to drop the leather curtain behind him. He stepped no closer to her. A slow, mocking smile spread across his lips. He was not sure who he mocked. For here was a prize. And the stirring in his loins for the maid before him made him understand why the Norman had risked so much to have her.

Her skin was as fine as silk from lands he could not name, and her eyes…by the bones of his ancestors, he had only seen the green of her eyes in precious stones. Eyes that still watched him as if she knew his thoughts and awaited his final judgment.

Or was he misreading her frozen pose? Did she feel the same wanting, the very need he had to touch her? His quickened heartbeat and breathing told him that the Norman would never have her.

Desire for a woman had never come upon him with this swift, striking force. He was afraid to move, afraid she was but a vision that would disappear from his sight. He shook off the fanciful thought. She was real enough. The long fiery tresses hung tousled about her as though she had just risen from a tumble with a lover and he had tangled his fingers within the cascading wealth of hair to draw her closer.

Backlit as she was by the fire, he could see her slender form beneath the coarsely woven robe. Her ripe breasts rose and fell as her breathing deepened with the silence stretching out between them. Her fingers appeared to be trembling as they sought to grasp the rope belt, as if it would be some protection from him.

''All good deeds are rewarded,'' he murmured, breaking the silence. His gaze was bold, raking her appraisingly.

Gilliane started at the sound of his voice. Her earlier thought, that he had come to rescue her, gave way to dread as she finally recognized the desire in his gaze. Or was she mistaken? Did he think her the reward for having rescued her?

Alone! And trapped! He could ravish her, slay her, and none would know her fate in this desolate place if rescue was not his intent. She broke off staring at him, her gaze skimming the small room.

When she had first entered the dwelling, she'd been surprised to find it empty, with the fire burned low as if its owner had only stepped out minutes before she entered. The place was clean, and the air redolent with the aroma of the dried herbs hanging from the wood pegs wedged into the stone walls. A pitcher of cool, sweet water stood on the small table, along with hard cheese and half a loaf of fresh bread. And a candle, which she had quickly lit, unable to believe that she was truly alone in a safe place.

She had felt safe until minutes ago, when this Highlander entered. She thought of the small dagger she had to protect herself, but that was tied to her shift beneath the robe.

Her gaze met his and just as quickly skittered away, lest she give him an idea of where her thoughts were taking her. But she could not stop herself from studying him covertly, sensing, the way an animal at bay must sense, that any sudden move on her part would bring more danger.

For he was dangerous. She knew she was not mistaken about that, there was a savage strength in the tall, lithe body. The broad shoulders and long arms had to make him a dangerous foe. His clothing was finely made. Despite the smudges of dirt and a few rips, she knew the rich sheen of good cloth. His narrow waist was adorned by a leather belt holding his sporran, a pouch the Highland men favored to hold their coins. The dirk beside it had a simple design on the handle, and like the clan badge that she could not quite make out, gleamed with silver.

It frightened her that he still held his hand on the hilt of his broadsword. There were tales told of the wild, savage men that swept down from the mountains and glens of the Highlands. Men who stole and raided, who raped and murdered. Men who spoke strange languages, and who, it was whispered, worshipped in the old ways of the Picts and Celts and Norsemen that had come before them.

Had she run from one devil only to die at the hands of another?

She was about to ask him to declare himself, but he spoke before she formed the right words.

"The villagers spoke of the witch of the wood, and surely I've discovered her dwelling. But you, fair maid, you cannot be she. Or maybe you are, for I swear I'm—"

"I am not a witch!" Gilliane crossed herself.

"I've heard you whisper no chant, no spell at all, but I swear I'm ensorcelled," Jamie said as he stepped closer. A hint of a smile creased his lips when she sidestepped to keep the small table between them.

Gilliane glanced at his muscular legs and the black boots where the fire's light caught the gleam of metal. Dear Lord! How many weapons did he carry?

"Be not afraid of me," he whispered, forcing himself to stand still.

Her gaze was drawn to his face. The candlelight wavered and shone on the deep, rich color of his hair, a mahogany as dark as found in the Highland wood. This close to him, she could see the weathered swarthiness of his skin, but she judged him to be young. He was as handsome as any hero of her dreams.

Ruggedly masculine with dark brown eyes, a straight nose and a mouth that was carnal in its shape. She knew no other way to describe it to herself, for she wanted very much to touch his mouth, to feel its warmth against her own. She was ashamed of her sinful thoughts. He was a stranger, and she still knew nothing of his intent toward her. Even this reminder could not still the unaccustomed heat that coursed through her. She took a deep shuddering breath, longing to turn aside from his gaze, but his eyes compelled her to look at them, at him.

Had his eyes grown darker still as she stared? They were set beneath thick, dark brows, and lined with such long, richly dark lashes that she felt a stir of envy.

So completely had he captured her attention that a cry escaped her when he touched her. She had not known he had moved so close. He spoke of being ensorcelled by a witch, but surely he had lied, and was the devil himself to beguile her to silence and stillness and into forgetting her danger.

She jerked from the hand he placed on her arm. "Touch me not."

"I canna help myself." The mocking smile returned to his lips. "But don't be denying that you feel it, too."

She readied the lie, but could not speak it. She knew something strange passed between them, something that set her blood on fire and made her dizzy with its strength.

"I've frightened you," Jamie said, "and that was never my intent."

"I am not frightened so easily, good sir."

Jamie thought the lift of her slightly rounded chin charming, and her mouth was shaped for a man's kisses. A flush stole across her cheeks. He had to force himself to remember that he needed her to free his aunt. But every heated drop of blood within his body cried out in denial that any other man should touch her. And as much as he wished to cast aside what he read in her gaze, he could not. There was innocence there, innocence and bewilderment over the desire he thought she felt, too.

"You called me 'good sir,' and so I shall strive to be. Come away from this place, lass. I freely admit that my word is my honor, but alone here with you, I might not keep it."

"Do you think me a fool to go with you when I know there are men searching these very woods for me?"

That she dared to show him stubbornness tried his patience.

"Aye, I'll name you fool for telling me that much. I've come from Sister Ellen. She reached Inverness and told the tale of your flight from Deer Abbey. My man and I have come searching for you and offer," he stated with a short bow, "our protection."

"Sister Ellen? Is she all right? They caught up with us just outside the wood, and she begged me to flee while she tried to lead them away from me, but they split up and two nearly caught me. This is my fault. I should have...no, no, I could not go meekly. I could not."

Her impassioned voice led Jamie to think of other passions, and he stifled his annoyance with himself for so easily being distracted.

"Please! Tell me what befell Sister Ellen?"

"She's being tended at the priory."

"Tended?" She could not keep horror from her voice. "She was injured?" Gilliane glided with innate grace to where Jamie stood, and without thought for what she was doing, placed her hand on his arm. Her immediate fears for herself were cast aside with concern for Sister Ellen. "Do tell me, pray! What happened to her?"

"Gently lass, gently now. Calm yourself, Lady Gilliane. I swear to you she took no injury from those who chased you both. She suffers mostly from exhaustion."

His voice was dark, deep and gentle. Fear ebbed from Gilliane. But other emotions roiled too close to the surface. She knew she was losing control of herself. Terror, anger, despair, flight and fright were too powerful to stand against when one was battered as she had been. A small keening sound escaped her.

Jamie watched her head bow as if she could no longer hold it erect. He could not see her eyes, but her lashes fluttered as if she were about to faint. A pale sheen tinted her skin and his own words came back at him—*she suffers from exhaustion.*

He had to wonder if this place had addled his wits that it had taken him so long to see how truly exhausted Lady Gilliane appeared.

Remembering the ordeal that Sister Ellen had related, Jamie focused his considerable tender concern for the slender woman, who trembled. He slipped his arm around her, believing she was at the end of her strength.

Her sudden struggles against him caught him off guard. She truly was no match for his strength, but then, he exerted little force to subdue her in fear of hurting her.

Jamie's touch seemed to snap something inside Gilliane. The strange warmth coursing through her veins, added to all that had happened, made her feel trapped within his arms.

She fought harder to get free.

Jamie tightened his hold. "What possesses you, lass? Stop kicking me!" Exasperation toned his voice when she refused to listen to him. "I said I meant you no harm. Now cease before you do yourself some injury."

"Unhand me!" she cried out. "Unhand me at once!"

Gilliane pushed at his hard, muscular chest and tried to kick him again. Her borrowed novice's robe became entangled around her legs and caught on his boot knife. She twisted and started to fall. Jamie's quick motion saved Gilliane from injury, but brought him to the floor beneath her.

As in the first moment they'd gazed upon each other, time again appeared to stand still.

She no longer struggled against him. He no longer attempted to restrain her.

But neither moved. Both seemed to sense that to move would be to break this absolute awareness, this total absorption with each other.

Jamie had wanted to touch the silken tangle of her gloriously colored hair from the moment he had seen it and her. Seemingly of their own volition his strong, long fingers slid through her hair to clasp her head and draw her lips to his.

He did not know if fear or outrage for the liberty he was about to take held her rigid. But he could not seem to help himself. At the last moment, he lifted her head slightly and lightly traced the shape of her jaw with his lips. There was an absolute, concentrated stillness to him as he drew in the scent that was hers and felt the delicate shuddering ripple of her body stroke the full length of his.

"Thy taste is sweeter than the fine wines of Aquitaine, fair maid. I would steal no more from you," he whispered.

Jamie could not hide his aroused state. He was not accustomed to denying himself anything he wanted. Right now, the slow, unhurried tasting of her skin flooded his own easily heightened senses. But he was a man, not a boy, and so held control over his desire. He loosened a bit of her hair so it fell like a silken curtain around them. Then he waited, a moment, two, but there was no cry of protest. She appeared as deeply enthralled as he was.

Gilliane felt lost. Her blood heated and seemed to swell her body. A sigh shivered forth as the full carnal shape of his mouth tested the pulse madly beating in her throat. His breath heated as it fanned suddenly sensitized skin. She felt powerless as tiny tremors flowed deeper and deeper inside her. It was his gentleness that held her, even as a part of her knew this was madness. A wicked madness that stole her will to fight him. But it was wrong. Wrong to allow him to hold her thus, wrong for him to kiss her throat. She tried to summon the strength to make an effort to free herself.

Her thought of escaping him went no further, for his lips came tasting hers. Not with force. No harsh demand. Naught but teasing brushes of his lips against her own. A tiny kiss at the corner of her mouth, another on her bottom lip. And warmth, gentle warmth that enticed her to be still. She had no way of countering a practiced seduction that softened her body against the hard, muscled planes of his. She had understood enough of the overheard talk of the village women to know a man's passion, once aroused, was not easily turned aside. Yet here were very tender kisses that begged no more of her, that invoked her own desire to respond. And it was his very gentleness that allowed the thought that here could lie love....

In the sudden blood-thrumming silence, shivering fear and thrilling longing melted inside her. His mouth's courting of her own was an alluring play, an awakening of her senses to the pleasure a man and a woman shared. She lost herself to the softness and warmth of his lips. Her every indrawn breath was filled with the scent of leather and horse, and a woodsy aroma she could not name. It pleased her. Everything about this Highland warrior pleased her. But she sensed the darker passion barely held in check within him before his kiss changed.

His hands holding her head tightened to keep her still.

His lips no longer gently courted hers, but demanded and claimed as no man had ever done.

Gilliane's hands clenched the sleeves of his linen shirt. Her legs trembled and her toes curled tight as her body softened and sank in shivering wonder against his.

Time, and the world that waited outside, disappeared from her thoughts.

There was only the Highlander, and these new intense feelings that overcame all reason.

Her wild shivering swept through Jamie, and with it came the realization that he had never wanted a woman half as much as he wanted this fair maid. A searing fever raged just beneath the surface of his control. He had tasted innocence in the first touch of her lips, and then enticed her to give her mouth fully to him. He had to end this now. End it before he stole what was only her right to give.

Jamie eased her head back, ending the kiss as gently as it had begun. Their labored breaths mingled. He looked into her green eyes, dark now, wide with desire and perhaps curiosity, but not fear. He thought of the Norman who waited to claim her, realized that, if not him, then others would want her. He knew then that no other would have her while he had breath in his body.

Desire was so thickly layered between them that his voice, when he finally spoke, was dark and husky with the force he exerted to keep his passion under control.

He whispered one word to her. One word he had never spoken to another woman.

"Mine."

Gilliane, frightened by her own wild emotions, slowly regained her sanity. For surely all this had been a madness that seized her. The intensity of his gaze and the promise in his dark voice alarmed her. She attempted to pull free, but he would not release her.

"You cannot claim me. 'Tis madness you speak."

"Aye, lass, 'tis true. But I swear to you now, it will come to pass."

She recalled with painful clarity Guy de Orbrec's driven will to have her. She looked into the beguiling Highlander's eyes, the man who had given her the first taste of passion, and knew he would be killed if he tried to keep her.

Despite her dreams and longings for someone to save her, Gilliane knew her life was not drawn from the tales of great romances that had been her father's passion. She had only herself to depend upon.

She shook her head, not knowing that he was a Gunn or that their clan motto was I Claim, I Hold.

With words she denied him. "Nay," she whispered, "'tis never to be. I have promised to take the veil if Lady Ailis is freed. 'Tis a sacred vow, Highland man. Not even you can expect me to break it."

She saw the doubt in his eyes at her lie.

Chapter Six

Jamie went stumbling from the stone hut, his hand tight on Gilliane's wrist as he dragged her behind him up the slope to where Crisdean waited with the horses and their prisoner.

"You found her then, Jamie?"

"I found something, mayhap the witch of the wood you were afraid of." His answer was curt, ridden with anger, and insulting besides, to both the lady Gilliane and to Crisdean for his concern.

"Aye, I found the right one." His speech went from his mind as he stared at Crisdean. Surely his man had marked the great length of time he had been gone from his sight? It could not have been mere minutes. Or could it? Was Crisdean holding his scolding tongue because of the maid?

Jamie glanced up at his mounted clansman. There was no expression of worry that Jamie had been gone for long. He turned then to gaze down into the glen and found that there was only darkness below, hiding the hut and even the symbol of the snake carved in stone.

For good or ill, some force had held sway over him in that dwelling, and he needed to know what it was. He had not argued with Gilliane over her denial. There had been no point in arguing over what would be. And he knew the truth deep in his bones. But it bewildered him why he did. He had never whispered that word to another woman, had never wanted to. To have spoken thus within minutes of meeting Gilliane, of only tasting one kiss from her lips, resembled true ensorcellment.

Gilliane's soft, excited voice exclaiming over her mare drew him from his dark and puzzling thoughts.

"Thank you for finding Fleur."

Crisdean snorted at hearing the mare's name, and he shared a look with Jamie, both thinking that only a woman would name a horse of fine blood Flower.

Gilliane saw the glance that passed between them. "Her name comes from the marking on her haunch of the lily flower. See," she added, flipping over the decorative edge of the saddle blanket to show them the mark.

"'Tis time we were away from this place," Jamie reminded them in a sharp voice.

Gilliane sent him a pleading look, feeling that his anger should be directed only at her.

"Jamie, the lass cannot ride the mare," Crisdean pointed out. "The beastie's been hard used and you'll break her wind if we are forced to ride hard."

"Jamie?" Gilliane asked, a suspicion forming of who he was.

"Aye, lass. That's Jamie Malcolm, the—"

"The fool who's keeping you standing about on a chill night," Jamie finished, with a warning look for Crisdean to hold his tongue. He could not even explain to himself why he wanted to hide who he truly was, but since leaving the glen, his natural cynicism had returned. The act of kidnapping for ransom was nothing new to him. The Highlanders did it all the time. He did not doubt that his

aunt had been taken and was being held for a ransom that
would beggar most clans, but where was the truth of Lady
Gilliane de Verrill's tale? She might be a part of this Norman lord's plot to gain easy wealth, or be a part of the
Gunns' troubles with the Keiths. Strange alliances came
about when the clans feuded. Until he was sure of this
young woman, he would withhold his identity.

Jamie gave short shrift to the nagging thought that her
rejection of his claim had anything to do with his suspicions.

"Come, my lady," Jamie said with a hint of mockery,
"you'll ride before me. My clansman is right about the
sorry state of your mare. And seeing how you care for
her, you will not want her damaged beyond future use."

He held out his hand to her, and noted her questioning
look before she stepped close to him. Despite wanting to
touch her earlier, he now found himself reluctant to do
so. But with Crisdean eyeing him, Jamie had no choice
but to put his hands upon her.

He had judged her slender and now felt for himself the
slim waist. Her height was tall for a woman, the top of
her head reaching the square cut of his jaw. From the back
of the saddle he untied his wool cloak and placed it
around her shoulders.

He did not answer her murmured thanks for the en-
folding warmth that surrounded her. He mounted behind
her and let Crisdean, leading their prisoner, go ahead.

But as they followed along the ridge of the saddle away
from the Glen of the Snake, Jamie could not stop himself
from looking back.

"Crisdean," he called out softly, "do not make for
Inverness. I've no wish for our prisoner to be seen by any.
Once we cross the Findhorn, find a place to make camp."

"Is that wise, Jamie?"

"Do you question my orders, Crisdean?"

"Nay. I thought only of the lass. Will she be able to ride so long and so far?"

Jamie's gaze grew hard. "She is not your worry. Need is a hard master and one that must be obeyed. She can sleep if she grows too weary. Truly, Crisdean, let us ride. To tarry when there are others about is foolish."

Crisdean's answer was to set his spurs to his mount and ride away from Jamie's strange angry mood.

Gilliane took courage in hand to speak. "You told me Sister Ellen was tended at the priory in Inverness. I wish to see her. I also wish to know where it is that you take me. That man that is bound? He was one of the three who chased me and Sister Ellen. What will you do with de Orbrec's man?"

"Roast him over a slow fire until he's told all he knows," Jamie snapped.

"Nay, you put your soul in peril—"

"Hush. I won't roast him." What Jamie did not add was that his brother Micheil was more than likely to do it.

What had made him snap at her was the need to gain her trust without giving away more than he learned.

"Sister Ellen is well on her way to the Gunn stronghold. The clan chief will decide what is to be done for his aunt."

Gilliane drew Jamie's cloak tightly around her and wished she could ride pillion, for the Scot's broad shoulders would block the wind. But with his angry mood, she dare not suggest it.

"You never told me where it is that we go."

"To Halberry Castle. The Gunns will wish to hear your tale."

"'Tis no tale, but a nightmare."

He made an encouraging sound, hoping she would tell him more but the night was cold, and he felt the weary sag of her body against his own and did not push her to talk.

The night and the ride were as long as Jamie said, and yet he pushed them on until they crossed Culloden moor after sunrise.

Hunger and thirst drove them to stop at Beauly Priory, one of three Valliscauliar houses founded by Alexander II over one hundred and fifty years before.

It was Gilliane who told this to Jamie while they waited for Crisdean to bring them food to break their fast. She told him a little about the other two priories, Pluscarden and Ardchattan.

"It was my father's work that allowed me to learn of such things. He transcribed from Latin, Greek or French whatever papers came into his possession or were sent to him by nobles."

"Sister Ellen mentioned that you learned of his death when de Orbrec's men came after you at the abbey."

"Yes."

Gilliane's throat closed with unshed tears. She was grateful to see Crisdean walking toward them carrying a tray, but saw the dismay on Jamie's face when he spied the monk accompanying him.

"The good father insisted that he come and give his blessing to our sorely afflicted clansman, Jamie. I did explain our reason for refusing to break bread inside."

Jamie quickly took the hint. "The poor man, good father. As you can see, we've had to restrain him because of the sudden fits. I fear he might hurt himself or others."

"But my son, the gag—"

"We travel with a clanswoman and old Cob here, ah, 'tis said that with the fit comes the foulest of curses. 'Tis a sore trial to us all when he is in the grip of his ailment. But here,'' Jamie said, dipping into his sporran and drawing forth two sovereigns, which he pressed into the monk's hand. ''Take this for our food and for a Mass where your prayers will aid our own that his affliction is soon gone.''

''Bless you, my son. Bless you for your kindness. Do enjoy our poor fare. I will go and pray for all, and for a safe journey.''

''You lied to the holy brother!'' Gilliane exclaimed, after the monk had left them alone.

''What would you have me do, mistress? Tell him the truth? And if any follow us, he'll be quick to tell them when we passed here. This way he'll keep quiet for the sake of the gold I gave him.''

Jamie helped himself to a wooden bowl of porridge. Crisdean poured out watered wine for them, and Gilliane took one of the richly browned barley bannocks and spread butter on the baked round.

While she daintily nibbled the edges of the bannock, she kept thinking of Jamie's glib tongue in speech with the monk. Last eve's foolishness was just that. The man was a practiced liar and she had best remember it.

Jamie gave Gilliane no choice about riding her own mare, now rested, but put her up on Killen when they were ready to set out again. Once away from prying eyes, he demanded that Crisdean relinquish his cloak to cover the bound Cob.

They swung wide around Black Isle to follow a narrow track that took them farther north with every bone-jarring, wearying mile.

It was a brutal pace that Jamie set, one that he and Crisdean were accustomed to, but which exhausted Gilliane to the point she barely remembered him lifting her from saddle at day's end.

She tasted cool, sweet water and ate a little of the hard cheese that Crisdean had bought from the innkeeper in Inverness. She refused the share of cold bannock he offered with it.

Gilliane lay down wrapped in the thick, soft wool of Jamie's cloak. Her bed was layered with moss, while nearby, the soft murmur of water tumbling over stones should have lulled her to sleep. She closed her eyes and pretended to rest, but the thought of what Lady Ailis must be suffering allowed her no peace. She would do everything and anything to get her free from de Orbrec, but right now all she could do was pray for her. Perhaps it was the soothing rote of prayers that brought her sleep, or simple exhaustion. She knew not, only that sometime in the night she awakened, feeling overly warm.

The stars above were faint pinpricks of light as she stirred fully awake. She started to sit up, then realized the warmth came from the bodies of the two men, who lay to either side of her.

"What's amiss that you woke?" Jamie asked in a soft, rumbling voice. "If you're still cold, we can't have a fire. I have no way of knowing if we are followed by de Orbrec's men."

"Aye, I understand that. And naught's amiss," she said in a whisper. "When I first woke, I foolishly thought myself safe in my own bed, and then knew it could not be. I merely wondered where the warmth came from."

"Don't take offense, lass. I swear none will hear of this from either Crisdean or myself. It was for your comfort only and no thought to dishonor you that we lay beside you. Now, try to sleep," he added. "We've more hard riding on the morrow."

"I wish it were easy to do. I cannot help but worry for Lady Ailis's fate at de Orbrec's hands. He is a cruel man and will not respect her office."

That she gave voice to the fear Jamie had not put into words made his answer curt. "She is a strong Gunn woman. I will not say you are foolish to worry, but by now de Orbrec will know that if he harms her, he dies."

Gilliane heard the promise in his voice and remembered when he'd promised that he would claim her. She felt in need of comfort and thought of his warm arms around her, his kisses taking her from worry and guilt and the sadness that plagued her. It was on the tip of her tongue to confess her lie about taking the veil. She kept silent, knowing it was her only protection.

Jamie saw that the horses were calm, and closed his eyes to seek his rest. He found himself listening to Gilliane's uneven breathing. Unbidden, those lost minutes in the stone dwelling came to mind. He'd wanted her then as no other woman before her. That feeling had not changed. He caught the sound she quickly stifled.

So much had happened so fast that he knew she'd had little time to mourn her own losses, and the fear for his aunt only added to her burden.

To claim a woman meant more than possessing her body. Her needs and worries had to become his own.

"Lass, 'tis small comfort to say I'm sorry for all you've lost."

The tears that Gilliane had been fighting suddenly brimmed in her eyes. "You are kind to comfort me when I have brought this terrible trouble to your clan. My deep regret of not being with my father when he died hurts the most."

Jamie knew he should not turn or acknowledge the quiver in her voice. He warned himself, but rolled onto his back, then shifted to his side so that he faced her. But Gilliane had moved even as he had, and was lying on her back, staring upward.

He cupped her cheek but did not attempt to force her to look at him. "Cry if you've a mind to," he whispered. "I'm told I have broad shoulders to bear the weight that would bow another's."

"I must not. If I give way to tears I shall lose whatever strength is left me. I promised myself there would be time enough for grieving when this is done. Only…only there are so many more to cry over now." She sniffed, but made no move to brush away the tears that clung to her lashes.

"If only dear Lady Ailis had not offered me shelter. I should have stayed and fought for our serfs, whom de Orbrec has likely seized for his own. And the servants in the manor house must be in terror of him. Then those poor nuns without their abbess… Sister Ellen is apart from them, and sore tried." Gilliane turned to look at him. She freed one hand from the cloak, hesitated, then touched his beard-stubbled cheek.

"I have been a sore trial to you, too," she whispered. She was well aware that Crisdean, and beyond him, Cob, might be awake and listening, but she had no choice. Riding as they had all day made conversation impossible. And she had one fear that preyed upon her.

"Please, if I ask…no, I must say it. Do you know the chief of Clan Gunn well? Will he slay me for what has befallen his aunt?"

"Slay?" Jamie half rose, realized that he'd yelled, and lowered both his body and his voice. She had jerked her hand away, but he recaptured her soft, pale hand within his own. Even this innocent touch sent a shaft of need through him, and he silently cursed his unruly passion.

"Calm yourself. Fear not the chief. He'll not slay you. How could any lay blame upon you for this Norman's despicable acts?" As much as he desired her, she had presented him with a chance to voice his suspicions and hopefully lay them to rest.

His murmur became softer as he leaned close to her. "None could blame you—unless you were aware of his plan to take her hostage and hold her till your return with the ransom he demanded?"

His accusation stung her to the quick. She was too shocked to cry out. But she refused to allow his belief to go unchallenged.

"You thought I knew de Orbrec's plan? You dare believe that I am a part of it? That I put Lady Ailis's life at risk for riches? This Norman is all that is loathsome to me."

Her voice shook; her hands curled into fists. He had tainted her with his suspicion. What more could she do than proclaim her innocence?

Gilliane made a strong and successful effort to steady herself. "Better, far better, to accuse me of being in league with the devil. For I swear on all that is holy, he would be more welcome to me than Guy de Orbrec."

It was this last passionate denial that finally convinced Jamie of her innocence in his aunt's abduction and the claim for ransom. He knew, and thought she must, that it was a great sin for a woman to speak openly as she had done against even the most monstrous of husbands. And if Sister Ellen had had the truth from Gilliane, de Orbrec's claim of a contract signed by her father was as good as a marriage performed by a priest.

But thoughts of the marriage contract turned him to her vow to take the veil. She could not, for that vow was empty. The contract held sway over all.

His continued silence, far from comforting her, generated the fear that he did not believe her at all. She withdrew her hand from his. This time he did not stop her.

She wanted to turn her back and leave him to his vile suspicions about her. Why should it matter what he believed? But if she could not convince Jamie that she was innocent of any wrongdoing with de Orbrec, how could she make the chief of Clan Gunn believe her?

"Gilliane, Sister Ellen said there is a marriage contract signed by your father with de Orbrec?"

"Another falsehood. The man is a liar! Why do you wish to believe I am a part of that man's evil? He murdered three wives because they bore him daughters. I ran at my father's order so as not to become the fourth."

"I did not say I believed it, only voiced a suspicion I had, and you put that to rest. But if the contract is real, then your vow to take the veil is empty. That contract will be broken with de Orbrec's death. Oh, yes, my lady, he will die for what he has dared to do. But you would be committing a sin to hide away behind abbey walls."

"My father refused de Orbrec's offer of marriage and…" She paused, looking away from his penetrating gaze. If she admitted that she'd lied about the vow he would believe nothing she said. But she would not compound the lie by repeating it.

"Believe me or not, Jamie Malcolm or whatever your name is. I have told you the truth about de Orbrec. Cease these accusations. You are not a woman alone, prey to whatever man thinks to seize her!"

She did not care that she shouted the last. What was once comforting warmth against the night's chill now was a stifling prison. She sat up, shoved aside his hand, scrambled to her feet and glared down at him. Anger was her only weapon.

"I find your manner offensive. Mend it before you seek me out. And keep your twisted beliefs to yourself."

Chapter Seven

Jamie was stunned by the venom in her voice. He felt the power of her glaring eyes and thought her a vision of a Valkyrie the old Norse traders told their tales about.

She carried no shield or sword, wore no breastplate of metal or helmet of protection, but her fierce, proud stance was armor enough.

The breeze stirred, lifting one or two long tendrils of her hair. Wild, she appeared to his eyes, wild and ready to do battle with the feminine weapons he desired both to conquer and claim for his own.

But Jamie knew that if he made a move toward her, she would never trust him, or come to him again. And he wanted that. Wanted it with each heated beat of his blood. He had to force himself to remember he was not alone here with her. Yet the ache to touch her increased to where he had to lace his fingers beneath his head to keep himself still.

He could not harbor suspicions about her after what she'd told him. No woman would revile a man by naming him a murderer if she cared for him. Yet if what she claimed was true, then surely, he reasoned, someone would have brought this charge against the Norman lord.

Could a man kill three wives with none to question their deaths? The village priest at the least, or other nobles in the area would raise more than a question.

Jamie admitted his confusion. She appeared guiltless. Why then did he not proclaim his belief in all she said? Was it her beauty? Or was it the strength of his desire that made him wary of trusting her?

It was fool's play to go on with this.

But she stood, watching him and waiting for some word.

"Have a care, mistress, that you do not stray far. Although the night is quiet, the land is never safe."

Gilliane turned from him and walked toward the small burn. Her anger with him ebbed as she went. She could not force him to trust where he would not. She could not make him believe her. Perhaps the fault lay with him. Jamie might have some incident in his past that affected his trust of women. It seemed the best reason she could find, and while it discontented her, she clung to it.

She found a thick stand of grass near the horses and spent what was left of the night there.

In the morning Gilliane was anxious and unsure how to behave. Chrisdean, the first one she saw, offered no sign that he had heard the conversation in the middle of the night. He shared out the last of the hard cheese and cold bannocks, and each of them took a turn drinking the sweet water of the small burn upstream from where the horses watered. She decided to take her cue from him and pretend nothing had happened.

Gilliane's decision to ride her mare met with no opposition. She felt a sense of freedom having her own mount, but she truly was not free. They rode close together, entering onto lands controlled by Clan Ross, sometime enemies of the Gunns.

As the morning mist burned off they followed another of the narrow twisted trails, which led them along the rocky shore of a river, then took them high on gray, forbidding stone pathways where the sun barely shone. She remembered claims of those who were raided south of here, claims that the Highlanders fairly disappeared before their very eyes into their lands. She understood now how that could be.

Rocky as it was, there was a sameness to the land slowly awakening to spring that left Gilliane with time to think. And study the fine figure of Jamie ahead. He rode in the lead and paced the horses carefully over the rough terrain, his every move cautious to ensure their safety. The sun revealed reddish glints in his thick chestnut hair.

Gilliane was not sure when the thought firmed in her mind that Jamie Malcolm not only belonged to Clan Gunn but very likely was one of Lady Ailis's nephews. She wanted to ask him if it was true, but he had positioned the still-bound and gagged Cob between them, with Crisdean bringing up the rear.

They came upon the blackened ruins of some shepherd's hut, where Jamie called a halt. He dismounted and came to help her down.

Gilliane held on to his shoulders after he set her on her feet. She looked up at him, expecting him to be looking down at her. She found instead his muscles hard with tension and his gaze focused beyond her.

"What is it? What is wrong?"

"There's a party of men on the flat below, six by my count, and I know not if they are friend or foe. Stay close to the horses. I need to speak to Crisdean."

"Do you see them, Jamie?" Crisdean called out.

"Aye. I don't like the look of them. We're on Ross lands, and while we're not fighting with them now, there's a few of that clan that will spill Gunn blood as soon as not."

"We could wait until nightfall, Jamie. Then slip away in the dark."

Jamie looked over the shelter, scanty for them and for the horses. The riders below would know of this place and might ride by.

"Much as I would like a quick skirmish to loosen my sword arm, we can't take the risk. Lady Gilliane and Cob must be first brought to safety within our own lands. Still, there are only six of them...."

"I know that gleam in your eyes well, Jamie. Six of them to two of us is near even." Crisdean's look was hopeful, almost encouraging, but he, too, understood their priority.

"It sours me to turn and run. But there's no other choice." Jamie stood by Crisdean's side, watching the riders below as his clansman did. "Can the mare make a good run of it?"

"She's had a day's rest. The lass isn't heavy. I'm more worried about Cob's horse. He's of better stock than expected for a man-at-arms to ride, but the poor beastie's been gelded. You believe and I agree the heart's cut out of the animal when that's done. The animal's been hard ridden, first from the Norman's keep south of the abbey, then chasing the lady and good sister."

"He can't be mounted pillion on Killen or Mhor. We both need sword arms free. We'll take the chance. And we've almost run out of time. See, they're turning up the track. Even if they're just a hunting party...no, there's too much risk."

"Jamie, you're scheming."

"Aye. Take the lady Gilliane and Cob back the way we came. I'll ride down toward them. They'll be sure to give chase. Once I lead them away from here, you can safely cross the track across the heath. I'll meet with you after nightfall.''

"Jamie, we can all ride together. There's no need for you to show yourself.''

"There is a need. The life of my aunt depends on having the lady safe and sound to present. You need Cob to tell of this Norman's keep and the amount of his force. I charge you with seeing that both are brought to my brother.''

Jamie clasped Crisdean's shoulder, silencing any further argument. He wished he had his shield and spear, but they were packed with the other men's on the cart they'd abandoned when they gave chase to the Keith thieves that stole the furs.

He approached Gilliane and told her what he planned.

Something about the set of his jaw warned Gilliane not to protest. "Take care, Jamie,'' she whispered.

"Obey Crisdean in all things. He'll see to your safety.''

"Better he should see to your back. But then you do not trust me to bring myself and Cob to your clan. No, 'tis sorry I am for burdening you now with my foolishness. Is there no other choice for us, that you must put yourself to the fore and fight them?''

"They'll find our tracks and chase us down. Using myself as bait will draw them off.'' Jamie did not know why he explained it to her, when he was not in habit of doing so. But then, he'd never had a maid who dared ask him about any decision.

He lifted her to her sidesaddle, handing over the reins.

"Go with God, Jamie.''

"Aye, an' you, my lady.''

Crisdean led Cob's mount and herded Gilliane before him. Jamie stared after them for a moment, wishing he had had a sweet taste of the maid's lips. He mounted Killen, loosened his sword and rode down the track to meet the party of riders.

He missed having Crisdean by his side, but counted on Killen to give him whatever aid he required as he closed upon the six, who had spotted him and were now trotting their horses toward him.

Closer now, Jamie saw that, like him, they were without full armor. He had guessed right in thinking this a hunting party. He set his spurs and Killen leaped forward with a burst of speed. Jamie guided him directly at the center of the riders, until they had no choice but to split their group or be run down by the stallion.

A few quick twists secured the reins to the saddle, leaving Jamie's hands free. He uttered no sound, no battle cry, but the hard gold glints in his brown eyes showed his willingness to use the sword he drew.

"What do you on Ross lands?" demanded one of the men.

"Does a Sutherland account to a Ross? Does a Gunn? Or a Keith?" Jamie shouted back, hoping to confuse them as to his true identity.

At the slightest pressure of his knees, Killen spun on his hocks, rearing high enough to paw the air with his powerful forelegs, but not so high as to unseat his rider.

Jamie had worked long hours teaching his favorite warhorse to respond to the sound of the sword being drawn, to the slightest touch of his legs, to the softest murmur of his voice.

Killen's hooves hit the ground with a jar and he raced back toward the regrouping riders, tearing up the heath as he went. This was what the stallion had been bred and trained for—to kill and disable his rider's enemies. Killen veered for a black horse that snorted and pawed the earth, whinnying in challenge. The gray stallion used his teeth to savage the other horses's hide, swinging his massive head from side to side, allowing no other steed to close upon him.

Jamie, too, cleared the space around them with his swinging sword, striking a few blows. But he was not trying to kill any of these men, just engage them long enough for the others to ride to safety. Once more Killen raced free, turned again, but this time, Jamie held him for a moment.

"You've grown fat 'round your winter fires. You give me little sport." His voice and then his laughter mocked them, but he hoped that none would notice that each turn and run drew them away from the track that led up to the burned hut.

Jamie did not wait to see the effect of his taunt. He rode over the rocky ground toward the wood, drawing them farther and farther away from the track. Killen gave him the speed he demanded, and they soon outdistanced their pursuers.

If any of the men's training had been equal to Jamie's own, he would not have escaped as easily. Once on the other side of the wood, he barely made out their frustrated shouts at having lost sight of him. By his reckoning he had engaged them less than an hour. It should have been time enough for Crisdean to get the others away, but he had to be sure.

Jamie chose those nearest to him, and rode closer. He cried out, *"Buaidh no Bas!"*—Victory or Death, the clan cry of the MacDougalls, just to confuse matters more as he sped around the periphery of the forest, and this time he cried out the Latin motto of Clan Ross, *"Spem Successus Alit!"* Racing around the edge of the wood yet again, he gave another yell, Clan Sutherland's rallying cry

"Sans Peur!" He heard the confused shouts of the men being called back, and decided he had best leave before the hunt for him intensified.

He rode off, satisfied with the mischief he had made, for there would be a wild tale told this night in the keep at Easter Ross, built much like his own home on a huge promontory.

As an added reward, Jamie's rushing through the wood and then around it flushed out the game the Rosses had been hunting. From the alder, pine, oak and birch trees came a herd of red deer and all manner of wood fowl, hiding his track. He thought he heard the squealing grunt of a wild boar and almost envied the hunters their sport if they went after it. But he hastened to catch up with Crisdean and Gilliane. He wondered if she had a sense of humor and would appreciate his mischief.

He was even more pleased when he came upon the hunters' rough camp and was able to rifle their food stores before they returned. He swiped a bag of grain for the horses and a full skin of wine. Although he had no love of cold oat cakes and hard cheese, they were foods that would not spoil, and he took a healthy share of them. Jamie rode hard and soon reached the River Alness, where he searched for a shallow spot to ford. He could see where his party waited, and found the place to cross.

Gilliane turned her mare toward him as Killen's hooves sent a spray of water flying. "Are you unhurt?" she cried.

"I tried to tell her, Jamie, that no harm would befall you."

"And none has. I've food, but let's ride from here."

Jamie was in high spirits, and Gilliane's concern capped his good mood. Crisdean laughed when later that night, Jamie told the tale of what he had done. They had found shelter in a natural corner of rock, where it was deemed safe enough to build a small fire.

Gilliane wanted no part of their merriment. "You could have been killed if they caught you," she said, pointing her finger at Jamie. "I understood your need to draw them away, but why did you risk yourself?"

"Lass, think. What's sweeter than life after a risk won?"

"And do you always win?" she asked.

"Aye. So far I have. I didn't go blindly about what I did. I judged what they would do, and was proven right. We've wine to warm us, and food, and while I could desire something else, this does fill the belly. We're safe and closer to Halberry Castle. Tomorrow night should see us within its gates, and none too soon. I've been near a week in these clothes and am galled to the devil by my own sweat."

Gilliane withdrew a little. Jamie's reminder could go for her as well. There had been no time for bathing before she ran from her home, none at the abbey, and these days and nights of riding brought home her disheveled appearance. She had to look worse than a serf girl of the village. Would the Gunn chieftain even believe her?

It showed her exhaustion to have that foolish thought. Sister Ellen would be there before her, smoothing the way. Had not the good sister claimed that she knew the chief's wife?

Remembering her earlier speculations about Jamie, Gilliane leaned toward the fire again and waited until he finished his whispered conversation with Crisdean. The clansman left them then, and she heard Cob bitterly complain that the gag was to be tied again.

"Crisdean will take first watch," Jamie explained when he saw that she looked in the direction Crisdean had gone.

"We need a watch?"

"As a precaution only. I know you thought me reckless, but truly I am not."

"Will you answer me with the truth if I ask one question?"

"That depends on what you ask, Lady Gilliane."

"Are you the lady Ailis's nephew, Jamie?"

Jamie gazed across the fire at her, surprised to find her watching the flames and not him. "'Twas an omission that served. Aye, she is my aunt."

She looked up at him then, unaware that her dark green eyes appeared to hold mysteries for the man who watched her every expression with avid enjoyment. The firelight teased him with its play upon her hair, gilding it one moment, the next hiding its glory in shadow. There was a smudge upon her cheek, and he wanted nothing more than to brush it from her skin, but it was not the time nor the place to play at seduction.

He noted the faint blue shadows beneath her eyes and chided himself for not thinking of her comfort.

"Come, Lady Gilliane, I stand accused of being reckless with your welfare. Let me make a bed for you."

"Who accuses you, Jamie? Not I. I admit that I am tired, but do not wish to sleep. You never asked me why I sought shelter at the abbey at my father's order. I wanted you to know that when I was little, we lived in France. Your aunt and mine were at the convent together. I can remember visiting them there, and hearing tales of Lady Ailis's home in the wilds of Scotland. When my father's brother died, after having gained the manor and farms near Tomintoul, we came here to live. I always remembered your aunt's kindness, as well as her stories about her family. Sometimes she shared news from the few letters she received."

Jamie poked at the fire. ''You make no mention of your mother. If I trespass upon painful memories, forget that I asked.''

''The little I know about her was told by my father and his sister. She was an orphan Father met and fell in love with, but she died of childbed fever after giving birth to me. I did not lack for a goodwife's guidance. Aunt Jeanne, although already in the convent, found a good woman, a widow fallen on hard times, to serve as my nurse. Old Giselle did not wish to come with us. I was twelve then, and already ordering our home.''

''You were an only child and, I think, a lonely one.''

''Lonely? Perhaps,'' she replied, taking care to observe him. ''I had charge of the household at a young age, and then I had the great romances to read. Why did you say that?''

''There is a bittersweetness to your smile and a slight shadow in your eyes. Or,'' he added with a soft laugh, ''is it the firelight playing tricks with my eyes?''

Gilliane shifted her position, moving closer to the fire. ''I hope I do not insult you to say that you remarked about it because you yourself were lonely?''

His smile disappeared and he seriously studied her. ''Such sharp observations must stand you in good stead. A middle son must work hard to find a place for himself. Micheil clashed with Da over almost everything, but there was a bond between them that none could break, as he was the first son born. And Davey is the youngest, so we all protected him.''

''And your sister? The oldest, was she not? Your aunt believed there was not another maid in these lands as beautiful as she.''

Jamie turned from the fire and looked into the darkness. How could he explain the jealousy that so beset Bridget that she'd lied to them all and led the clan into a feud that lasted more than ten years?

"I have brought painful memories to your mind. I had no wish to upset you."

"You did not, Gilliane. Bridget was indeed the most bonnie lass, but she died last year." He heard her apology, but sought to change the subject and found a ready question.

"Is it true that beyond your aunt in France there is no family to protect you from de Orbrec?"

She had lulled herself into forgetting that accursed name, and here Jamie set it before her. "It is true. But that need not concern you or your family. I will do whatever is needed to see Lady Ailis free from his wicked clutches. And lest you think my calling him wicked is a maid's drama, it is not. I accused him of murder to you, and stand ready to do the same to any who will listen."

"But you never saw him do the deed, no matter what you believe to be true?"

"Aye, and there is the greatest of my problems, for none of the others that he married had family to worry over their deaths."

"A pattern of murder? For gain?" Jamie demanded.

"In my own case there is little enough—the manor house and the farms entailed to it. The coins are few, if any are left. When I fled my father's bedside it was done in the middle of the night, and I took nothing but my mare and the clothes I wore." Her voice broke on the last, and she turned from him.

But Jamie wanted to get to the heart of the matter and could not allow her emotions to interfere.

"And you swear that this contract de Orbrec claims to have, signed by your father's hand, has no binding power, no validity at all?"

Instead of answering him, Gilliane bowed her head. Her long tangled hair hid her from his sight. She fumbled with the knotted cord that held her soiled and torn habit closed. She finally grasped her small dagger and brought it forth.

But Jamie did not rest his gaze upon the gleaming, deadly little dagger she held. His gaze fastened on the velvet, shadowed cleft that her torn shift barely concealed.

"Sweet saints!" he muttered when he found his voice. He looked up then, and saw what she held. "Do you mean that paltry blade to be your protection?"

"Nay!" said Gilliane. "I will swear upon it!"

Chapter Eight

Jamie had a lusty nature, which many a willing lass was eager to satisfy. But he had been on the road for more than a week, and there had been no time to see to his needs. No opportunity. No one had ever aroused him as did the lovely Gilliane. And he had barely sampled her charms.

Bewildered, Gilliane continued to stare at him. "My protection? What threatens me here with you that I should require protection?"

Jamie gnawed his bottom lip. Could she truly be so innocent? Did she not see what state she brought him to? Heat built, and with it his frustration.

"Jamie?"

"From me. You need protection from me if you do not cover yourself. Quickly now."

She looked down at herself and saw what the parted cloth revealed. With a cry she clutched the robe closed. Heat rose and flushed her skin. She was mortified that he thought her so brazen as to do this apurpose.

When she regained the courage to look across the fire at him, his eyes were closed, his head bowed and resting within the spread fingers of one hand. His every breath appeared uneven, but she could not utter a sound.

Gilliane swallowed. She stared at his mouth. She longed to forget what he'd said, to take some insult from what he'd implied, but the very shape of his mouth with its sensuous fullness beckoned forth wicked thoughts. She did not understand why a man's mouth, most especially Jamie's, should be so finely molded and promise so much passion. What a delight it would be to have the kisses from his mouth belong only to her.

The heat inside her seemed to climb to an alarming degree that she should, even to herself, admit such a shameful thing. The priest said all such thoughts were lust and that was a sin. Even if one was married. She had never thought to question it before, but did so now. How could it be a sin to desire the man you had promised yourself to before the altar?

But there, a little voice pointed out, is your mistake. There is no promise before the Lord or anyone else between you and Jamie. Nor is there likely to be.

Gilliane rushed to stand.

"Where are you going?" Jamie demanded.

"Where I will offer you no temptation," she snapped.

"Are you still breathing?"

"Are you mad? You can see that for yourself."

"Then stay, Gilliane. Distance will only make you cold. Stay by the fire. The fault is not yours but mine. I apologize for making you uncomfortable with my unruly nature and uncalled-for remark. Come," he offered with a smile. "Sit and tell me what reason made you draw forth the dagger."

She stared down at the blade she still held, then recalled why she had it. "I drew it to use the hilt as a cross, to make a vow of truth."

"Oh, de Orbrec," he said, in such a dismissive manner that he could see her anger.

Green eyes flashing, Gilliane rounded the fire and fell to her knees before Jamie. "Do not ever take that man lightly. He is evil, I tell you. You would think to best him in an honest way, but he is sly and would try some trickery that could cost you your life."

"Do you desire his death?"

"No!" she cried, trembling.

"No?" Jamie repeated very, very softly, his body stiff with tension. He did not trust himself to touch her, and her expression appeared earnest, yet again the suspicion formed that by her own words she damned herself.

"Perhaps you would care to explain yourself, Lady Gilliane."

She felt chilled by the coldness of his eyes, and even more so by the tone of his voice. She sat back on her heels, sighing while she struggled to find the right words.

"I lied to you," she began.

"Somehow, that admission comes as no surprise to me."

His sarcasm hurt. She forced herself to ignore it. "I do desire Guy de Orbrec's death, but to admit even that is a sin I shall need to confess. Just as I shall confess that I pray for his death, but not by anyone known to me. Let the wasting sickness that brought my father's death take him. Or the pox, a more fitting end for one so evil. Or let some heavenly guided sword find its way into his black heart in the heat of battle. I revile him." She lifted the dagger with its two precious moonstones set within, holding it very carefully by the blade.

"I lost my rosary. This forms a cross and will do for my vow."

"Gilliane, don't. I need no vow. I should not doubt

you.'' Jamie knew why that even came into play. He wanted to bed her, and all else was tinted with that lustful need.

I will destroy myself if I thrice question her every word about de Orbrec.

Jamie tossed more wood on the fire, thankful they had not been followed by de Orbrec's men or the Rosses. He looked around for Cob, displeased with the thought that the man had overheard their talk. It took a moment to remember that Crisdean had left him near the horses. If the man tried to escape, the horses would rouse whoever was on watch.

Gilliane appeared to sag in place. ''There is little more I can do, Jamie, to make you believe me.'' Her eyes met his without any hint of evasion.

Jamie nodded, although to what he agreed he was not sure. Thankfully, she had not wrung a promise from him against killing de Orbrec. The man must not be allowed to continue preying on innocents. For touching a Gunn woman, the Norman had to die. Jamie came to his feet with a quick, graceful motion and held out his hand to help her rise.

''It is late and you are weary. Come, see the thick moss bed Crisdean fashioned for your rest. We added the horse blankets for warmth. Not sweet smelling, my lady, but the best comfort we can provide.''

''Stop treating me as if I will break, Jamie. I am stronger than you know.'' She not only laid her hand in his, but gripped his fingers as she rose and stood before him.

''You mock my care of you, Gilliane? Do not. I will treat you as you are to me. Precious.'' His voice grew husky and intense. ''Very precious, my lady.''

With those few words matters between them changed.

The hand she held was no longer a steadying point. The disquieting light in his brown eyes and the tension in his hand made her breath quicken. Not only her breath, but her whole body, she realized as he slid his other hand beneath her hair and cupped the back of her head. Now, she thought, now he would kiss her and she would have what she had longed for.

But Jamie's long fingers merely stroked the sensitive skin of her nape as he lowered his head and brushed his lips across her cheek.

''Sleep well,'' he murmured before releasing her to step away.

Bemused, Gilliane swayed where she stood. She had wanted his kiss and received one. There was no cause for anger, but guilt came. How could she think of dallying with Jamie when her whole purpose was to help free Ailis? It was Jamie's fault that she forgot the reason she was there. Jamie, tempting her with wicked thoughts of desire and kisses. But he had called her precious. Precious indeed. He would not think so if he knew she had lied to him to protect herself. And how dare he think she could sleep well with guilt and worry plaguing her?

Her retreat from the fire brought Jamie's sigh of relief. He had not handled that with his usual finesse. He knew she wanted him to kiss her. The desire was in her lovely eyes. The maid was pure temptation to him, and had he given in to his own need to taste her lips again... No! He had an equal desire to do her no dishonor.

Until she was his he would not claim her. The quiet night allowed him to be ruthlessly honest with himself. He had to put aside any and all suspicions that she'd lied to him. He felt he could, but there remained a nagging conviction that she hid something from him.

He wanted a clear mind to think over all she had told him and everything she had sworn was true.

Each time he believed he honed in on some half-truth, his thoughts turned to seeing her the first time and his senses replayed his first sweet taste of innocence from Gilliane's mouth.

It was more than desire that prompted him to claim her. There was her quiet strength and sweet nature, with hints of a temper that would make life lively.

Round and round went his thoughts, until he grew disgusted with himself.

He was selfish to the extreme in thinking of dallying with a noble-born maid like Gilliane when he should bring his thoughts to bear on his aunt's plight as hostage. If all that Gilliane told him about the Norman lord was true, then his aunt was truly in danger. He remembered too well the hot tempers that flared when she and his father had clashed over some matter. And later, when Micheil became clan chief, their fights over her care and wardship of Seana nic MacKay, who was now Jamie's sister by marriage, were as legendary.

He felt himself sink into a coil of despair. Surely his aunt, growing up as she had with his strong-minded, controlling father, would know the ways around a man like de Orbrec.

Or would she?

While unbeknownst to Lady Ailis that she centered in her nephew Jamie's thoughts, both he and his brothers figured high within her own. She had no doubt that they would come to rescue her.

Her initial shock at being carried off like a sack of barley soon gave way to righteous indignation and to the infamous Gunn temper at being so abused. Of course, the whole of her wrath was expressed in the silence of her mind, for she had been kept gagged and tied for the whole journey southwest to de Orbrec's stronghold.

Castres Keep was a forbidding sight to Ailis's eyes. The keep stood on the high, steep bank of the river, which protected it on one side. The other three were protected by deep ditches. New stone walls were being built to surround the inner keep. The walls gave an odd appearance, with the partial wooden palisades still erect, the uneven stone walls rising between them.

The gatehouses that controlled entry were of stone, and when the guards manning them recognized the banner of their lord, the drawbridge was lowered and the portcullis lifted to allow them to pass. The first small bailey was strewn with filth, bringing a roiling nausea to Ailis that she fought down lest she choke.

Her horse was led forward toward slowly opening gates that must have been hewn from great trees left whole, so massive were they.

The stench of the outer bailey carried over into this one. Her gaze passed over the donjon, its height impressive, as was the size of the hall attached to it. What Ailis focused upon was the sullen silence that greeted their entry, and the fearful, bruised faces of those servants present, who backed to the sheds or walls.

She could hear penned animals from beyond the bailey, but once more her gaze was drawn to the cringing figures of the grooms coming forth to take hold of the horses.

Marche came himself to lift Ailis from the saddle, but cramped from the continuous bindings, she could not stand after the rope binding her ankles was cut.

She bitterly resented being swept into Marche's arms with her hands still bound and the gag yet in place, then carried like some war prize or baggage up the steep wooden stains that led into the long hall.

Flaring torches lit the dank hall. The smell was a little better. She saw dogs prowling the rushes for bones or scraps. Here, too, the servants shrank back to walls as Marche walked toward the roaring fire in the great hearth. A finely carved chair sat before the blaze, its back to the hall, and a small table beside the chair held a finely wrought goblet.

"My lord, we are returned."

"I had word of your coming an hour ago. Your man tells me we have a hostage with a rich demand for ransom."

"They defied your order. I acted as I thought best."

"Will they pay it, Louis?" The question was asked as the man rose from the chair and turned to face them.

Ailis could not stop her eyes from widening. If this was Guy de Orbrec, he was truly a creature welded by Satan's hand as pure temptation for all who gazed upon his face.

The old Roman coins that filled one of the treasure boxes in the storeroom at Halberry Castle could have used his face for the handsome profile etched upon the silver and gold. Was his comeliness the reason those poor young women had fallen so easily into his clutches? Face and form were without warmth, beautiful but uninviting, for she could see into his eyes, and there was no soul hidden within their black depths. Coal-black like the thick curls that tumbled over his forehead. No scar marred his perfectly sculpted features. His form was slender, dressed in rich cloth heavily embroidered with silver thread.

Her gaze went again to his face, almost as if she could not believe her eyes. Fine brows arched smoothly over large, almond shaped eyes. The nose was thin, perfectly straight, and the mouth a classical cut that neither smiled nor moved as Ailis stared at him. Vain. The man was vain about his handsomeness. He enjoyed holding his still pose while she gaped like a country maid.

Truly, the sight of him had thrown her off balance, and all the planned speeches to demand her freedom and return to the abbey died. She recoiled, if only inwardly, from the black charm of his smile.

"Welcome to my keep, Lady Ailis," de Orbrec said in a rich, warm voice.

And then he turned to Louis. "You have been remiss in allowing our hostage to greet me properly. See to it!"

Ailis expected the gag to be removed, the ties cut, but what she got was Louis's strong hands on her shoulders pressing her to her knees. Her knees! As if he were a king, that she had to bow her earthly body to him! Outraged, Ailis fought against the hands that held her.

"Do you, a woman of the cloth, go against the Lord's will?" de Orbrec demanded with mock sternness. "Are not women subservient to men? 'Tis a shame, Louis, that you cannot see the eyes. I believe they shoot the flames of hell at me."

Ailis cringed at the laughter that followed, and her body, although strong through continuous hard work, had been deprived of sustenance, rest and water for almost a day. She felt herself weakening in her struggle to remain standing.

"Down, I say," de Orbrec demanded again. "No woman stands within my presence. On her knees or her back, 'tis the place for worthless females. I grow impatient, madam."

Then Ailis understood. He wanted her defiance. It would allow him to take harsher measures to have his order obeyed. Evil—so Gilliane had called him, and so

Ailis felt him to be. He stood gloating as she physically resisted.

"Perhaps she is one of those women who enjoy being beaten." The Norman stroked his chin. He shook his head. "Louis, you disappoint me. Have I not shown you how best to bring obedience? Kick her feet out from under her and she will fall quick enough."

"But, my lord, she is—"

"A woman and no more. A hostage worth some coin. I will not kill her. Bah! I lose my taste with this one. Secure her in the pit."

He turned his back as Louis shifted his grip on Ailis and led her to a door on the far side of the hall.

"Do not resist him, madam," Louis whispered as he pulled open the stout wooden door. "You will only make your time here hell for yourself. He will not kill you, but you will pray for death."

Ailis shuddered, in part at his words, and in part at where he was leading her. Down the stone steps into the lower levels where most Scottish keeps had their pit prisons. Halberry had one, but in her time of living there, she had known of no one kept within its small damp space.

So deep was she in her own thoughts, Ailis had not realized that Louis had a torch, which he set in the iron wall bracket while he pulled on the metal set in the floor. Ailis felt cold sweat break out on her body. Pit prison!

She turned and raised her bound hands to him. She begged with her gaze to be untied.

"It will be dark down below. I will see to securing a candle for you and food. Now, it's best you go quickly, for you've angered him."

He slit the rope that bound her wrists, and the gag as well, but before Ailis could take a breath, he was pushing her down the wooden ladder into the pit.

She stood at the bottom and watched as the light faded and the hatch slammed shut. There she stood, leaning against the wood, shuddering and fighting tears.

She felt stripped naked. Her habit, her office, her place in the world as she knew it had been ripped from her. She was as any other female, the one thing she had fought against all her life: chattel to be disposed of by a man.

Guy de Orbrec could not bring her to her knees, but her despair and her need for a renewal of her faith did.

And so she began her prayers. *"Ave Maria, gratia plena, Dominus tecum…"*

Chapter Nine

They came deep in the night to Halberry Castle, which allowed Gilliane to rouse long enough to be impressed by massive stone. There was an immediate welcome when Jamie called out to the guards on the walls. Within minutes the drawbridge was lowered over a trench cut from rock. Halberry had been built on a promontory that jutted out to sea. The sharp tang of salt air breathed life into Gilliane's weary body.

Jamie carried her before him on his horse and lowered his head to whisper her awake. "We are home, Gilliane."

Home. She heard the word, but home to her was a small manor where a groom would run to hold her horse. Here all seemed confusion as dozens of men milled about the bailey. She shrank against the warmth of Jamie's body when he was hailed from the far end of the open yard.

There was welcome here, strong and warm, with each voice calling out for Jamie's notice. He released her into the arms of one of the grooms, his gaze and attention on the young man running across the bailey.

"Davey!" Jamie cried.

In the light of the flaring torches that sprang up all over, Gilliane saw the family resemblance between the brothers.

This young man, then, had to be the youngest. Jamie clasped him as soon as he had dismounted, and the grooms—it took two to hang on to Killen's bridle—led the stallion toward the stable.

With his brother close by his side, Jamie made his way through the press of talking, gesticulating men, greeting everyone he met.

Gilliane stood alone, staring after him, wondering what she was to do. Jamie appeared to have completely forgotten about her.

She barely kept him in sight, but saw the two dogs that leaped for his attention. Monstrous in size as they were, she feared they would knock him over.

Jamie laughed as he fondled them both equally. "Lord, Davey, what have you been feeding them? Gently, Jennet, and you, Cudgel, be still," he ordered. It took a sharp rap to their long snouts before the animals stopped leaping at him, but the wagging tails of his brother's dogs, nearly the size of ponies, beat painfully against Jamie's legs.

"Where is Micheil?" he asked then. "I know the news I bear is none to the good, but surely our brother and chief will come greet me."

"Be not angry. Och, Jamie, Micheil is sore wounded. 'Tis a hurt that will heal, but he's taken a fever, and Seana's like a mountain cat with a cub an' will no' allow him to move about. Be thankful," Davey added with a deep and heartfelt sigh, "that you've been away. Between Micheil's black temper and that witch woman he's taken to wife, the keep rings with curses and cries."

Jamie threw back his head and laughed. "She made him crazed from the day he met her and knew not that he sought to seduce his own betrothed." He flung his arm over his brother's shoulders. "My men?"

"Safe, as is the good sister that accompanied them.

Truly, Jamie, Micheil's in a raging temper over this kidnapping of Aunt Ailis. And the woman? Where is—''

''Sweet Mercy! Gilliane!'' Jamie drew away from his brother, pushing and shoving aside any who stood in his way. He found her standing where she had been left, swaying on her feet, eyes filled with exhaustion and a little fear as he came forward.

''Gilliane, forgive me.''

She had no chance to respond beyond emitting a tiny shriek as he swept her up into his arms and carried her through the crowd of men, who fell silent and cleared a path as they approached.

Warmth assailed her once they reached the great hall. Stout logs blazed in two huge hearths. Bright, bold tapestries hung from the wooden rafters to keep the sea dampness at bay. She had little chance to see more, for Jamie hurriedly crossed to the stairs that wound upward, calling over his shoulder for someone named Peigi.

The shaft of jealousy that pierced her was unwarranted, but Gilliane suddenly feared that Jamie had a woman of his own and called her to him. Gilliane fought her exhaustion and the cradling safety of Jamie's arms.

''Still your struggles, Gilliane. It is not much farther. I know they'll have a place ready for you.''

A moment later Jamie set her down before a wooden door. ''Bide here. I need to see how my brother fares. And Peigi will be along to see to your comfort.''

''Jamie, wait.'' She grabbed for his arm. ''Sister Ellen? Where is she?''

''Here. Well, somewhere about. Peigi will find her for you. Just wait for me.''

Gilliane trembled where she leaned against the stone wall. Jamie had gone to see his brother—the chief of Clan Gunn, and the man who held her fate within his hands. It would be upon his order that she would be sent back to the Norman, sent into his clutches to free a Gunn woman.

Merciful Lord, she prayed, help me find a way to free Lady Ailis and keep myself free as well.

Gilliane leaned her head against the stone wall and stared at the flaring torch that lit the winding stair. She felt leached of any strength to fight, to think, even to pray.

Jamie closed the door to the anteroom softly. He disliked leaving Gilliane before she was settled, but his own selfish need to be sure that his brother had truly taken no serious wound overruled his desire.

The room was furnished with riches from their storerooms, which Micheil had thrown open to his bride. True, she had given him his heir before they'd said their final vows before the priest, but the long, long betrothal was as good as marriage in many eyes.

Seana had lost no time in refurbishing these rooms. Rushes were gone from the floor, and in their place rested the brilliant-hued carpets of red and blue, gained through trade or piracy over the last two hundred years.

Two elaborately carved wood chairs, their seats softened by costly velvet cushions and foot stools, were drawn close to the stone hearth, where a fire burned brightly. Tall candlesticks made of twisted iron held thick candles that lit the corner of the room with a soft glow. A small side table held a silver wine flagon and goblets on a tray.

Jamie glanced at the wall hangings covered with scenes of gardens and maidens fair attended by tall young lordlings wooing with harp and lute. The colors had faded, but he remembered them well from his childhood, for his mother and her maids had worked the cloth and sewn for hours to create these tapestries.

The room was warm and peaceful. He felt the tension drain from him. And then he remembered Gilliane. He was sure that Seana would not mind if she waited in here.

Jamie poured wine into two goblets and carried one with him to the door.

Gilliane was no longer there. He rightly assumed that Peigi had come to fetch her. He closed the door and drank the wine himself, not only to relieve his thirst after the leagues they had traveled that day, but also to fortify himself to see his brother.

He refilled the goblet and took it with him to the door on the far wall. He knocked softly.

"Come!"

The highly irritated voice of his brother Micheil beckoned him to enter. Jamie loved him, and respected him, for Micheil had borne the heaviest weight from a young age, not only of fighting their enemies and waging a blood feud, but for having honored his blood oath to their father.

Jamie schooled his face to hide his thoughts as he approached the bed. The thick velvet hangings were tied back. A fire was lit and smaller branches of twisted iron had burning candles to allow him to see clearly. To his surprise there was no sign of his sister by marriage.

"Alone, Micheil? I thought from what Davey told me, that I'd find that witch woman hovering above you, counting your every breath."

Jamie went to the chair pulled close to the bed, and removed the embroidered cloth from its cushion. He saw that his brother was propped up by a profusion of pillows. He set the cushion aright and sat down.

"So where is she?"

"With the bairn. He fusses when she is not there to tuck him in with a last kiss, or song, or whatever else his little heart fancies. She's spoiling my son with her indulgences and I—''

"You," Jamie interrupted, "haven't the heart to curb her. None of us do. Sweet saints, Micheil, after losing him—och! I do not wish to remember those black days."

"They have not ended, Jamie."

Jamie sensed more than saw his brother's growing agitation. "Micheil, dinna fash yourself. There's worries enough happening now without reliving the past."

"Aye, I know it well. More than you ken. But I worry for her, Jamie. Having the bairn ripped from her arms only hours after his birth, and then lost to her until we discovered him in…our sister's arms, and her ready to plunge them both into the sea, would unbalance the mind of a saint. 'Tis painful to recall it. Dinna look at me so, Brother. You know I'm right."

"Aye, you are. You weren't yourself then, either. But give her time, Micheil. She'll soon see she and the boy are safe here. Tell me instead, Brother, how it is that your arm's bound tight to your chest. I thought Da taught you better how to fight."

Smiling as his brother's face grew a ruddy color, Jamie sipped his wine, satisfied that he had turned Micheil's black thoughts away from the past.

"Da did teach me better, you young fool." Micheil's piercing blue eyes took in his brother's tired face, the dark shadows beneath his eyes and his dust-laden clothing.

"Tell me—" Jamie started to say.

"Tell *me*," Micheil demanded at the same moment.

Jamie gestured with the goblet for Micheil to go first.

"You've had no easy time, Jamie."

"True enough. I'm sure you've had most of the story by now, and I'll tell you the rest, but first I want to know how you took your wound."

"You're a stubborn piece of work, Brother."

"Aye." Jamie laughed. "Runs in the blood, don't you ken. I've sent a man to watch this Norman's keep. Oh," he said, rubbing his forehead, "would you believe me so tired I can't remember who I sent?"

"I believe it." Micheil lifted his left hand to push at the unruly lock of black hair that fell over his forehead. He alone favored their father in looks. His glacial-blue eyes that so resembled the deepest part of a loch fixed on his middle brother's face.

He was heartsick that his dearest dream of bringing peace to his clan was nigh impossible with the blood debt that the Keiths demanded. He was sickened, too, by the need to tell Jamie their enemies' latest vow.

"How much did Davey tell you?" Micheil asked.

"Very little. He feared this fever you've gotten, but he didn't have a chance to tell me more because I had forgotten Gilliane…the lady Gilliane de Verrill," he hastily corrected, seeing Micheil's start at his using her first name. "I can tell you true, Brother, I understand why the Norman wants her to wife." Jamie drained the wine from his goblet.

"Jamie," Micheil warned in a soft voice, "dinna set your heart on her. She's the means to win our aunt's freedom. I'd no' have you forget that."

"'Tis my chief that speaks?"

"'Tis both your brother and your laird who demands this from you."

"So be it." Jamie rose and almost kicked the chair aside.

"Jamie, you cannot leave without telling me what befell you."

"I'm not leaving you. I only go for more wine to wash the dust from my throat."

"Bitter dust?"

"Dust of the long ride, Micheil. I've no desire to quarrel with you. I rarely do."

Micheil sank back against the pillows. His whole right side ached from the tight binding and the bruises he'd taken. What manner of maid was this Lady Gilliane that his brother took quick offense at his warning? He nearly growled with his impatience at being laid up at such a time. And Jamie knew nothing of their other guests or the reasons they had come.

To cool the heat in Jamie's eyes, Micheil spoke first when he returned and once more sat beside the bed. "Since I know your patience is greater than mine, and that you'll wait me out, I'll tell my tale first. We rode out to drive off a band of Keiths raiding the north farms. What the devil they wanted with bone-and-hide animals that had no chance to fatten is beyond my ken. But it turned out to be a cleverly laid trap for us. Once we closed in and fought with them, another band of those betrayers came up behind us.

"I swear to you, Brother, I know not how we escaped with our lives. I still shudder to relive those moments. 'Twas my life they wanted more than any other. I was fighting off two of them when I took a blow to my back—how like those cowardly whoresons! I rid myself of the two, but two more came from behind and knocked me from Breac's saddle—no mean feat that. I saw them attempting to broach my horse, and ran forward when again they attacked. Between their horses and swords, I fell with a sickening jolt. My collarbone's broken. It took three of my men to beat them off me.

"Now this fever besets me, and it comes and goes. Seana and Peigi conspire to keep me abed, and Davey abets them, but there is much to see to, and I cannot do it from here.''

"Seana's cozened you into a soft prison, Micheil. But you know she does it for love of you. And Davey has had a soft spot for her from the very first. Much as I hate to press you now, we need talk of this ransom for our aunt and this Norman who dared take her.''

"And the maid? You have her here safe?''

"Aye, she's safe. And she's fair, Micheil.''

Jamie looked away, but his husky voice once more sent an alarm through Micheil, who attempted to raise himself up. A choked growl escaped him. Pain shot through his body.

Jamie jumped up, nearly spilling his wine when he leaned over to press his hand against Micheil's good shoulder.

"Calm yourself. I took your warning, Micheil. There is no need for another.''

"'Tis my own frustration at being laid low that caused this.''

"Well, don't be a bletherin' fool, Micheil, and seek to undo all the good your wife has done. If she finds you upset, your Seana will have my head on her platter. And Micheil, I've a sore need for my wits now.''

Micheil grabbed his brother's arm. "Aye, more than you know. This ransom of our aunt will fall to you alone, Jamie.'' Micheil calmed himself and motioned his brother back to his seat. "I've yet to deal with the families of Niall and Fiona. They've come seeking to reclaim their bodies for burial in their own plots. I've a mind to turn them away without what they've come for, but it's foolish to make them pay for acts of betrayal against the clan that they had no part of.

"It galls me to deal honorably with them. When I think

how we harbored that viper Fiona, as she filled our sister with her poison—as well as my bed. And Niall, that bastard, encouraging them both every step of the way..."

"Micheil, see to yourself. Leave off the blame for Fiona. You couldn't have known what jealousy would drive her to. And what difference can it make to grant their families the peace of having their bodies laid to rest where they will? You're chief of the clan. And the good of the clan must be set before your personal desires."

"Will you tell me my role now?"

"Nay! Bury your black temper, Micheil. I've said I'll not quarrel with you. But all this leads me to think that there is something you're not telling me."

"I sued for peace with the Keiths. Aye, I know we talked against my doing so, but the guilt of the lad's death lay heavily on me. George sent his answer. He'll not rest till he has our three heads hanging from his wall."

"The lad killed himself by his attempt to escape, Micheil. We told him no harm would come to him. Didn't his father or clan teach him what it meant to be hostage for the clan's good behavior? Where lies the fault for his death? Had we a strong king there'd be a place to bring complaint without fighting the same battles over and over."

Jamie gulped his wine, trying to cool his own temper. Of all times for Micheil not to have his full strength, this had to be the worst. He could not admit that to his brother, for it would inflame his very dangerous temper. With all the clan needed to fight off the raiding Keiths, there'd be few enough men for Jamie to have with him when he went to ransom his aunt. He knew he would not take many. He intended to challenge de Orbrec to personal combat, but none need know of his plans as yet.

A pair of very sharp eyes noted the flushed look on

Jamie's face and the more ruddy complexion of Micheil. On soft slippers she entered the room silently.

"Jamie, what have you done to him? I knew I should not have left you two alone."

Jamie stood and moved away from the bed. "Aye, blame me. But 'tis his own temper that makes a sumph of him to move as he cannot."

"Who are you calling soft and stupid?"

Jamie hugged Seana and whispered, "He's in the devil's own temper and I swear 'tis not all my fault." He released her and stood back as she neared the bed. Seana, if it were possible, grew more lovely each time he saw her. Jamie kept silent as she scolded her husband. The scold was lovingly given, and to his relief, he saw that Micheil's scowl had disappeared.

Seana wore no veil, claiming it reminded her of the nearly ten years she had spent in the abbey with nuns, her husband's aunt chief among those who'd held her captive. But she had forgiven those who had played a part in the terrible clan feud between her family and Micheil's. Her honey-shaded braids swung free as she set the bed to rights.

"Micheil, I swear you need a keeper. An' don't be giving me your black looks or that devil's temper because your brother is here. You can lie still or he'll be out on his ear for undoing all my good work. Och! You're worse than our son. Stop squirming about. You'll loosen the binding, and if that break sets wrong you'll never hold a shield again."

She barely kept tears back as she scolded, for to lose Micheil after all they had been through would be to lose her own life.

Seana turned to Jamie. "'Tis truly beyond my ken how he thinks to heal without giving himself time enough. I know you need to talk to him, Jamie, but please, cannot the rest wait till morn?''

"Seana! Cease!" Micheil ordered. "Leave him be. Tend to your woman's duties. Have his bed freshened and a hot bath sent. And food. Oh, and the maid'll need seeing to.''

"Mo ghraigh," she whispered. The look in her misty gray eyes fringed with thick lashes held Micheil for a moment before a wicked smile curved her lips. "Aye, my heart, will you give up soldiering to be teaching me the ways of a mistress of her own keep?''

"Nay, 'tis no' what I meant.''

"All has been seen to. Peigi has taken the lady Gilliane in hand. I put her in the inner tower room, where she'll be warmer. As for your brother, all is ready and welcome in his chamber. Now, won't you rest, love? No more can be decided this night.''

"She is right, Micheil," Jamie said before his brother spoke against his wife's wishes. "I'll come break my fast with you if Seana will give me permission to enter her rooms.''

"The lack didn't stop you from coming tonight.''

"How such a lovely face can hold such a tart tongue is enough to plague my thoughts, dearest sister.''

"Go on with you, Jamie. And yes, come join him in the morning.''

"Will you be letting me have a look at my nephew then?'' Jamie backed toward the door as he asked. "I swear that Heth must be crawling by now.''

"Jamie, come back. I'm not done with you.''

"Sleep well, Brother.''

"Jamie! 'Tis your chief that—''

The rest of Micheil's speech was cut off as Jamie

closed the door. He left their quarters to seek his own room.

Then he would find out where Peigi had put Gilliane. He needed to see for himself that she was well cared for. More he would not admit to himself.

Chapter Ten

Gilliane had been led to a small chamber she would have to herself. She stared gratefully at the first bed she had seen in days.

The plump pillows invited her to lie down. She removed Jamie's wool cloak and folded it, laying it atop the chest set against one wall.

Clan Gunn was rich indeed to have costly carpet laid over the stone floor. It felt soft beneath her feet as she moved to stand before the fire, to receive its warmth.

She started nervously as the door opened. The old woman, Peigi, who had brought her here, entered the room, followed by serving men carrying a huge wooden tub and leather buckets that steamed with hot water for her bath. More men came after them with buckets of cold water. The moment they were gone, Peigi closed the door behind them and, to Gilliane's surprise, drew the latch.

"I'll no' be havin' me Jamie payin' ye a visit while ye're indecent, my lady."

"Oh, Jamie will not come. He is most concerned about his brother."

"Aye, that's why the fool left ye alone. Dinna think I'll be letting him get away with forgetting his manners."

Gilliane could not help smiling. Somehow she had not expected to hear strong, stalwart Jamie spoken about in such a manner.

Peigi drew a stool nearer the fire and set down her burden.

''Lessen' ye be thinkin' I'd speak with disrespect for him, I'll tell ye true that I swaddled his bottom. He's near my own boy, like his brothers.''

She came forward and helped Gilliane discard her travel-stained robe, then drew the fine linen shift from her.

Gilliane sat on the small wood chair near the fire while Peigi pinned up her hair.

'''Tis a pity I canna wash it now, lass. Ye'd be sittin' by the fire till dawn to dry it. Go on with ye, lass. Get in. An' dinna think I won't have a talk with me Jamie over his careless care of ye.''

''Nay, Peigi. It was not his fault. None of this is.''

''Och! Ye've a sweet nature to defend him. Go on now. Get in the tub lest the water cools an' ye take a fearsome chill.''

Gilliane sank into the hot water. A sigh of bliss escaped her lips as her aching body was soothed by the water's heat. She could no longer think about what was to come, but simply put herself into Peigi's capable hands.

Peigi used a cloth with fine milled soap to wash Gilliane's back, but she handed both over when Gilliane asked for them.

While Gilliane washed herself, Peigi heated stones at the fire's edge, then carefully wrapped them in cloth. She placed them beneath the covers to warm the sheets.

Gilliane felt the tension of the last few days drain from her. This was the life she'd had before de Orbrec made his infamous demand. This was part of what he had stolen from her—this simple enjoyment in feeling clean, safe, warm and well cared for.

Guilt assaulted her. The Norman would care nothing about Lady Ailis's comfort. Gilliane prayed that someone within his keep would find the courage to ease Ailis's lot while he held her.

The water cooled. She stood and Peigi rinsed her. She shivered as she stood by the hearth while Peigi used thick cloths to dry her.

Peigi then pulled a soft wool bed robe from the chest, telling Gilliane the lovely shade of green came from the dye of the broom plant.

"Our laird's own lady sent this for ye, lass."

Tears welled in Gilliane's eyes. It was a simple kindness, but her emotions were overwrought and she could not even answer Peigi's plea as to why she cried.

"'Tis lovely." She sniffed, rubbing her fingers over the flowers embroidered around the loose cuffs.

"Lovely it might be, but ye'll be catchin' yer death less ye put it on."

Gilliane slipped into the robe and realized that the laird's lady was a bit shorter than she, for the hem barely reached her ankles. She wrapped her arms around her waist, wondering how she could every repay the Gunns.

Peigi opened the door and beckoned in two maids, one carrying a tray and the other a small side table to set it upon.

"This be Cuìni," Peigi said, pointing to a young girl with a shy smile and a single thick, wheat-colored braid. "The other one's Nora. They'll see to havin' the tub emptied and removed. An' no dawddlin', mind ye," she added as warning to the maids. "Now, lass, best sit before the fire. Have the mulled wine. The recipe's secret, an' near a hundred years old. I can promise ye'll sleep well if ye drink it. An' eat,'' she admonished, going to the door. ''I'll be back to see ye to bed.''

Gilliane nodded. She took her seat before the fire. She lifted the silver-chased goblet and drank deeply of the wine which instantly warmed her. The taste was rich with spices. She understood now what her tired mind had been telling her for some time. The clan Gunn would have no trouble in raising the ransom, a thing she had feared to even speak aloud.

She ignored the work of the maids, who used the leather buckets to empty the tub of water, then summoned the men to remove it from the room.

Finally alone, Gilliane sat and stared at the flames. She admitted to herself that she felt lost without Jamie's strong presence. Had her flight and de Orbrec's threat so weakened her that she feared to be alone?

She did not even know how to summon one of the maids to bring her to Jamie.

Bring her to Jamie! What was she thinking? Such an act would surely draw the wrath of the chief and his lady down upon her.

Why the wanton thought of needing Jamie near? Gilliane refused to seek an answer. She only knew the need was there. She drained the goblet, feeling a heat spread to chase the chill from her.

Gilliane did not hesitate to refill her goblet. She glanced at the rest of the tray. Half a cold fowl; a dish of some crumbly yellow cheese; another with salted salmon and thick slices of buttered bread; a small wooden bowl of cracked nuts and raisins—this was a feast after the poor fare she had shared with Jamie and Crisdean.

Naught tempted her to eat, but then she thought of short, round Peigi with her small dark raisin eyes and that motherly, scolding voice. Gilliane forced herself to nibble the bread and cheese.

Finishing the second goblet of wine, she was about to pour out the last of it when Peigi returned.

"Lass, ye've no' eaten? 'Tis late, but I'll stir the kitchen wenches to find somethin' more to your likin'."

Gilliane found she was having some difficulty answering. She blinked and saw that Peigi was leaning over her.

"Och! I've made the wine too strong for ye."

"'Tis fine wine, Peigi," Gilliane managed to reply at last. "Very fine wine. I am warm for the first time in days, and I have no worries now—no thoughts at all."

Peigi smiled and brushed her hand across Gilliane's forehead. "There's a good lass. Come, I'll be helpin' ye to bed now."

"But 'tis warm and cozy by the fire." Gilliane reached up and managed to catch hold of the old woman's hand. "Peigi, tell me about Jamie."

"That's the way of it? Och, lass, dinna be settin' yer heart on that one. Ye'll be breakin' it for true if ye do."

Embarrassment added to the flush on Gilliane's cheeks. She looked away from the dark eyes that seemed to read more than she wanted them to.

"I have not repaid your kindness well, Peigi. 'Tis sorry I am to have asked. I was so sure that you would all blame me for what befell Lady Ailis."

"How, lass?"

"If I had not run at my father's bidding—"

"Dinna fash yerself so. I heard the tale. Ye could do naught else. None will harm ye here, lass. As for our lady, we all pray for her safe return. I know her well of old. She was still a maid in her brother's home when I came to give me service here under the old laird. I was a wee maid then and sent to serve the lady Ailis. Oh, she was a merry one. Merry unless she crossed her temper with her brother. How the stones would ring with their fightin'! She'd have none of the men he offered to her. Our lady wanted no man to have a hold over her, an' in the end she had her own way, taking the veil.

"This Norman that holds her, will he harm her?"

Gilliane's grip tightened on Peigi's hand. Fear came rushing back until she shook with it.

"Lass, lass, what's beset you?" Peigi cried out.

"Sweet saints, Peigi! What have you done to her?" Jamie demanded as he stepped through the door.

"Naught! Naught, I swear. I but asked of the Norman who holds our lady."

"Jamie!"

Gilliane's cry brought him swiftly to her side and he scooped her up into his arms, holding her tightly. "'Tis all right, Gilliane. He can't harm you here. And he dares not harm a hair on my aunt's head."

"Jamie, Jamie, you know not what you say. Her hair is shorn," Gilliane mumbled against the warmth of his neck.

"Aye, 'tis true enough," he answered with a laugh, but his gaze caught Peigi's. "Fetch me some barley-bree."

"But I've given the lass mulled wine, Jamie."

"Fetch me the whiskey, Peigi. Quickly. Can't you see how she's shaking?"

He sat in the chair, cradling Gilliane against him. "She's a carlin—an old woman—that Peigi. Fine and strong, but there's times when I wish she'd still her wagging tongue."

"Do not blame her," Gilliane whispered, snuggling against his chest. The heat of his body lessened the sudden coldness of hers. Here was where she had wanted to be and where she'd dared not allow her thoughts to drift. But

he had come when she needed him. He was a man a
woman could place her faith and trust in. A man a woman
could love. The thought slipped far too easily into place.
Time and events made her dependent upon Jamie. She
could not trust herself to believe what she felt.

"'Tis my own guilt that made me behave so," she said,
when he made no attempt to speak.

Her admission sobered Jamie. He, too, had bathed and
eaten, but he had indulged himself in a drink more potent
than mulled wine. He had taken a few drams of their own
home brew, a malted Scotch so thick a man could float
an egg upon it.

"You've naught to feel guilty about, lass. You swore
you had naught to do with de Orbrec's plan. I believe
you. The guilt belongs to that Norman and his men."

"Jamie! You cannot understand the guilt I feel. Here I
am, safe and warm and welcome in the midst of your
family. Your poor aunt is likely confined without any
comforts. They say he has a pit prison. Oh, Jamie, would
he put her there?"

"Stop, lass, stop. We canna know." The anguish in her
voice sent his mellow mood fleeing. "I swear to you I'll
have her free. Now hush. You'll make yourself ill."

"You are sweet to comfort me yet again, Jamie."

"Nay. I've my own guilt plaguing me. If I hadn't been
robbed of the furs by those Keiths, I would have been at
the abbey that day."

"But Jamie," she protested, holding him tightly, "you
could not have known what was to happen."

"And you did?"

"I knew he would send men after me. I never believed
that he would dare take your aunt and hold her for ransom."

"So there you have it, lass. We both feel guilt over

something that neither of us could have known. And if you continue to put yourself on the rack over this, you'll make yourself ill. And I need you, Gilliane. I need you...."

His voice trailed off in a whisper. He was sober enough to realize the danger of remaining here with her.

The heat of their bodies released the lavender scent clinging to her skin. Jamie was far too aware of her slender body pressed so trustingly against his. She had a supple, feminine strength that would mate perfectly with his male power. His gaze drifted over her, the bed robe offering little protection, clinging as it was to the curve of her breast, hip and thigh. Her fire-warmed richness surrounded him.

"Gilliane," he whispered, his body fully aroused as he gently touched her chin and slowly lifted her face to his. He thought of his admission that he needed her, and knew the bone-deep truth of it. He had claimed her as his and he would fight anyone who tried to take her from him.

She saw through tear-filled eyes how firelight sharpened the planes of his face, the straight nose and firm mouth. She could not meet his gaze, but watched instead how the play of the flames burnished his dark hair with reddish and golden lights. Her hand came up to cradle his cheek, her thumb resting lightly on his lips, but the temptation proved too much and she traced their shape, feeling his breath's ebb and flow. She wanted so much to blame her wanton touch on the mulled wine she'd had, but that would be a lie.

Jamie held her tenderly, with her head resting on his chest, against his heart, his arms nestling her. Gilliane sensed her body softening as he very slowly rocked her, his undemanding gentleness lulling her into the false assumption of safety, as if nothing could assault her.

She closed her eyes.

Jamie drew a sharp breath. She appeared lit by a warm bronze fire. A few loosened tendrils of her hair curled about her pale face. Her thick lashes lay like golden smudges on her silken cheeks. But his gaze was most strongly drawn by the sensuous shape of her mouth. He wanted to touch those lips as she had his.

The gentle rocking ceased. Gilliane did not open her eyes. His lips brushed her hair, her temple, her brow, and still she made no move to pull away, no protest.

His arms tightened as he drew her closer still, held her hard against him so that his skin was on fire where her taut nipples pressed his chest.

She trembled at the touch of his lips against her soft mouth, which lifted instinctively, blindly, to mate with his. His hands moved caressingly over her, stilling any fear before it could take hold. He wooed her mouth with tiny kisses to the corner, with the heated glide of his tongue on her bottom lip.

"Sweet, sweet," he murmured. "You've the taste of warm honey."

One hand slid beneath her braids to lift and hold her head as he claimed her mouth with barely leashed passion.

Her lips parted slowly beneath his searching mouth. His hand soothed her restless move with a gentle touch that enticed her dormant passion to arousal.

Jamie slid the bed robe aside to bare one shoulder. She whimpered softly as his mouth trailed kisses down her neck to her shoulder, where he tasted the incredible sweetness of her skin before returning once more to lay claim to her lips. He felt a deep hunger stir within him and knew that Gilliane responded to the same. It was that bewitching spell that she had cast over him from the first moment he had seen her. He was lost to his reeling senses.

Gilliane was lost in the heated play of his carnal mouth. She was moaning, her gentle whimpers of pleasure breaking into breathy gasps when his lips left hers.

"Jamie?" The poignantly innocent eyes she raised to him would have melted stone.

But Jamie was not stone; he was heated blood that drummed one thought and need into his mind—to carry her to the waiting bed and satiate both their senses and bodies until neither of them could move.

Her head fell back against his hand, her mouth a most tantalizing promise.

But Jamie's sharpened senses heard the scrape of a shoe on the stone stairs and knew his time alone with the lovely and tempting Gilliane was at an end. He gently drew her robe up to cover the bared skin, regret darkening his eyes. He eased her up to a sitting position and whispered a warning of Peigi's return against the delicate shell of her ear.

Gilliane, bemused by the passionate kisses and now his sudden withdrawal, had not Jamie's skill to dissemble before Peigi's eyes.

It would have done her no good to try. She could not hide the reddened lips, nor the lambent look in her green eyes.

Peigi did nothing to hide her disapproval of Jamie taking unfair advantage of the maid. She did not say a word as she handed over the barley-bree he had sent her to fetch. But she refused to move from their side as he held the edge of the cup to Gilliane's lips and encouraged her to sip the whiskey.

Gilliane turned her head aside after one sip. She held herself very still, afraid to move or to speak. She was still in thrall to those passionate minutes spent in Jamie's arms, knowing full well that she should not have allowed him the liberties he took, but not knowing how to fight him and her own desire for more.

After one burning taste he had stopped pressing the whiskey on her. There was no longer any chill to chase; if anything, she was too hot.

She barely held on to Jamie when he rose with her in his arms and carried her over to the bed. He held her, but did not meet her entreating gaze as Peigi removed the now cooled stones from the bed. He set Gilliane down and she wanted to cry out for him not to leave her, but there was Peigi, coming between them to settle the soft covers over her.

"Sleep with only the sweetest dreams, Gilliane," Jamie whispered before he left her.

Peigi bustled about, snuffing the candles, adding a log to the fire. Finally, lifting the tray, she whispered her own wishes for a good night's rest, and Gilliane was alone.

Gilliane slipped her hand from the cover and touched her lips. They felt different, slightly full, still warm. She could both feel and taste the velvety heat of Jamie's mouth on hers. Within her was a hunger that left her shaken by its intensity. The passion between them made her head spin.

She heard again his dark whisper saying that he needed her. She dismissed the fleeting notion that he'd meant her presence being needed to ransom his aunt. It was the man who whispered of need to a woman he wanted.

Could Jamie learn to love her? And what of her own growing feelings for him? Could she call them love?

Or was she confusing the desire he aroused with those tender feelings dear to a woman's heart?

She had acted the wanton with him and it was wrong. Even worse was the fact that Peigi had witnessed the result.

Rolling to her side, Gilliane stared at the bed hangings. It was more than past time for her to be honest with herself.

Her emotions were in turmoil. She wondered if Jamie thought she'd flung herself at him for protection from de Orbrec. But that alone had not drawn her to him. There was an innate gentleness in Jamie that only added to his masculine strength. Even his admission of his own guilty feelings tonight had been made with the thought of easing her distress. How much easier for him to keep silent and let her wrestle with the burden of her guilt for bringing this trouble to Clan Gunn.

And she could not deny the ache of wanting him.

If she gave way to her own desire for Jamie, and they made love, de Orbrec would never want her for a wife. No other man would.

But to use Jamie in such a fashion would be an act of desperation, a small voice whispered.

"Desperation, aye," she said aloud.

Dare she take such a chance? There would be nothing to stop Jamie from taking what she offered and still return her to the Norman.

And what of his tender regard for her? What if this was the beginnings of love? She would spoil any chance to have Jamie's gift of love.

Was there anything short of death that would release her from this coil?

Her inner voice was silent. Just like her tears.

Chapter Eleven

Davey was the first of the family to enter the great hall in the morning. Jennet and her mate, Cudgel, had awakened him for their morning run. Davey did not mind the teasing he incurred over naming his female hound after a small horse, for she was of a size for a child to ride, while her mate Cudgel earned his name for reiving any stick he found, no matter in whose possession it was.

As he entered, Davey saw at the far end of the hall a cloaked figure—obviously female, but unknown to him. She slipped out the servant's door before he could stop her.

Moibeal, one of the maids, crossed behind the high table, carrying two leather buckets of water.

"Lass, did you see the maid leave?"

"Aye. She's the one that came with Janet. Welsh she is, with nary a word to say to any."

Davey could not recall her appearance, but then, like his brother Micheil, he had been upset by the raking up of painful memories with Janet's coming to reclaim her sister's body.

Yet he was intrigued enough to follow after her. Once outside in the early morning mist that held the salt tang of the sea, he found no sign of her. Shrugging, he dismissed his curiosity and called his dogs back to him. He opened the door to the servants' entrance and sent the dogs to plague the cooks. There were matters of grave import to be discussed with his brothers this morn. All else must wait.

But instead of following the dogs inside, he closed the door behind him and walked to the gate of the kitchen garden. He was about to open the latch on the gate when he felt a great weakness flood his body.

Davey had to close his eyes to stop the dizzy spin that came upon him. It was ever thus when the sight visited him. He staggered backward, slamming his hand against the stone wall of the tower. He was unmindful of the scrape on his palm, which drew blood.

The sudden pounding in his head was far too strong for him to fight against. He knew he should not fight it—that only made it worse. But this helplessness that overcame him at times frightened him. He had nearly lost his life once when the sight came upon him near an icy stream and he had blacked out for hours before he was found.

He could not stop the images that formed in his mind. Half the time he could not make sense of what was being revealed to him.

Some called this a gift, and others named it a curse. Davey knew he would consider it a blessing if he could ever learn to control it.

He fell to one knee, his hands tunneling through his thick brown hair, holding his head tightly. His mouth opened with a silent cry.

The mist cleared and he saw a sword, its steel blade glinting with a powerful light. He recoiled to see its blade edge running red with blood.

Davey squeezed his eyes tight, wanting to see more,

needing to know who wielded the sword, and most desperate to fathom whose blood stained it.

The pain in his head increased. The image began to fade. He threw up his hands in supplication, in a desperate bid to recapture what he'd been shown.

He felt a light touch upon his head, and a voice like soft notes of music whispering for him to go gently now.

The mist was still before his eyes, blinding his normal vision. He heard and felt but could not see who it was that guided him to stand, or brushed his brow with so soft and tender a touch that fear left him.

He suddenly felt the solid wood of the garden gate at his back and leaned there gratefully.

"All things come. All things pass. All will be known when it's time."

He reached out blindly. "Who are you?"

There was no answer, and seconds or minutes later—he had no way of telling which—he saw that he stood alone.

Davey was shaken. Never before when he was gripped by the sight had there ever been anyone with him.

Had there truly been someone now? Surely that voice he'd heard could not belong to an earthly being?

Oh, but he longed to hear it once more, sweet and melodious as any song, and strangely comforting, too.

He found a great reluctance within himself to return to the great hall. He wanted to stay here, to be near where this latest vision had come upon him. He caught himself repeating the words whispered to him.

"All things come. All things pass. All will be known when it's time."

Jamie was the one he most often shared his visions with, taking comfort from his brother's acceptance, and his help. But he did not want to share this with Jamie, or with anyone else.

A bloodied sword? What meaning could it have?

Moments later he realized he appeared the fool, leaning as he was against the kitchen garden gate as if waiting for an early morning tryst with some lass.

The noise of the bailey reflected back from the stone walls and hit him like a blow. From the pens he heard the lowing of cattle, the bleating of sheep and goats, the grunting of pigs, and nearby, the voices of men and women moving about their morning chores.

Davey shook his head, and in doing so, shook off the lingering effect of his gift. He entered the keep as he had left, and stood by the servant's hall as he sorted out clansman from servant, well aware that he searched for the cloaked figure of the Welsh woman.

But the mysterious woman was not there, nor did he see Jennet and Cudgel. He wondered if they had sneaked up the stairs to his room.

The long trestle tables and benches were being set in place. Davey saw that none of his family had arrived to break their fast. He did spy Niall's mother as she came down the stairs, and he quickly stepped back, unwilling to engage her in conversation.

Davey never again wanted to hear his cousin Niall's name mentioned within these walls. He knew his brothers felt the same, for Niall had been that most foul of men who betrayed his clan and his cousins for his own gain.

Micheil's compassion allowed Niall's mother to make her plea to have his body returned, although she was well aware that he could not be buried in consecrated ground, since he had taken his own life when confronted with his treachery.

Davey felt his own compassion stir to see the brokenhearted woman who'd lost her only son be shunned by the clansmen near her.

He glanced impatiently at the stairs that would bring his brothers down to break their fast. Still no sign of them. When he looked outward at the hall, he saw that Niall's mother, Mary, had the company of another come to beg for the return of a clan traitor's body. He had been surprised to see that Uallas had sent his younger daughter, Janet, to recover the body of her sister, Fiona.

Davey answered a few greetings, but all could see he was distracted. The servants were bringing in the steaming bowls of brose, a thick oatmeal, along with wheels of cheese, crocks of butter, trays of fresh baked bannocks and pitchers of ale. With all the bustling about, the sweet scent of thyme rose from the rushes strewn across the stone floor.

He looked again at the stairs, wondering if Micheil had taken a turn for the worse, only to dismiss the thought as soon as it formed. Seana would have sent for him if that were true. More likely his brother was indulging in watching his son. As for Jamie, his exhaustion would keep him abed.

Undecided if he should stay or seek his brothers out, he stepped aside for the progression of servants bearing the trays for the high table. Then Davey took his own place, to await whoever would join him there. He was curious, too, to see the lady Gilliane.

He hailed Marcus and Gabhan when they arrived, beckoning them to him. He could question them about the lady who raised the Norman's ire.

So with the echoes of the sea lapping at the rocks below the promontory where Halberry stood, strong against all, and with the smell of the salt tang coming from the high slits in the wall, Davey heard what little they had to tell. He heard more when Crisdean joined them.

High above, too high to hear the sea, and where the scent of it was faint, Jamie finished telling Micheil all that had befallen him. Before Micheil could question him, Jamie turned his brother's thoughts with his own query.

"Tell me, what you mean to do about returning the bodies?" Jamie helped himself to the thinly sliced, salted salmon, for he and his brother sat in the anteroom with a heavily laden tray between them to break their fast. The newly laid fire burned brightly. Jamie blessed Seana for leaving him alone with Micheil, knowing it was best he vent his spleen where none else could hear him.

But far from shouting in anger, Micheil's mood turned pensive. "I harken back to our pagan beliefs, Jamie, and truly hope those traitors will enjoy a rebirth. Hopefully to another clan."

"You're talking of the old tales?"

"Aye, those from the Norse raiders that intermarried with our people. I remember Da telling us of Valhalla, the heaven of the warrior, and from our Celtic forebears there comes that beautiful legend of *Tir-nan-Og.*"

"The Land of Eternal Youth," Jamie added in a musing tone. "And don't be forgetting the legends of other-worlds that wait—*Magh Meala,* the Plain of Honey, or Silver Cloud Plain and the Country of Promise."

"Aye. All the pagan heavens, where the noblest and the fairest of brave men and lovely women can be found. With palaces, Jamie, ringing with music and laughter."

"And wine, Micheil, all the sweet wines and wonderful food." Jamie smiled, his eyes alight as he met his brother's gaze.

"Best not be forgetting that the tales of luxury and sensual orgies also include something else dear to my heart. Warfare still goes on there, for what heaven can there be without a good sword to hand?"

"Have a care to yourself, Jamie. I know your love of a good fight. I cannot do without you. As for what you asked, I'm disinclined to give over the traitors for family burials that would give them any honor."

"Micheil, I caution you to think again. Uallas has ever been loyal to us. He treats honestly with us for the furs he barters and trades. You can't be denying that he has enriched our coffers over the years. What harm would come if he has his eldest daughter back for burial? She can't go into the clan plot at St. Magnus's Chapel. There is another reason I urge you to consider this request with favor."

"Go on, Jamie," Micheil said in a soft voice as he watched his brother over the rim of his gem-encrusted goblet.

"Don't be taking offense."

"If you don't tell me, Jamie, how am I to know what I will do or say?"

"You'll not be fit for riding out to protect our lands. I must go south to recover our aunt. If you enrage Uallas over this, might you not turn his thoughts to making a devil's bargain with the Keiths?"

"You're thinking of those you caught stealing our furs?"

"Aye, Micheil. I find it passing strange that the Keiths should have known about my trip to Inverness. They could have been watching," Jamie said quickly, seeing the hard set of his brother's mouth. "And I need to look into the possibility of their having known of my plans ahead of time."

Micheil rubbed his forehead. "Jamie, it sickens me to think we haven't routed the traitors from our midst."

"You're not alone. Where did you put the three Keiths I sent back with Marcus and Gabhan?"

"Into the pit, were my orders. Surely you did not think I would treat them with honor?"

"Those cowards! Never!" Jamie declared. "I thought to use them when needed to trade hostages. And that time will come, no matter how I wish it otherwise. Leave them for a moment and hear what I've planned for this whoreson Norman. I'll bring the maid and the ransom, but I intend to challenge him to personal combat."

"Sweet heavens! Say 'tis a jest!"

Both brothers turned to see Lady Gilliane at the door. She held the back of one hand to her mouth as if to still further cries of protest. Her gaze targeted Jamie with a silent plea for him to answer her.

But Jamie's eyes were far from warm or welcoming. If anything, the dark brown gaze bore a hard gleam.

Micheil looked from his brother's stony countenance to the fair maid frozen in the doorway, then scowled. Neither seemed inclined to speak, much less make the necessary introduction.

Moments slipped by and neither maid nor man appeared aware that he watched them. Micheil cleared his throat; it gained him no reaction. The scene would be comical, he thought, if the matter they discussed did not have such grave implications. Why had the lady Gilliane protested Jamie's proposal?

He knew he would never have an answer if he allowed their staring match to continue. "You must be Lady Gilliane de Verrill," he began.

"Aye, 'tis she," Jamie muttered.

"My lord." She directed her speech to Micheil and made a graceful curtsy to him. "Thank you for your kindness and welcome to your home. 'Tis heartsore I am that I come under a black cloud.''

Jamie said no word in her defense, for he was still mulling over her cry when she'd heard his plans. Had she been listening at the door all the while?

Jamie thought of Gilliane's sweet surrender to his kisses last eve. He wondered if she thought him so poor a warrior that he would fail in personal combat with the Norman.

He felt Micheil's desire for him to speak, but he drained his ale instead.

Gilliane used the few minutes to recover from the shock of hearing Jamie's plan. She knew she had to offer some explanation. Both brothers were waiting for it. She had no rights here, most certainly no right to protest any action that Jamie planned against de Orbrec. She had to remember that she was here on sufferance, a pawn to be used to free their aunt.

"I beg your pardon for entering without your permission, but the door was ajar," she pointed out. Her head bent in seeming submission, but her voice, while low and sweet to the ear, held a note of desperation.

"Your lady wife sent me here to answer your questions. I also need beg your pardon for my...my outcry. I allow my own fear of the Norman to color all to do with him."

"But here you are under our protection, Lady Gilliane." Micheil saw that she accepted his words, if not completely, and wondered again what had passed between her and his brother. He studied her openly, for the slender maid stood proudly now. He had granted Seana permission to dip into his sister's chests when needed, although it pained him to think of Bridget. He had to approve Seana's choice of clothing for the maid. The dark green tunic with a pale green *bliaut* flattered her coloring. Her only adornment was a simply wrought belt of gold links that encircled her hips over the folds of soft wool.

He shot a quick look at his brother to see if he found her as pleasing to the eye, but Jamie wore an expression that could only be regret at her presence here.

Her skin was pale; her green eyes meeting Micheil's gaze were wary. Micheil smiled, and it was a smile of such warmth that it had seduced many a maid to his will before he had found and finally claimed his heart's mate. But he was still man enough to appreciate beauty, and to admire the wealth of copper hair that hung in two thick braids to her thighs.

A lovely prize, he thought, and that only added to his confusion over Jamie's continued silence.

"Offer our guest wine, Jamie," he ordered in a soft, but nonetheless firm voice.

"Please, am I forgiven?"

"Lady Gilliane, there is naught to forgive."

"You are both merciful and most gracious, my lord."

"We do not stand on ceremony within these rooms. My name is Micheil."

"And mine is James! This is the lady Gilliane de Verrill and we are in Halberry Castle, home to the clan Gunn! Enough!"

Jamie knew well what mist had formed as he watched the byplay between Gilliane and his brother. He also knew the ugly beast that reared its head had no place here, not a whit of foundation. But his jealousy had grown. He was ashamed of the words as soon as they were spoken. Without apology, he abruptly left them.

"You seem to cause my brother to behave in an unusual manner."

Gilliane glanced behind her at the open door where Jamie had disappeared. "I am glad to hear his uncertain temper is unusual.'' She turned to face Micheil. ''Perhaps your brother does not trust me overmuch.''

''Not trust you? Nonsense!''

''Perhaps.'' She shrugged. ''I do not think he believes me when I tell him that the Norman is sly. Jamie is an honorable man and would meet de Orbrec as such. I fear for him should he pursue the thought of personal combat.''

''You are young to make that judgment.''

''I am one and twenty.''

''And still unwed?'' Micheil asked, masking his surprise, for he had thought her younger.

Micheil's expression of sympathetic warmth invited her to confide in him. She saw no reason not to tell him the truth.

''I had no wish to marry, and my father would not force an alliance upon me. My father was a scholar and his best works were translating the great epic tales. His was a soft, dreaming nature. He believed love must come first before two people commit to sharing their lives. A belief I hold. Our manor lands are small, but two good farms, not a holding that many would covet.''

''Many would covet you for a wife, Lady Gilliane.'' Micheil spoke without thought, and then quickly recovered to add, ''All women wish to marry. Land holdings are not all men seek in marriage.''

She remained still, but he caught the tiny lift of her chin, showing a stubborn nature. He cursed himself silently for getting involved in this discussion with her. Jamie! 'Twas his fault! And Micheil would not be forgetting that.

But there was something enchanting about her that bade him keep her here longer. He found no guile in her steady gaze.

"You are wrong, you know. Women wish to marry when there is a man who shares their dreams and touches their hearts," she stated bravely, emboldened by Micheil's interest.

Micheil sensed she believed what she said. He was grateful that his wife was not there, for she would have taken Gilliane's side in this. He had one less worry that this maid might entice his brother into marriage. No sooner had the thought come to mind than Micheil recalled that Jamie had certainly acted the jealous fool.

He would have to ensure that she was not left alone with Jamie, whose seductive ways he knew too well, else he would be honor bound to see his brother brought to the altar, willing or not.

Micheil had not lightly offered his protection to this maid, and once given, his word was law.

"Come, I've kept you standing there too long. Sit beside me. I fear my family has abandoned me, and my wound allows little freedom to move about with any comfort. You can tell me more about this Norman who holds my aunt. I can assure you, Lady Gilliane, that I will not treat your grave misgivings about de Orbrec with disbelief."

Gilliane came forward, eager and willing to tell him what he wanted. She hoped that he, in turn, would tell her more about Jamie.

Chapter Twelve

Jamie rode out alone, having recognized his unprece-
dented behavior for what it was. He could not believe he'd
acted the jealous fool! Only once did he turn on the moor
and look back at Halberry, and wonder if Gilliane was
still with his brother, using her bewitching charms on him.
Jamie forced thoughts of her from his mind. Anger settled
to mere annoyance that she interfered with his duties.

Gilliane, he decided, was a maid given too much to
dreaming. Strangely enough, he understood. He, too, for
a time, while young, had read the Latin classics available,
most notably Virgil's *Aeneid* and other tales where
knights lived by their honor. Stories that told of one love
held for a lifetime, of knights who righted every wrong
and went into danger without a thought to themselves.

He had encountered the real world at a young age. A
world of war, of clan feuds, of killing and death. His was
a dual nature, for he was proud of his skills as a fighter,
yet on the other hand, sickened by the need to spill blood.

Jamie did what was demanded of him, as clansman and
as tanist, but he knew he still yearned for something more
to give meaning to his life.

These lands he rode over were good ones. Not as rich

as some, but certain practices put into place by his great-grandsire, and adhered to by those who'd followed as clan chief, had brought riches into the Gunn coffers.

Serf and crofter alike were to be protected at all costs. In the good years, when the harvest was bountiful and the herds fat, less than the full *calpiches* owed were collected by the bailiff. When the harvest and herds were lean, the storehouses in Halberry were opened and foodstuffs doled out as needed. Contented people, they worked their lands, husbanded their animals and fished the seas, and the clan thrived.

There were those who scoffed at the Gunns' coddling, but the serfs' and crofters' eyes were sharp for strangers lurking. In their need to protect their crops from burning or their herds from raiders, they were quick to give alert to the patrols Jamie ordered to ride out each day.

Jamie cursed when he thought of the Keiths so foolishly raiding animals that were little more than hide-covered bones. A waste! A waste of time, of men. Far smarter to wait until the herds had fattened, to gain some profit for the effort of reiving them.

For all his desire to avoid seeing anyone, Jamie slowed his horse when he heard himself hailed by one of the herders. He changed direction and slowly rode over to where an old man stood leaning on his staff.

"Duncan," he greeted him. "How fare you?"

The old man lifted eyes still a young, sharp blue despite the fact that he carried over sixty winters on his slight frame. His white hair straggling to his shoulders framed a deeply weathered face.

"Lad, 'tis true what they say aboot our lady? She is taken?"

"Aye, Dundan. But fear not. I'll have her back where she belongs 'ere long."

Jamie showed no annoyance at being called a lad, for he and his brothers all were lads to Duncan. They had made mischief aplenty in years gone by, scattering his sheep from moor to forest.

"Yer word's a bond, lad. Ye've heard the new jest?"

"About the Keiths, I'd wager."

"Aye. Seems when they're gettin' ready to make mutton pie, they tell all that first is needed to steal a Gunn sheep."

Jamie laughed, and then said, "But Duncan, that holds true for us as well. Be it roasted sheep, lamb, beef or chicken."

"Reiving's a way of life for us. But no' the killing they bring with it."

"Keep a watch for us all, Duncan. You've seen the new patrols I've set to ride our lands?"

"Aye. They come 'round." He looked off, still leaning his weight against his wooden staff. "Jamie, ye've a look of trouble aboot ye. Many a time, one or other of ye came with the need to talk."

"And maybe I will, Duncan, when I've first sorted it out in my own mind."

"Keep well, lad. 'Tis yer deep thoughts that make ye a fine tanist. Many's a man can wield a claymore and cleave a man in two, and he'll no' be troubled by the killing. No' ye, lad. Yer da saw that in the three of ye. He was right. No' one of his sons is a mindless beast. That'll preserve our clan. Be off with ye now. I've work to do."

Jamie took no offense in his summary dismissal. He was too surprised by Duncan's mention of his father having spoken to him about his sons. Canny old man to sense in part what was troubling him.

He set his spurs to the young stallion, Dearg, named

for his red-brown coat. Jamie used him for pleasure riding now, but soon he would begin training him to the ways of war.

Off to the west he rode, heading for the tiny Loch Stemster. On its south shore was his favorite place to be alone, among the standing stones.

A cool breeze blew off the water as Jamie dismounted and tied the reins, leaving enough slack to allow his horse to nibble the blades of new grass.

He stepped into the U-shaped setting of stones. Forty there were, and he remembered as a small boy riding his pony here, filled with awe as he stood before each towering stone. He walked toward the most northerly stone, which had an ancient cist built against it. The burial chamber lined with smaller stones had stood in this place for hundreds of years. No one was sure who had built it or who had set the six-foot-tall stones in their strange shape.

There were tales of circles of standing stones, not only here in Scotland, but in Wales and England as well. Some said they were for celebrations, and others claimed they were arranged for dark rites practiced at the full moon. At Mid Clyth there was the Hill of Many Stanes, where nearly two hundred and fifty stones were laid out in precise rows.

Jamie glanced around, and noticed as he always did the absolute silence that dwelled in this place.

No bird called, for no feathered predator or prey flew over this place. No deer browsed its grasses or shrubs; no hares ran their courses here. Never had he found the pawprint of a fox or wolf.

Yet there was peace for him here, despite the eerie silence.

He felt guilty that he had stolen this time, when there was so much he needed to do. But he wanted to fix his plans in his own mind before he shared them with Micheil.

He sat down with his back against a stone. No sooner had he breathed a sigh of ease and closed his eyes than the image of Gilliane's face came to him.

He was obsessed with her! There was no other answer for it. He needed to use her as a bargaining tool to free his aunt, but he knew he would never turn her over to the Norman. He wanted time with Gilliane, time to see if this desire for her went beyond a clamoring of bodily need.

Jamie opened his eyes and looked around. He wanted to bring Gilliane here, share with her this place that he had never wanted to share with another. She would understand the power of the silence that drew him here.

Jamie needed her to draw out the Norman, yet he could not, when done, return her to her manor house. What was to stop de Orbrec from taking her then? His challenge for personal combat could not be to first blood drawn, it had to be to the death.

If Gilliane was wed, the Norman would no longer have any claim, real or false, upon her.

Wed?

Had he lost his reason, to conceive of such a thing?

For who else would wed Gilliane but himself?

Daft! Of all the daft thoughts for him to be having…and yet, it was not so incredible an idea, after all. He was of an age to seriously consider taking a wife, and while physical desire made for a strong bond…

Wait!

Jamie had to stop himself from pondering any reason for marriage. He knew well his skills in battle, but he was not so foolish as to think he could not be killed.

Where would that leave Gilliane? A young widow dependent upon his brother's care. And while Jamie knew that, for his sake, Micheil, and even Davey, would watch over and provide for her, his death would serve her no good purpose.

He could no longer sit, nor find the peace that had always been his in this place. Thoughts of Gilliane served him no good purpose, either. Once again he made himself prey to frustration, guilt and desire. Aye, desire…he had stirred that fire until he burned with need for Gilliane.

Jamie mounted. He turned his horse for home when he suddenly sensed he was no longer alone. A quick look over his shoulder revealed four horsemen bearing down on him. He waited a few minutes more, to be sure his eyes were not playing tricks on him, for the men were Keiths.

Jamie wore little in the way of armor but for his cuir-bouilli, leather that had been dried, hardened and boiled, by soaking in hot wax until it was strong enough to withstand and even deflect blows by sword or lance aimed at his back or chest. He had only his small round shield with him and his sword.

What he had going for him was the element of surprise. The Keiths were gaining on him, and he thought they expected him to turn tail and run.

Jamie did the opposite. Drawing his shield, he set it on his left arm and with his right hand drew his sword. He then set heels to his stallion, toward the oncoming riders.

Shocked at seeing the Keiths so deep on Gunn soil, he let his rage carry him, intent on attacking the four men.

One rider drew up, and Jamie thought the man must have sense enough to wonder if they had ridden into a trap, for surely no sane man would attack them if he was alone as Jamie appeared to be. He was closing fast on the other three, who had not stopped their headlong rush toward him.

Thundering hooves shattered the silence and peace of this ancient place. No clan cries came, nor those of challenge to battle. There was only the labored breathing of the heaving beasts, ready to battle.

At the last possible moment, Jamie urged Dearg up, and the stallion responded to his demand with powerful grace. He veered slightly, came to a skidding stop, and with a pivot, raised his forelegs as he screamed his challenge to the Keiths' horses.

The short, round shield allowed Jamie to use his left hand to control the rearing horse, and to keep his seat. He feared that one of the Keith swords might broach his horse, a common war tactic that would not only upset the rider but kill his mount.

He lashed out with his sword, striking one shield, his knees constantly pressing the horse to move him away from harm. Two of the Keiths came upon his left, where the short round shield offered little protection to back, side or leg.

Jamie was hard-pressed. He slashed from side to side with his sword in an effort to clear the space around him long enough to urge his stallion through, so they could turn again on the group of Keiths. Guiding the horse with his knees, he faced his attackers yet again. Nor had he lost sight of the fourth horseman, who kept his distance and merely watched his clansmen fight.

Jamie thought at first that the three Keiths were holding back, perhaps with the thought of taking him prisoner and using him to trade for those clansmen he had captured. But when he saw the murderous intent on their faces, he quickly rid himself of that idea.

Jamie fought in earnest now. One man gave forth a great cry as Jamie's sword caught him between neck and shoulder. Jamie thrust again, and the man toppled from his horse without another sound. Jamie then swung his shield at the face of another, barely dodging the thrust of his sword, so it missed piercing his ribs.

With a deft twist of his body, he warded off a blow that would have severed his right leg, but his counter-stroke forced him to lean sharply out from the saddle, exposing his left side. He felt the blow, and the stinging slice of the sword blade, but ignored it as he twisted back and swung his shield full strength into yet another Keith's face.

Sweat stung Jamie's eyes, his blow did not land as he intended. The curved edge of the shield caught the man beneath his nose, breaking it, and smashed the lips curled into a snarl. Still the man's sword lunged at Jamie, or perhaps he aimed at his horse. Jamie ended the man's life before he succeeded in any further harm to man or beast.

Only one more left. He was not tiring, but he was beginning to feel light-headed from the loss of blood. He had to finish this one quickly.

The air rang with the clang of steel upon steel.

The Keith was good—not an admission Jamie wished to make, but the man was of a height and weight and skill to equal his own.

Slash and parry. The moves and countermoves were a deadly dance. Jamie felt the wet seep of blood that soaked his tunic and spurted anew with each move he made.

At first the sound was faint and seemed far away. But the repeated cry caught his attacker's attention. Jamie, intent only on ending the fight, parried a thrust and quickly brought his sword around for another strike, but the man was gone, raking his horse's sides with his spurs as he raced to join the one who had remained apart.

Jamie spared a brief thought as to why the man hung

back. Not that the reason mattered. He could not go after them. He wanted to, but he swayed in the saddle.

And then, wiping his eyes, he saw what had chased them off. One of his patrols rode at breakneck speed toward him from the south.

Even before they reached him, he heard their hails to yet another patrol, riding hard from the north. How then had this small group of Keiths approached? Jamie meant to have answers before the sun had set.

He met the captains' gazes with his own hard stare and with the point of his sword waved toward the dead Keiths.

"Take you this refuse and bring it to our borders. Let them serve as warning to all who would dare trespass on Gunn lands."

He saw Tormod and Simon nod to each other before they in turn commanded Peadar, Tomas, Alec and Paul to do Jamie's bidding.

Both also noted Jamie's pallor and his blood-soaked side. It was Tormod who spoke. "We act your escort if you can ride."

"Aye, I'll hold my seat," Jamie answered, barely doing what he claimed.

He motioned for Simon to take the lead, and saw that Tormod fell in alongside rather than behind him. He felt his strength failing and did not wish to talk, but one last thing had to be said.

"Ride with me as far as the sight of Halberry. Then do you both go and find out how those Keiths entered these lands. Do not return to me until you know, and if there be a traitor among those set to guard the borders, bring him before me."

"Aye," Simon answered.

Chapter Thirteen

Jamie dismounted stiffly and forced his aching legs to walk across the open courtyard. He waved off all offers of help, unwilling for word to be brought to Micheil that he was sore wounded. Stiff, tired and sore, he climbed the outer stair. It seemed that everything that could ache did. He curbed his uneven temper as he made his way across the hall and beckoned a maid to his side.

"Bring hot water to my chamber," he ordered, "and wine. And tell no one I am returned."

But it was too late for that warning. Seana, with Gilliane in tow, came from the storerooms into the great hall.

"Jamie!" Seana cried out as she spied him stagger in his walk. "What ails you?"

As Seana lifted her skirts to run across the hall to Jamie, Gilliane followed, but her longer legs allowed her to reach his side first. The young maid-servant backed away.

Gilliane acted without thought and reached out to steady Jamie. Her hand came away almost instantly, sticky with blood.

"'Tis naught," he murmured when he saw her pale face and widened green eyes. The very last thing he wanted to deal with was a fainting woman.

But Gilliane surprised him. She turned to Seana. "My lady, 'tis your place to order his care, but I beg to be allowed to tend his wound. I am not unskilled. And he has done much for me, while I have little in the way to repay him."

"I believe we should first have him carried to his chamber," Seana replied, then turned to the hovering servant.

"He's already asked me for hot water and wine to be sent. I'll go quickly."

"And I'll not be carried. Gilliane, lend me your shoulder, so I can walk on my own."

"Stubborn, thick as the stone of these walls ye are, Jamie Gunn!"

"Aye, Sister," he said with a grin. "But you love me well."

Gilliane could not smile, could not speak, but only stare at Jamie. When he still made no move toward the stair, she forced herself to say, "Please, let me tend you. Your wound still bleeds."

"I told you 'tis naught. A mere prick that gives me little pain."

Seana frowned at the underlying anger in Jamie's voice, but thought it best that she leave to order what was needed from the stillroom. Just before she slipped through the archway to the stairs that led downward, she looked back to see that Gilliane remained with Jamie. Seana shook her head over Jamie's stranger behavior, vowing to speak with her husband about it later.

Once Seana was out of sight, Jamie stopped, and perforce Gilliane did, too. She turned with a questioning look. "Do you need more than me to help you now?"

Her soft voice washed over him, sparking the desire only banked by the fighting. "Nay. I wish to know what you think you're about, offering to tend my wound. 'Tis not your place as guest here.''

The warm welcome she had received from his brother and wife, even those who served her, faded beneath the glare of his dark eyes. She could not understand why it angered him.

''I spoke the truth. I only wished to repay you for all you have done for me. If you do not wish me near, I will call another. Just name who it is that should tend you.''

''None. Come, we waste time.'' Jamie said no more as he led the way up to the top of the tower. The door to his chamber stood open, and when he entered, he saw that one of the scullery boys knelt by the hearth, coaxing the coals left from the morning's fire to flame anew with tinder sticks. Once the flame rose, he added peat, then a fat log.

''Leave us,'' Jamie ordered.

''And I pray you, sit down,'' Gilliane said as she entered. The room was chill with the shutters open to the sea breeze.

She realized anew that the clan Gunn had wealth, for the large bed had hangings of rich green velvet. A large, ornately carved chest rested against the wall. Two others of plainer design sat on either side of the hearth. A low-backed chair with a green velvet cushion and a covered footstool was angled to one side of the fire. In the corners of the wall against which the bed was placed stood tall candle holders. The stone floor was covered with several small carpets, their designs and colors faded.

Jamie noted her interest in them. ''They were my mother's. And the small tapestry was her first completed work.''

This was a softer, more gentle side to him than he had revealed to her. Yet when Gilliane turned to look at him, there was something in his dark gaze that made her uneasy.

She could not know that she was caught in a shaft of sunlight that turned her hair to flame. The very pale, silken look of her skin made her eyes a more vibrant green. As his gaze moved past her parted lips and swept over the curve of her breast, Jamie felt desire coursing through him. It only served as a reminder of how long he had been without a woman. He looked at her face again, though a veil of dark lashes half lowered to conceal his thoughts. His wound forgotten, all he could think of was the taste of her mouth, and how perfectly her body softened to fit his. He should be shamed for thinking of violating a guest, but half his mind had already laid claim to her as belonging only to him.

He was saved or damned—he could not decide which—by the trail of servants that followed Seana into the room.

Seana cast a quick glance at Jamie and then at Gilliane. Both seemed frozen in place, and she wondered what words, harsh or otherwise, had passed between them. Sensing she would not be answered if she asked, she set the tray she carried down on the flat top of the chest nearest the door, and then made way for those bringing in the tub and bathwater she'd ordered.

"All you need to tend his wound is on this tray," she said, addressing Gilliane before she turned to Jamie. "I cannot understand why you are still dressed." When he offered no response, she moved toward him. "Perhaps it is best if I take that chore upon myself. When you have bathed, I will send the lady Gilliane back to tend your wound."

"Aye," Jamie agreed. "Perhaps that would be best.

But if you intend to stay, do not plague me with questions.''

Gilliane started for the door, although she felt hurt that Jamie refused her service. She was pushed back inside with the arrival of both Micheil and Davey.

''Where...'' Micheil started to say, only to see that Jamie still stood upon his own two feet, and was not wounded to the death as he had envisioned. ''Conspire against me, will you?'' He sent a dark look to his wife.

''Do you direct that accusation at me, heart of mine?''

''You, him, all who thought not to tell me that my brother returned wounded from an encounter with Keiths on our lands.''

''Cease, I pray you, Micheil,'' Jamie said in a calm voice that belied the stir of temper in his gaze. ''I am not a lad who wants your protection over every cut and scratch. I came to no harm—no real harm,'' he amended quickly as he saw both Seana and Gilliane about to protest. ''You all are making much ado over little. And you must tell me, Brother, who ran to you with a tale of my encounter.''

''Have you forgetten, Jamie, to whom you speak?''

''Please, please, let his wound be tended,'' Gilliane said, ready to stand between the brothers.

Seana, of a like mind, for she had witnessed their flaring tempers more than a few times, stepped to her husband's side.

''Come away now, Micheil. Let Jamie have his bath. I am sure he intended to come and tell you all that is needed.'' She motioned behind his back for Davey to come forward and help her divert another quarrel.

Micheil, finally sensing that he had insulted his brother's pride, nodded, but at the door turned. ''Come to me as soon as you are able, Jamie.''

Jamie gave him a curt nod.

Davey, who had stood silent all the while, motioned to the servants to leave, then stepped close to Gilliane. "Do you go also. Let me deal with him. I would venture he took his wound over some carelessness of his own, and snaps at all because of it."

"But he did not snap at me," Gilliane protested.

"He will. Trust me in this. I know my brothers well. Neither means to set off the temper of the other, but at times they canna seem to help themselves."

"Then I will leave." Gilliane could not resist adding to Jamie, "Should you wish for me to tend your wound, please send word."

Davey closed the door behind her. "Your bathwater cools. Let me—"

"Will you stop! I'm not helpless." But when Jamie attempted to lift his arms to remove his leather, he felt the tear of his flesh.

"Proud, proud Jamie," Davey muttered as he hurried to help his brother disrobe. "Sweet saints, 'tis a long, wicked gash that bleeds anew." As he examined the cuir-bouilli, Davey realized the sword had slipped between the side straps, for the leather was cut there. He turned to show his brother, but Jamie was already in the tub, his head thrown back and his eyes closed.

"Davey, I sent Simon and Tormod to find out how the Keiths slipped through the patrols. Find Crisdean or Gabhan and tell them to seek my captains out."

"Aye, I'll do it. Do you want me to send the maid to you?"

Jamie did not answer, but Davey, who closely watched the expression on his brother's face, noted the tightening of his lips.

"She's a comely maid. That hair makes me think of

flame. Did you take note of the color of her eyes?'' he asked Jamie in a bland voice.

"I deem it wise,'' Jamie said after a lengthy pause, "not to think of her hair or the color of her eyes. I deem it wiser still not to dwell upon any thoughts of Gilliane.''

"You must be sore afflicted, Brother, for you have never before lied to me.''

"Davey, leave me.''

Without another word, he did so.

When Gilliane left Jamie's chamber, she fled first to her own, getting lost on the way. Then, feeling confined by the walls, she sought out the kitchen garden. The stone path curved around the newly turned beds, and the earthy air competed with the tang of the sea. She paced to the far end, confused by the panic at seeing Jamie wounded, then the joy of being allowed to tend him, only to end with the feeling that he did not trust her, not even to see to his wound.

But he desired her…. She could not forget how she'd tossed and turned in bed last eve, while her lips burned from his kisses. And sleep would not come no matter how she tried to think of all else but Jamie.

She wrapped her arms around her waist, for, foolishly, she had come out without her cloak. Although it was spring, in these northern lands of Scotland, so near the sea, the day was chill.

It was wrong of her to think of Jamie with the desire that burned within her. Wrong, too, she reminded herself, to give him liberties that belonged to one's betrothed and none other. She had come here like a beggar maid. All she wore was borrowed finery, though generously and lovingly given, she did not deny.

The scrape of a boot on the pathway made her turn. Davey stood there, holding out her cloak.

"You forgot this. The day's too cool to be without."

She stood still while he slipped the wool over her shoulders. And when he made no move to leave her, she turned to him. "Was there something more you wanted?"

"'Tis to ask you to forgive Jamie's temper. It was not meant for you. Being of an age together, we three brothers at times forget that we are men grown."

His warm smile and kindly eyes begged her to smile back, and she did so gladly.

"He has much on his mind," Davey continued, taking her arm to walk the paths with her.

Gilliane could not repress the pang of envy she felt. She was alone, without family to care about and dependent upon strangers for her very life. The envy was for the family love that lay so protectively over Halberry Castle.

"Lady Gilliane, please do not take what I ask amiss."

"Ask or else how will I know what you wish?"

"Has my brother Jamie treated you with all honor due a maid in his care?"

"Mother of Mercy!" she cried, jerking her arm free of his. "What are you accusing me of?"

"Nay! Not you. I but wish to discover the source of Jamie's anger. So I need be bold. Did my brother attempt to have his way with you?"

Gone were the smile and the kindly eyes. Here, too, she saw the dark temper that seemed to mark the three brothers. She shook her head, sending her braids swinging, though her verbal denial was a whisper.

Davey made a courtly bow. "I beg forgiveness. I assure you I meant no insult."

Gilliane bit her lower lip. She wanted someone's counsel, for the burden of what little she had confessed to

Micheil this morning weighed heavily upon her. But she could not take yet another of Jamie's brothers as a confidant.

Gilliane needed to get away from him, from all of them. She backed up a few steps, as if to flee, then realized how foolishly she behaved.

"Have you a chapel here?" she asked.

"Aye. Please," Davey said, holding out his hand again. "You must think I've the manners of a lout. Allow me to make amends and take you—"

"Nay! Just give me directions."

"As you will." Davey explained where the chapel was, built against the far wall that backed onto the sea. He watched her leave him and wondered if he had erred in questioning her. Perhaps Jamie's bath had cooled his temper and he would talk to him now. There was no harm in trying. And Davey had yet to speak to anyone of what had befallen him this morning with the strange vision of the bloodied sword.

But when he returned to Jamie's chamber, it was to find that his brother's wound had been tended to by Seana, and that Micheil and Jamie were deep in discussion of how and when they would pay their aunt's ransom. Davey refused to join them in a cup of ale, but listened to their plans.

"I'd not wait," Jamie said in answer to Micheil's idea of leaving in a few days. "I'll leave the ordering of the patrols and all else in your capable hands. I will take few with me. Ten men to act as escort, and the lady Gilliane."

"Jamie," Micheil said in a measured tone, "let me be sure I understand you. Do you mean to give her over to the Norman?"

"I've tarried long over the answer to that. Truly, Brothers, I cannot in good Christian conscience do so."

"Methinks 'tis no' your conscience that led you to that conclusion."

Jamie merely smiled at Davey. "I'd not lie to you. She draws me strongly. But I will need make the appearance of complying with the demand that she and the ransom his man named for our aunt will be his to claim."

"You'll risk her?" Davey asked, ignoring Micheil's scowl for interrupting again.

"There'll be no risk." Jamie sipped his ale and then continued. "I've already explained that I mean to challenge him to personal combat for the insult offered our clan. You know I will fight to the death, lest the lovely maid never be safe from his threat. Not only her, but others who catch his eye. He's claimed three wives already. I cannot fault her for refusing to be the fourth. I'd not have a woman of our clan given to him when, as Lady Gilliane explains, he is obsessed with having a son."

"If this damn feud with the Keiths did not drag on, I swear I would seek justice for her at court."

"Och, Micheil, there's none to be had lest you'd carry chests of gold to buy it. When has the king ever bothered with justice for us? An' don't be denying that having the king set his eyes to our wealth would please you."

Micheil tossed back the last of his ale and set his cup aside. Davey waited, and when he saw that Jamie was done speaking, he broke the silence that had fallen between them.

"I willna allow Jamie to go without me."

Jamie paled at his younger brother's tone. He turned to where Davey leaned against the chest. "Has it come upon you again, Davey? Have you had a sighting that warns against what I would do?"

"I wish I could answer you. I truly know not what it was I was shown this morn. Does it bode ill or victory for you? I ken not. A bloodied sword was all I saw.'' Davey thought about what had followed, but held his tongue. He could not explain that part of it at all, and found there was a great reluctance within himself to share it.

''I for one,'' Jamie stated, ''will take it as a sign that my cause is just, that the sword you saw was mine. But it pains me, Brother, that you should yet suffer these sights, for I know what they cause you.''

''Aye!'' Davey snapped angrily. ''An' I'll be an old man grown gray still sharing with naught but you two.''

He refused their pleas to stay, and neither Micheil nor Jamie could find the words to soothe their youngest brother.

''Leave him be, Micheil,'' Jamie said at last, his weariness evident, that he could not devote the attention he had always given to Davey after one of his visions. ''There is another matter upon which I would have your counsel.''

''Another matter? 'Tis not enough we have before us?''

''It concerns the maid, Gilliane.'' Jamie went on as if Micheil had never interrupted him. ''I would wed her.''

''You what?'' Micheil came out of his chair at no small pain to his injury. ''Are you truly daft? Have you lost whatever wits the good Lord graced that thick skull with? Marriage? You?''

''Answer me this, Brother. After you kissed Seana that first time, did you truly have a choice of mate? Sit down before you fall down. Aye, and if you'll calm yourself, Micheil, I will tell you why I wish to wed her.''

Chapter Fourteen

In Castres Keep, Louis Marche used torchlight to guide him to the cover of the pit prison. It was time for his nightly visit to the nun. There was no need to set a guard over the pit, for the woman could not lift the cover. He set the torch in the iron wall holder and, straining his muscles, lifted aside the cover. There was a rustle of cloth and then he saw the woman.

With one hand Lady Ailis shaded her eyes against the sudden flare of light that formed a pool on the floor of the pit. She knew not if it was day or night, but was sure it was Louis who stood looking down upon her. He was the only one she had seen since being carried here.

She waited silently, having quickly learned that her questions to him would go unanswered, and only serve to anger him. She fingered the beads of her rosary, continuing with her prayers while he just stood there for some reason of his own.

"Do you have water?" he asked at last.

"Aye. I'd have a bath, too, or even a bucketful."

"Make do with the skin I filled for you." He tossed it down and saw that she caught it. Her strength was not yet depleted. He also knew that if he were seen, de Orbrec would have him whipped for disobeying his orders. Marche's reflection upon what he had done in taking her hostage made him desire to cover himself with a few acts of kindness, which cost him little as long as none found out.

He started to pull the thick stone cover into place, then stopped, for he thought he heard her whisper.

"What? What did you say?"

"I said bless you, Louis."

"Keep your blessing for yourself. You'll need it."

When the darkness was complete, she had no reason to be brave. Once again her hope was crushed that she would be freed of this place.

There was room to stand, but little to pace. If she stretched upward she could just touch the cool stone that sealed her prison. If she had a stool or something else to stand upon, she would try lifting the stone. But she knew it was a wasted dream. She had heard Louis grunt when he'd set the tightly fitted stone in place. The air was stale, yet she had found by feel the chinks between the stones that showed evidence of others who had been held prisoner in this place.

Ailis fought off the despair that threatened to choke her.

Other than a straw pallet and a bucket to relieve herself, the pit was empty. She did not count the vermin that infested her bed. She was blessedly thankful that there were no rats, but then she did not spill a crumb of her food, for who knew when that madman de Orbrec would cease feeding her?

She walked her rounds of the pit, measuring her turns by the feel of each damp wall.

Ailis had small things to be thankful for, and she knelt to pray. Her faith that she was not abandoned, that her nephews would come and ransom her kept her strong.

But being constantly alone with none but Louis to exchange a few words with proved hard.

She chided herself. "You are not truly alone. The Lord will not abandon you. Have faith," she whispered. "Faith will carry you through this."

Lord Guy de Orbrec sprawled in the high chair overlooking his hall. The remains of his meal littered the table where he alone sat to eat. He watched the man who entered skirt the lower trestle tables and quickly come forward to kneel.

Louis returned to the hall in time to see Radnor kneel before de Orbrec. He hurried forward to hear what the man had to say.

Radnor ignored his lord's curses at the length of time he had been gone. He swallowed, eyeing the wine that de Orbrec sipped. His own thirst wanted quenching, and the information he had was worth a bit of boldness.

"Well, let me hear what you found out, Radnor."

"I beg a drink first."

"Louis! See to it. I grow impatient with waiting."

Louis poured ale and brought it to Radnor. He disliked playing the part of lacky, but showed no sign of it. He knew too well the anger that simmered within de Orbrec, ofttimes erupting against one who had done nothing more than follow his orders. Radnor drank the cup dry and held it out for more. Louis refilled the cup, but as Radnor went to drink, de Orbrec exploded.

"Enough! Tell me what you have learned."

While Radnor spoke of his men following all who had left the abbey, he eyed the gleaming plate upon the high table, and his lord's fine surcoat of red samite with its gold embroidery thick about the neck and cuffs.

"Three did not return. I found two bodies, and believe

my third man dead. The reason for my delay is that I knew you would demand an accounting. I followed their tracks to Inverness.

"I learned a nun was given aid at the priory," Radnor continued, wishing he dared sip his ale. "Strangely, she met with several men of Clan Gunn. I believe they had the maid with them when they returned north with some thieves they caught."

"You believe, Radnor? You call this your best effort to discover what I wanted?"

"Nay, Lord. I beg mercy, for I have ridden without sleep. Give me a moment more to collect my thoughts." Radnor shivered. He was sure none saw him shake, none but de Orbrec, who wore a tight, knowing smile.

"The Gunns are a small clan compared to others, but none belittle their fighting skills. They are said to have great wealth, but keep closed mouths about their worth. I did learn that their fighting force is depleted by war—"

"War? Nay, you jest, Radnor."

"Beg pardon, my lord, but their feuds are fought as wars, with raiding and lives taken with each clash. I could not find out the reason for the feud with Clan MacKay, but it went on for years and led to the one they now fight with the Keiths. At times they have truces with the Sinclairs, Sutherlands and Ross clans, but ofttimes they fight them, too."

Radnor was so parched he had to quaff his ale.

"And what of the men you left at the abbey?" de Orbrec demanded.

"I left two there. Three I sent to Inverness to watch for the Gunns. We will have word in time."

"That was well done. Was it not, Louis?"

"Aye, my lord. Radnor proves himself to be more than a captain of men-at-arms."

Guy smiled and once more questioned Radnor. "You mentioned this clan's wealth. From whence does it come?"

"'Tis said they engage in trade, not all by the king's writ. Some wealth came from Malcolm, Earl of Caithness, and another named Angus, whose daughter Maud married Sir Gilbert de Umfraville."

"The Norman baron?" de Orbrec asked, jolted out of his sprawl.

"Aye. Other coin fills their coffers from the horses they breed. They are a king's envy to ride. At the alehouse there were many who gossiped about the Gunns, for they arc well known. The clan stronghold is a great stone castle on the coast of the North Sea. Some claim they trade with Normandy and the Flemish as well as the Norsemen. The rich furs the thieves tried to steal from them were said by the merchant to be from animals unseen in these lands."

"Smugglers, likely," de Orbrec remarked with a sour note. "If your tale is true, such wealth should not be allowed in the hands of those who do not appreciate what power it can buy."

"I heard naught of smuggling, my lord," Radnor quickly said. "All their trade is done openly. They have little to do with the court since the old lord died. I did hear other news that should please you well."

"Radnor, all you've told me should please me," he warned in a very soft voice. "I'll indulge you. Tell me what you've saved for last."

"Those thieves they caught and took north were Keiths. 'Tis commonly known that the clan chief, George, vowed upon the death of his son and heir to see the three Gunn brothers' heads mounted on his keep's walls."

"Idle boast, more than likely." Guy drank deeply of

his wine. "If this chief meant to have their heads, it would be so. But they still live."

"Aye, my lord. I heard the Gunn chief is sore wounded and cannot ride. The one to come with the ransom and the maid 'tis likely to be Jamie. He holds the place of war leader for his fighting skills."

"Fighting skills?" Guy de Orbrec's voice grated. "You insult me, Radnor. Those wild Highlanders are little more than barbarians. What could they know of Norman fighting arts?"

"The family, my lord—" Louis started to say.

"That is of old, old times. Nay, this one won't be a threat."

Both Louis and Radnor knew better than to disagree.

Not one man who sat nearby and listened to Radnor ventured his opinion or added what knowledge he had. There were those in service with the Norman lord who could tell of the fierce Highlander's skills in battle. A few of the older men-at-arms had had fathers or grandfathers who had fought on the English side at the Battle of Bannockburn nearly sixty years before. The Scot victory had been so great it was still talked about. The flower of all England's knights and nobles, along with men-at-arms, had been beaten into the swampy ground they'd fought over. The English king, Edward, had been chased to the very walls of Stirling Castle. To the Scots went the rich spoils of armor and weapons, horses and gold plate. The very tents carried for the nobles' comfort, and all else that had been abandoned.

There grew a feeling within those seated in the hall that de Orbrec schemed for more than the return of his promised bride and the great ransom that Louis boldly demanded for their hostage.

But none whispered to his neighbor of this. 'Twas said

that de Orbrec heard all, for the dark lord he served had given him that power. Guy de Orbrec paid for their swords, silence and obedience. No more was asked of them. No more was given.

"Louis," de Orbrec said, motioning for more wine. "Have you fed our…guest?"

"Aye, my lord."

"Does she yet beg you for a candle?"

"Nay. Nor aught else."

A gloating smile creased de Orbrec's lips. "She does not sicken?"

"How can I say, my lord? She eats what's given and spends her time in prayer. Leastways, each time I open the pit she is on her knees."

"The place for all women," Radnor remarked. He was rewarded with de Orbrec's laughter and those of the men around him.

"Aye," de Orbrec said. "'Tis a position I favor for those who serve me. She'll have need of her prayers. Perhaps, to enliven your drudgery of her care, you should promise her a walk in the bailey, Louis. Who knows what that will bring you. There are those who say not all holy sisters keep to their vows of celibacy. Ah, what say you?"

"I say, my lord, that she needs flesh on her old bones and a veil over her face, for her eyes burn with the fervor of a martyr."

"Poor Louis. We have set you the sour chore." Guy rose and beckoned Radnor to him. "Come. I would have private words with you."

Louis watched with a bland expression as they left the hall for the lord's solar, built as an inner chamber behind the great hall. From the news that Radnor revealed, de Orbrec had heard something that set him to scheming. Louis based his judgment on the lack of the usual lengthy questions concerning the abbess. His lord relished knowing every word she spoke, every plea she made, and even wanted to learn the tone of her begging or her reaction to his orders of generosity or deprivation.

There had been far more of the latter than the former, so Louis had been forced to lie in order to give de Orbrec the satisfaction he craved.

Louis mulled over what had been said in front of him. There was no sparkling gem that had obviously drawn de Orbrec's attention.

Anger would not serve him. He would be told when it was time. Still, it rankled that his lord had taken Radnor, a mere captain, into his private solar where few, if any, ever attended him.

Louis knew the whispers among those who served in the keep as well as the village—that de Orbrec practiced his black arts within that room. In truth, he had never seen anything within the chamber that could not be found in any other lord's place.

He took a fresh cup of ale and sought the coveted spot to the side of the massive hearth where neither sparks nor smoke would blow. There he waited to be summoned.

The fire had burned low in de Orbrec's solar behind the great hall. He had sent Radnor from the room while he unlocked his strongbox and counted out sufficient coin for what he'd ordered done. The parchment was written and sealed—not with his crest, yet the one addressed would not mistake his valid offer.

Relocking the box and setting it back into its hidden niche behind the stone wall, he draped the tapestry back in place, then went to the door to summon Radnor.

''This bag of coins should see you there and back. Take no more than three men with you. If need be, buy horses, for there is no time to waste. I would have an answer to this,'' he said, lifting the rolled parchment and setting it on supple, oiled leather, which he rolled and tied to protect its contents.

"I know I need not warn you that this must not fall into any hands but those I directed. Now send Louis to me.''

Guy poured himself a cup of wine and sat in his great, heavily carved chair before the fire. He smiled as he thought of what he'd set in motion this night, and by the time Louis came to him, he was laughing.

"My lord, you asked for me.''

"Aye. Come in, Louis, come in. Join me with a cup of wine. We have a toast to drink.''

"We do?''

"Dolt! Didn't I just say as much? You are going on a journey and I wish you Godspeed.''

Louis hurried to pour some wine. Lifting the cup, and with confusion naked in his eyes, he waited for his lord to continue.

But de Orbrec was laughing again, and Louis wondered what had overset him, for there was a decidedly devilish gleam to his gaze, and the laughter had a wicked sound. Whatever de Orbrec planned, he meant ill toward someone. Louis drained a goodly portion of his wine and hoped it was not himself.

Finally de Orbrec ceased. "You'll share my mirth?''

"I would indeed, my lord, if you would but tell me what it is that I laugh about.''

"I have found a way to double your ransom demand to that clan.''

"Well, that's worth a toast or two.''

"Wait, Louis, wait. You've not heard how clever I am.''

"You are always clever, my lord. There is not a man in these lands who thinks as you." Louis had seen long service with de Orbrec and counted himself lucky, for his lord, against his nature, was most generous with him. Yet he watched him warily now and puzzled as to where de Orbrec led him.

As his liege spoke of his plan, Louis looked on without a hint of his own feelings. He had warred and survived and obeyed all that his lord had set before him, with little or no thoughts of honor. In truth, he admitted to himself, honor cost a man dearly, and he had come to like the chink of coins in his purse too much.

But two things assaulted his mind as de Orbrec finished to a close and waited for him to speak. The first, that he would be amply rewarded for having set this opportunity before his lord, and the second, that he could lose his life if all did not go exactly as planned.

"Louis?"

"A moment, please, my lord." The reward was great, far greater than he had dared dream. He smiled then and nodded.

"You are, as ever, right about this, my lord. This subtlety could have come from no other than your gracious self. You do me honor to let me drink a toast with you for this."

Louis knew he had struck just the right note, the perfect balance of not being too eager, for de Orbrec beckoned him closer and poured wine with his own hand. As Louis sipped the rich vintage of de Orbrec's private stock, sent from the vineyards in Aquitaine, he had to swallow the gorge that rose when he listened to the added refinements to the plan his lord then put forth.

"I would trust no other to see to this, Louis. I do believe when I have wed the maid that a trusted man should hold her manor.''

''I hear the two farms that are apiece with it are very rich.''

''Louis, Louis,'' de Orbrec chided, with steel underlying his voice. He toyed with the jeweled hilt of the dagger at his belt. ''Have you not yet learned that greed can kill a man.''

It was stated as fact, not a question, but Louis was quick to recover. ''Aye, my lord. But you misheard my intent. I did not consider more for myself, only that I remind you of the additional rewards that could be given for those who serve you well in all things.''

''And serve me silently, Louis. Never let us forget that.''

It was a well-aimed barb. Once again Louis swallowed gorge. Only this morning he had watched the tongue taken from one who would speak of their lord's business.

He had no intention of seeing that fate become his own.

But someday, he knew, this devil's lord would meet his fate, and he, who so rarely thought of prayer, prayed now that he would be long gone ere it happened.

Despite this thought, when de Orbrec finished gloating over his refinement, Louis agreed to see his will done by his own hand.

And pity the poor nun who would unwittingly serve him in this.

Chapter Fifteen

Far to the north at Halberry Castle, the weather, as was usual for spring, had taken a turn toward cold, with blustery winds from the sea setting the great tapestries swaying on the walls.

In a fair-size chamber that had once been a storeroom, Jamie looked around at those he had gathered to him. Most eyes were still on the map spread over the small, specially built trestle table centered in the room. A fire in the hearth threw out warmth, but did little to chase away the chill.

The chamber belonged to Micheil, who had joined them. He used the room to settle accounts or to share a private dram or two with those closest to him. And now Jamie used it to set out the final plan for paying the ransom and rescuing his aunt.

"I leave in two days' time to take the ransom, but I want to be sure that all know their roles. Timing will mean success for us. Marcus, you, Gabhan and Edam go on the morrow with our fastest horses. Seek out Colin. He'll have found a way to leave word for you. I need to know what he has learned about the Norman's keep.

"Crisdean, you are to guard the gold chest. I'd not see

it lost. Alec and Tomas ride with him. Just understand that I have no intent of this grand lord ever laying one finger on our gold.''

''And you'll ride alone with the maid?'' Crisdean made bold to ask, for no mention of her had been made.

''Aye, she rides with me and Sister Ellen. Nay, do not remind me how they will slow us. I have no choice in this. The good sister comes to tend my aunt, who is her own good abbess and will need not only another woman, but a sister of the cloth to see to her needs. Pray God that this bastard has not harmed her.''

''But you still mean to kill him?'' Gabhan asked, moving closer to the fire.

''I need her,'' Jamie answered shortly. He knew what they all thought—that he needed to show her in order to draw forth the Norman from his keep—but at that moment he met Micheil's gaze. His brother knew the true meaning of his words.

''Och, Jamie, but you could beat the devil at his own games,'' Micheil declared.

Before he answered him, Jamie asked if any had questions, and when none were raised, he dismissed his men to their beds. Only when they were alone did he turn to his brother. ''Your words were bold, and struck the right note, but fear drags my spirit for our aunt's safety.''

''As it does mine. It is ever thus. Once the battle is joined, Jamie, you will feel a lifting of your spirit. Do remember that you have right and God on your side.''

''Aye, I'll need it,'' he said with a false grin. ''Go seek your rest, Micheil.''

''In a moment. Are you still determined to talk of marriage with Lady Gilliane?''

He saw that Jamie cast his gaze upon the map and kept it there. ''I've already told you my reasons.''

"None I argue against, Jamie. Perhaps it is the way of it for us Gunn brothers. One woman and no other will do. When I spoke to her she impressed me as being a brave woman, coping with all she endured with great courage and honesty."

"I told you I laid my initial suspicions to rest. But there is still something she is hiding from me. I doubt her vow to take the veil, Micheil."

"Did you know she believes that a woman must trust the man she shares her dreams and gives her love to. She reminds me of Seana in that. Trust was the one thing she wanted from me—"

"And the one thing you could not, or would not give her," Jamie finished for his brother.

"Aye, 'tis true till she showed me that to live without her was not to be alive."

Jamie did not answer him. He thought of Gilliane, of his bone-deep need to know that within minutes he could go to her and hold her, or simply know that she was near. And what of her feelings for him? Could they ripen into love? The abiding, passionate love that Micheil and Seana shared? Jamie had not known that he wanted this for himself.

He closed his eyes and saw her face framed by that glorious tangle of copper-colored hair. Her fair skin tinted like fresh cream, and those green eyes that darkened when desire for him took hold. He smiled to himself, seeing that proud, rounded chin and that sweet temptation of her mouth.... His blood heated as he envisioned the only woman he wanted for his wife.

But he did not deny that Micheil had touched a sore point. Did she trust him enough to give him her love and share her dreams with him? He did not know. Silent curses spilled forth in his mind. Time was against him.

He had no time to play the courting lover when his clan needed him, when his aunt's life rested on his actions. He did not wish to lose Gilliane. He had to find time and a way to make her understand that.

Micheil sighed, and the deep, soft sound broke Jamie's silence.

"Time, Brother, I need more time to sort this out."

Micheil, worried, frowned at him. "Jamie, I seek to caution you, being newly wed myself. Seana loves me, of that I no longer harbor doubts, but still, she cozens me when she wishes her own way. You mentioned time. Can it be that time and circumstance push you into thinking that Gilliane is the only woman you want? You believe she lied to you about her vow to take the veil. I warn you, masking the truth is a woman's best weapon. Sometimes," he added with a wry smile, "what you believe is for your good and what she believes are not the same."

Jamie listened as he rolled the map and tied it, before sliding it into the oiled leather case. "Am I hearing you aright? You think I'm an utter fool to love and trust her?"

"Nay, Jamie, nay! I merely warn you that when the passion runs hot for a woman, good sense races away. And this is the first time I hear you speak of love. If she is truly your breath of life, I'll not stand in your way."

"Unlike you, dear brother, I will never be a slave to any woman," Jamie replied indignantly.

"No man ever is," Micheil remarked in a dry tone. "You were there and saw for yourself. I saw Seana and wanted her. Do you think any man sets out to love? Do you believe that when we do, there is a chance of freeing ourselves, short of death? Gillian is a beautiful young woman, Jamie. Sweet of nature, and I know you would never take advantage of her helplessness. Have a care,

Brother, that you do not permit her to use that helplessness as a weapon against you.''

''Aye. I ken your warning. All I can say again, Brother, is that from the first moment I saw her in that strange stone dwelling, I felt as if time had stopped for me. If I had ever dreamed of the woman I desired above all others, Gilliane would be she come to life. But that is a fanciful thought, belonging to our ancient beliefs. What more can I say, Micheil?'' Jamie shrugged. ''We are born of a race of mystics and dreamers.

''Something happened in that moment our gazes lifted to each other. I desire her, but the wanting is more than to slake the passion she stirs. Maybe she is my breath of life. And Micheil, as much as you hate hearing this, it must be said.

''If I should fail when I challenge de Orbrec, who would stand protection for her against the Norman's wrath? None. But if she is mine, she will have the clan.''

Micheil grasped his brother's shoulder for a brief moment. ''You will not fail. Now go seek your lady.''

Jamie had asked Gilliane to wait for him in the chapel. He had considered his chamber or her own, but he could not trust the desire that sprang to life so quickly and easily between them. He needed a safe setting to talk.

One would think, he mused, as he found a heavy, fur-lined cloak, that in a castle the size of Halberry, there would be many places for a private meeting. Not so. The great hall was filled with the pallets of servants and clansmen. Micheil's solar was private enough, but of such strong, masculine influence that talking war, not love, best suited the room.

His sister's rooms had been given over to the nun Ellen, as well as Janet and Mary and their servants. Jamie was thankful that group would be leaving on the morrow with the bodies they had come to claim. It was doubly good that they left before he did. The fewer who knew about this journey and his reasons for it, the safer it was for him and his men.

Jamie slipped through the kitchens, stepped carefully among the pallets laid nearest the fire, then hurried down the short hall that led to the outside door. Here he felt the sweep of drafts, and so was warned of the cold when he opened the door wide enough to slip outside.

He could see his breath in the air. He paused a moment to look up. It was a clear night, and the sky a dark velvet cast with the brilliant fire of diamondlike stars. His Gilliane, he thought, could wear that precious stone, but he would see her draped with emeralds to match her eyes.

He answered the softly given challenge from the guard near the postern gate, then hurried to the chapel.

The irony was not lost on him that he could not have found a better place to make vows or to keep his word of honor.

Jamie paused before he lifted the iron latch that would allow him inside. He reached up, as he did each time he came here and had grown tall enough to do this—touch the words chiseled in stone above the lintel.

"I Claim, I Hold," he whispered. This was not the only place within Halberry where their clan motto was carved for all to see, but it was the one that held the most meaning for him. Here the first of his line had had those words emblazoned when he had taken his bride.

The night was too cold for Jamie to linger without and for Gilliane to linger within the unheated chapel waiting for him.

He lifted the latch, a moment's hesitation holding him. Despite his speech to Micheil to see this through, there was a core of reluctance for what he was about to commit himself to do. Overriding that was the sense of rightness that allowed him no other course.

Jamie opened the door and slipped inside.

Only the finest wax tapers were used to light the altar. Jamie spied where Gilliane knelt in prayer. He imagined her there with the sun shining through the stained glass window that had come at great cost across the seas from Milano. A white dove of peace was centered within the blue, red and yellow panes of glass. His father had the window made to celebrate his marriage.

A tall wooden cross was mounted behind the altar. To one side was the stone carving of the Virgin, on the other the wooden statue of St. Columba, a missionary who had been instrumental in gaining the Scottish throne for King Aidan. Resting next to him stood the wooden likeness of St. Andrew, who, it was whispered, would one day replace St. Columba as Scotland's patron saint. Off to the right was a nearly mansize statue of Christ, and in its base a secret drawer that held several sacred relics.

Jamie made no sound as he moved forward until he stood behind Gilliane. The hood of the cloak was drawn to cover her hair, and even hid her profile from view when he stepped to one side.

He summoned patience to wait while she prayed, sparing a thought to kneeling on the padded prayer bench beside hers, to offer his own prayers.

As he moved to do so, his attention was drawn to the silver ring she wore, which glinted in the candlelight. The design—a seamless, unbroken circle with the twining of the endless knot—was Celtic. He knew that to be so, for within the coffers in the treasure room there were many pieces of similar design taken in trade or booty over the years.

But where had Gilliane gotten it? It had not been among the family jewels that Micheil had given to Seana. Gilliane had been wearing no jewels when he found her. The thought that someone had given her the ring brought a flare of anger. Jamie no longer respected her need to pray. He placed his large hand on her shoulder and felt her tense as he leaned close. ''Is it life or death you pray for?''

''I pray for no one's death.''

Not Gilliane's soft voice!

Jamie's hand tightened. ''Look to me,'' he demanded.

She obeyed and turned to face him, but the fall of the hood draped her features in shadow.

''Who are you? Where is Gilliane?''

''Gilliane?''

''Aye. The lady Gilliane de Verrill.''

''You are hurting me, my lord,'' the woman whispered, without moving to free herself. ''I know not the lady. I saw no one when I came here to pray. I bring no harm to any. I am a healer.''

Jamie glanced again at the ring she wore. ''That is a Welsh ring.''

''You err, my lord. Welsh and Wales are Saxon names given to my birthplace and my people. I am of the Cymry and my land is Cambria.''

''Celt?''

''Aye.''

''How came you to Halberry? Surely none here sent for you. I would know if that were true.''

''None sent for me. I came with Lady Janet on her sad journey to ease her grief.''

''Sad, was it?'' he scoffed. ''She came to claim the body of her sister Fiona, who betrayed her clan. There's a sorrow for you.'' Then in a softer voice, he added, ''Tell me, how are you called?''

"I am Meredith."

The awareness came upon Jamie that the tension had seeped from her; if anything, she radiated a calm that extended itself to him.

"Have you been long at your prayers?" He removed his hand from her shoulder and held it out to help her rise. Had she been standing when he entered the chapel, he would have known immediately that she was not Gilliane, for the top of her head barely reached his chin.

"An hour, no more. I swear I have not seen your lady."

"What notion could she take not to wait as I ordered? And she is not yet *my* lady. I was going to ask her—" Appalled, Jamie stopped and stared. He had been ready to confide to this stranger, this woman of the Cymry, his plan to wed Gilliane. He knew the tales of their powers and wondered if she was of the blood of the ancient Druids. He wanted to ask, but did not. A quick shake of his head helped regain his senses. She had backed away from him—not in a frightened way, but now he could not make out even her shadowed features.

"Come, I'll escort you to your chamber. While I trust my clansmen with my life, I'll not say the same for a maid's virtue at this hour of night."

"You are kind, my lord."

"Do not address me so. Micheil is laird here. I've no wish for his place."

"I meant no more than your due. I've not met many men like you and your brothers. But do not fear for me. Go seek your lady. You've matters of import to discuss with her and the hour grows late."

Jamie swallowed his protest. "As you wish. But promise me that if anyone accosts you, you will come to me."

"As you will."

The meeting left him unsettled. He had the strangest

feeling that he had not seen the last of the Welsh…no, the Cymry maid. He reached the great hall and sought the stair to Gilliane's chamber. The woman was forgotten when he saw Gilliane's door open, but the room was empty.

The large branched candlesticks were lit, the fire newly fed to last the night, but the bed hangings were still tied back and the cover undisturbed.

Vexed, he wondered if he had made a mistake and told her to meet him somewhere else. But where? His chamber? Sweet saints! He would be running all over the castle before he found her. He needed to see her tonight. Down he went, retracing his steps, careful not to step on someone's outflung hand or foot.

His room was empty, too. He had the thought that she might have gone to see Sister Ellen. He shuddered. Bridget's rooms were the one place he and his brothers avoided. Her death was too painful and the memories still fresh. He lit a candle and decided to wait for Gilliane in her room.

If anyone took note of his comings and goings they would believe him daft. Or bewitched. But he would have his way this night if it took him until the dawning to find her.

Chapter Sixteen

Fate was kind, for reason reasserted itself, and Jamie lost his anger on his second climb to her chamber. He knew there was a perfectly good reason why she had not waited in the chapel. All he need do was make himself comfortable and wait to hear it from her lips.

He sat in her chair, his booted feet at rest on the footstool, and helped himself to the nearly cooled mulled wine that had been left on the small side table. He did not want this time to think again of what he would offer her, but the flames lulled him into thinking of her hair. He smiled, knowing himself nearly obsessed with those copper tresses.

He sipped, drummed the fingers of his left hand on the arm of the chair and closed his eyes. His shoulder ached, but no discomfort would make him leave.

"Oh, my lord, I've kept you waiting overlong."

Her voice sent a sensual awareness through his body. Jamie opened his eyes, saw her cloak, and all his good intentions of hearing the reason for her delay went flying like sparks going up the chimney.

"Where the devil have you been?"

"I went to the chapel to meet you."

She neither sounded nor appeared defensive, and that set his ire aflame.

He glared at her. "Do you know that I have chased all over this castle in search of you?"

"Nay. How could I?"

"Well, I have. You were told to wait in the chapel for me, were you not?" Even as he spoke, Jamie thought to himself that this was the wrong way of going about making a proposal of marriage. Yet he refused to change the tone or recall his words.

"I received your orders," she snapped, wondering where his anger had sprung from. "I was also summoned to see to Sister Ellen. She is heartsick with worry over your aunt and did not wish to impose on Seana, who has more than enough to contend with. Mary and Janet have been at her all day. I do realize, my lord, that these small womanly matters are not of import to you, but I—"

"You have no damn standing in this clan to concern yourself over our matters!"

Her hand flew to cover her mouth and quiet the cry that escaped. A stricken look darkened her green eyes. Her head bowed as if its weight was suddenly too much for her slender neck.

The perfect vision of a submissive woman, as perfect as a man could wish, but Jamie, too, was stricken by the words he'd shouted at her. The cup, half-filled with wine, spilled from his hand, but neither he nor Gilliane took note of the wine soaking into the edge of the carpet.

He'd started to rise when she spoke.

"I wish you would say in plain words what it is that you expect of me, my lord. I offered to tend your wound and you sent me from you, only to order my company late this eve. Now, when I come, you take me to task for that which is not my fault, and then lay such cruel words upon me that I feel shamed to have ever accepted your aid.''

Soft, so very soft was her voice, but nonetheless each point she made struck home like a dagger well aimed, for it was all the truth. Clearly he had erred, but by the saints, he had never had his plans for a woman so fouled.

He was not going to die from her dagger pricks, no matter how well aimed, but it set the opposite mood of what he wanted. And Jamie hated to be denied when he had schemed to see her.

'''Tis not to be borne! I've made a porridge mess an' I canna abide the stuff.''

''What ails you?'' She glanced over at him at the sound of his muttering. She saw the overturned cup, the spilled wine and Jamie sprawled in the chair with one hand covering his eyes.

He looked away from her and set both hands on the chair arms to rise, but the grimace on his face made her hurry to his side. ''Stay,'' she cried out. ''You'll tear your wound.''

Gilliane fell to her knees beside the chair.

'''Tis no more than I deserve.''

''Tell me what is wrong! What have I done?''

It warmed Jamie considerably to know that she had such a sweet-tempered nature and was willing to accept the fault as hers. Temptation loomed bright for a moment to let it rest, but it was not his way to allow another to accept any blame for what he caused.

''Tell me, Jamie,'' she pleaded.

''You? You've done naught.'' He still could not look upon her face. ''Me? Och, lass, there's a tale to tell.''

Her hands tightened on the arm of the chair. ''Can you not tell me?''

"First I beg your pardon for my coarse and uncalled for words, Gilliane."

"Forgiven," she responded, so promptly that she had her wish. Jamie turned to look at her.

He cupped her satin-smooth cheek and tilted her face toward him. It was too soon for what he had to ask, yet there was no other way to fully protect her.

"You are most generous with me, Gilliane."

He started to shift his body in the chair and hissed softly with pain. Gilliane was right. If he did not calm himself, he would likely rip open his wound and set back the task he'd laid for himself. Her breath rushed out as if she had held it, and he wondered if she would hate him when he told her what he planned. That truly would be unendurable, and yet he knew he would endure her hate if need be.

The hood of her cloak had fallen back and now he gently pushed it off completely. He could no more resist tangling his fingers in the silk of her hair than he could disavow his clan. One was as necessary to him as the other.

"Gilliane, I ask more of you. I ask you to grant me patience to tell this in my own way and time. But while I speak, I want for you to remember that I wish no ill to you, only good."

Mystified, Gilliane nodded. The fire's flames made love to his face, shining on the rich mahogany of his hair, gilding the weathered swarthiness of his skin, the angle of his straight nose, the carnal shape of his mouth that invoked thoughts of kisses that set her to burning. The warmth that instantly flowed through her at the remembrances of what his kisses could do to her was sinful temptation to taste the forbidden again. Truly, she chided herself, she was a lustful wanton to have such thoughts when he made no move to join his lips with hers, and offered no sign that that was his eventual intent. If anything, Jamie appeared to be struggling with some trouble of his own.

She gazed up into his dark brown eyes, their sudden hot, fierce look so compelling that her breath came a little shorter. The warmth she had felt turned to heat that suffused her body. She knew there was no hiding the flush that crept from breast to cheek.

"Jamie," she whispered at last, almost desperate to break this spell that held her, "you asked for my patience. I give it freely, but please, the hour grows late and with your wound you should be abed."

That diverted his gaze from her loveliness to the bed. And Gilliane's gaze followed his. She was quick to turn away, but when she looked up at him again, she caught a hint of color over his cheekbones. Sure it was her own passionate imaginings, she dismissed it.

"Gilliane, you know we leave in two days' time with the ransom. You know also that I must take you with me, for there is none other who could pass for you. But before we leave Halberry, I would wed you."

He could protect her with marriage, but he dare not speak to her of love. If he failed in battle, Gilliane would mourn him, but she would be free to love another. The thought pained him more than he could bear. Gilliane, his Gilliane, with another man?

Despite his wound he leaned closer, ready to argue away all protests. Gilliane said not a word, nor did she blink.

"Did you hear me? I wish to marry you, Gilliane."

"Marry?" The word was hardly a whisper. She was afraid to move lest she shatter. Her eyes grew large and dark. "My vow—"

"There is no vow to take the veil, is there?"

She could not lie to him. She shook her head, but guilt plucked at her. Was it her own thoughts, her sinful desire, that had brought this about? Was she to resist him? And what could she argue to deter this madness? Truly, her growing love for Jamie beclouded her mind. She could not think clearly. Dare she laugh as if this were a jest? Should she cry out that she, as any other woman, longed to be loved? The last thought seemed to free her, for a bitter set came to her lips. Love? What woman found that first? None that she knew.

Jamie felt a cold knot of fear that she would refuse him—a knot that expanded with every breath he drew and released. She remained silent, unseeing and unmoving.

"Have I deceived myself in thinking that passion bound us? There are many who have made marriages last starting with less."

Gilliane drew a shuddering breath. "Why? Why would you ask this of me? You gave no sign...you...do you jest?"

"Only a woman could be fool enough to say such a thing! I am giving up my freedom. Do you think I'd jest about that?"

To his shocked surprise, Gilliane came to her feet and backed away from him. "Since your freedom is of such a great prize to you that it causes you grief to be without it, I will forget these cruel words and ask that you leave me."

"I'll not!"

"Of course you will not," she stated, entwining her hands before her. "First I am not to concern myself with your clan business, and now I may not send you from this chamber, since it truly is not mine. Perhaps it is best that I go to join Sister Ellen and the others. I can lay a pallet on the floor and know that there you will not dare to follow me.''

She started for the door as Jamie pushed himself free of the chair. Sharp pain from his wound spread inside him, but that would not deter him.

''Gilliane! I command you to return to me. I asked you to hear me out. Do you now take back your given word to do so?''

Gilliane bit her lower lip, undecided what to do. She did not wish to hear more of his insulting offer, and yet she had given her word to listen to him. And she could not forget how much this man had risked, and was still to risk, for her.

Hurt and disappointment left her poised near the door, still ready to flee. She had waited for some words of love, even if they be false, some tender sentiment or two. Not even an embrace…! Her anger flared, and she remembered something he had said when first they met: *All good deeds are rewarded.*

From that thought came her icy words. ''Tell me, Highlander, is my marriage some reward to be had before the deed is done?''

''Deed? What the devil are you bletherin' about? I go to kill or be killed, and sought only to offer you the protection of my brothers and clan!'' he responded with all the fury that was his to summon.

Gilliane lifted her chin, straightened her spine and tossed her head back. ''You will have no need of giving up your freedom. I have already made arrangements with Sister Ellen to go to the abbey.''

''You a nun?'' Jamie stopped himself from nearing her, afraid that once he put his hands upon her, not one word of sense would pass his lips.

''Aye. 'Tis my choice to make. I can bring the manor

house and two farms as my dowry. There are many willing to take me with that.''

''I'll have you with naught but yourself.''

Soft, so very soft was his voice, issuing forth those words. Gilliane raised a hand as if to ward him off, but then dropped it.

Jamie went to her then, closed the door, uncaring if any had heard them shouting, and taking her by the hand, led her back to the chair.

''Would you please sit down and let me begin again?'' The heat of his gaze belied the calm of his voice, but Gilliane had lost the will to argue. Would he really have her with naught but herself? She wanted to believe that, for Jamie was in truth all that she had dreamed of to have for her own.

''My words were harsh and hasty. A fault I admit and will likely keep admitting until I grow old and feeble.'' Jamie glanced toward the fire, knowing himself to be in a rage of need, and unwilling to slake that need with any but the woman who caused it. But he had to stop either quarreling or offending her by his speech. He took a deep breath to calm himself, and went down on one knee. Taking one of her delicately boned hands within his larger one, he once more started anew.

''I have never offered marriage to a woman. I want you to know that. I cannot speak of love, for love takes time to grow, but I have deep regard for you and care for your well-being, Gilliane. I desire you, and you, I think, return that desire. Wait, do not answer me as yet. I have made no jest. I know well how to judge my skill, and feel I will beat this Norman. But I know, too, that a chance strike of his will end my life. I truly do this to protect you. If you wish it not, I swear I will never importune you again.''

Is that all? she wanted to demand, but held her tongue. Where was her dream knight, come with avowals of love and undying faith and devotion? Where was the gentle wooing, the delicate dance of courtship that any maid wished for? Then reason reasserted itself. Jamie offered no dream, but the harsh reality of choices left to her...marriage or taking the veil. She lowered her head so as not to look into his eyes, and prayed for guidance to choose wisely.

The steadiness of his breathing helped to calm her. She set aside the desire she felt, and knew he spoke the truth— their mutual passion could bring only good to a marriage. It was more than some had to begin with, and she added to that all else he offered. And therein lay a bone of contention.

"Jamie, the advantage to this marriage would all be mine. I would have the care of your family and clan. And you—if you...nay, when you survive this combat that you insist on having with de Orbrec—"

His hand cupped her cheek, his thumb pressed to her lips to silence her. "Gilliane, look at me." It was only a few seconds before she did, and his breath caught at the light in her eyes as his hand slid to cradle her head.

"I would have you, Gilliane, and that is a far greater prize than any other to me. I want not for land, nor for wealth."

"And I have little enough of either to give to you."

"Give me yea as your answer, and I will be content."

She searched his eyes for guile, but found none, and yet she had to ask. "Jamie, if you could have me without vows said before the priest, would that be enough?"

"Never!"

Harsh and grating, the answer came too quickly to be

anything but the truth as he saw it. And then his voice softened as he spoke again.

"In this you must trust that I have more experience than you, Gilliane. Yes, I hunger to join my body to yours, but there is more to passion than a single sup. Do you remember when I first kissed you?"

"Aye," she whispered, unable to look away from him.

"I told you then that you were mine. Then you thought to deny me by claiming your vow to take the veil when my aunt is free. But that was the lie that you just admitted."

"You frightened me with your bold passion and, I admit, by claiming me as yours."

"But I no longer frighten you."

He did not ask, yet she sensed that he wanted her to confirm it. Gilliane shook her head. "Please, Jamie, listen. There have been no banns read. And do not take this amiss, but your brother as clan chief must desire a marriage for you that will bring added strength or some more desirable thing to your clan."

He did not know whether to be startled, angry or hurt that her thoughts so quickly turned to practical matters rather than the path he had been slowly directing her toward. He had so carefully leashed the desire she aroused in him, and wondered if it was his own growing inability to maintain a decent reserve to conceal his passion that made her sway away from it. He was too close to her; all he wanted was her lips yielding beneath his own. He tried again to order his thoughts, to recall all he had told Micheil of why he wanted this marriage.

"To set your mind to rest, Micheil offers no objection. You impressed him with your forthright telling of all that passed with de Orbrec. Furthermore, I would not be ruled by him or any other in choosing a wife. And my choice is you.''

"I am frightened, Jamie."

"Nay. Not of me. I swear I'd be tender with you, lass."

"And you won't leave me here to worry and wait?"

"I cannot, much as I wish to keep you safe. There's no choice for me. There is no other with hair like yours, 'tis *goud gléidh*.''

He smiled at her frown. "Gold, sweet lass, gold as the fire's glowing embers. Aye, a fire to warm a man. This man,'' he whispered, raising her from the floor and drawing her onto his lap. He felt the faint trembling of her body, but paid it no mind as he cradled her head within both his hands and brought her lips to his. "A fire for this man and no other.''

Gilliane set her hands on his shoulders, clutching the soft, well-washed linen shirtsleeves, ever mindful of his greater strength. The heated touch of his mouth came courting her own with a delicate play that brought a small moan from her. Now the thirst was quenched, and as greedily as he, she sought more. There flared anew the hunger that he had spoken of, that passion he so effortlessly drew forth from her. Reason fled along with doubts. How could this not be right? How could she deny the need to join with him and have him for her own? Love would come. She would make him love her.

But all too soon he drew back, his arms sliding down her back to keep her close.

"Och, lass, I swear I want your answer. If you are still afraid, Gilliane, I will tell you this. 'Tis oft the custom here in the Highlands to handfast. We can say vows, any you wish, with witnesses or without. Live with me then, for a year and a day. At the end of that time, should you wish to be free, I swear to you now, I'll not try to hold you.

"But if there is a bairn, 'tis mine to raise. I can offer you no more than my word of honor that I'll burn nigh unto death if I cannot have you to wife."

The declaration was sincere; at least she wanted to believe it so. Had to believe him, for she wanted him with the same burning intensity that mantled his cheeks with the heat of passion.

"What say you?" he whispered, nuzzling the tender spot below her ear. "You claim you've not given your heart to another, Gilliane. Be mine. Aye, be mine."

"And you, Jamie, will you be mine as well?"

"Aye," he said softly, kissing her cheek, her temple, the tip of her nose. "Aye," he said yet again, in a darker, more velvet voice, and then again, with passion riding high, he took her mouth with his and sealed their fate.

Chapter Seventeen

He tossed off her cloak and set about unbraiding her hair until she wore it as a mantle. He buried his hands within the silken flames, kissing her until she lay pliant and sweetly moaning in his arms.

The desire to bed her now was nearly too strong to resist. Equal to that need was the urge to whisper of love, not passion and desire alone. Although he kept his vow not to speak of those gentle sentiments dear to a woman's heart, he could show her with tender loving.

Fighting his aroused state, he eased his kisses to mere touches. The trembling that beset her slowly lessened.

"Gilliane, sweet, sweet bonnie lass, if I do not stop now, I will not be able to."

But he bent to kiss her again before she could summon will or sense to answer him.

She heard the low, sensual rasp of his voice whispering words in Gaelic. She tried to understand, but a storm of new sensations beset her and she only knew that she burned.

Her lips parted at his gentle urging, and his tongue teased the inside of her mouth, taunting and ravaging at the same time until she grew dizzy from the building pleasure he shared.

Along one side she felt the hard press of his body, that hard masculine length that shifted and turned with her as he freed one hand from her hair and began to caress her. A slow, heated ache consumed her, and she clung to him.

Her breast seemed to swell to fit the shape of his hand. A tiny, shivering moan escaped her lips when he nuzzled her throat and his thumb circled the nipple straining against the cloth that bound her.

Jamie plied the wiles of seduction with all the skill at his command. He caressed and kissed and loosened laces. He forced his head beneath her chin and, using his cheek, brushed aside the kirtle and shift cloth to bare her skin for his lips. Lower, then lower still, his warm lips kissed the curve of her breast, and his grip shifted so that his fingers could grasp the cloth and draw it aside. Then lower still, Jamie claimed the prize he had aimed for, and took her nipple into his mouth.

Gilliane thought she would swoon from the pleasure. He held her flesh with flaming delicacy, and she trembled at the brush of his hair against her bare skin. But these new feelings were naught compared to his mouth's gentle teasing with teeth and tongue. She trembled, she shivered and understood more of the hunger that cried out for this one man.

A cry came from her lips in response to a pleasure nearly as agonizing as pain. There was need in her to touch and kiss in return. She bent her head forward to find the flesh of his neck, and was rewarded with a low groan when she pressed her lips there. But this offered her little satisfaction. Then her lips moved to the same rhythm as his, tiny nips soothed with the languid pleasure of lips and tongue.

And then the rhythm changed to deeper, darker hunger. Gilliane lifted her hands from his shoulders and pressed his head against her breast. Her pulse raced and fires burned in her blood as a hot wave of strange, exquisite longing spread deep inside her.

Jamie was fast going past the point of prudence. The touch of her lips and teeth and tongue on the back of his neck was obliterating what little sanity he had left. A muffled moan came from him as he spread his legs and tried to shift Gilliane's body to come where he needed it. But she clung to his head with her warm hands when he tried to lift it. What else could he do but please her with renewed attentions to the dewed, wild rosebud nipple that pouted for more? And she rewarded him with soft little sounds of pleasure. She held him tight as if she could not get enough of the gentle savagery that aroused her near to his own state.

But he could not wait for much longer. He needed more than caresses, much more. Yet he was caught on the horns of a dilemma. He could not bear to release the sweet flesh he was teasing and tasting, but he had to move for he ached from belly to thighs.

Gently then, his mind made up, he removed her insistent hands and raised his head to take again the honey sweet lips that beguiled him. He plundered. He teased. He ravaged, then hungrily demanded. And when she offered him a whimper of capitulation, soft and breathy and as needful as himself, he judged the time was right.

"Gilliane, Gilliane," he murmured against her mouth. "Let me ease myself. Let me ease you, lass. I swear I'll not despoil you." Even as the words left his mouth, Jamie wondered at what he was doing. Near begging? Impossible! He never pleaded. Never begged.

But when she lifted her head and he saw her eyes, he

was glad for every word. Her eyes were those of a dark forest glen, deep, deep green, almost black with desire.

With a soft sob, Gilliane knew she would not resist him. Her body trembled as if it would break if he did not hold her. Heat pooled into flame that his kisses and touch both quenched and raised to new heights of desire.

Jamie held her tight and stood with her in his arms. His mouth teased hers, to be sure there would be no protest. But he broke the kiss as he laid her on the bed. With the power of his gaze alone he held her still, ignoring the small tearing of his wound as he divested himself of leather belt and thigh-length shirt, shoes and breeks, until he stood before her naked. But here, too, his reading of the slight shift of her body told him not to give her time to take fright. His manner had been smoother, certainly more sure, but never had such a raging passion taken hold of him as for the enchanting woman who awaited him.

"Jamie?" Her quavering whisper deflected his urgency and allowed him to approach the bed, to lean down and kiss her with a great deal of tenderness.

When his lips released her mouth, he helped her remove kirtle and shift, desiring to see his prize. A few minutes more would bring him all he wanted.

The wavering firelight and glowing candles revealed a strangely vulnerable Gilliane. But sweet, sweet saints, she was bonnie! He could not stop himself from devouring the sight of her ripe, rounded breasts, the small flat belly, the cream silk flanks and the pale reddish-gold mound of curls.

"I swear I'll be gentle with you, lass," he whispered when he found his voice, and came down to lie beside her. He tried to ease the breathing that sounded as if he had run the length of their lands in full armor. And he took pride, too, in her own proud lift of her head, for he wanted no frightened fawn in his bed.

"Are you not pleased with me, Jamie?" The words cost her a great deal to say, but he had made no move to kiss her, no move to touch her, and she thought his desire for her had fled.

"If you pleased me any more, lass, I'd expire. You're more lovely than I envisioned. Aye, you please and tempt me to use you as a fully wed woman. But I'll no' be forgettin' that you're an innocent maid. I swore I'd be gentle, and I will."

For some reason, rather than delighting her, his words of her being too innocent to fully please him struck a jealous note, for within her, love for Jamie gathered and grew. Surely no bride had ever been so tenderly wooed. He did care for her. Caring could grow into love.

Gilliane reached up to touch him, arrested by the sight of her small, pale, fragile-looking hand against the darker and more powerful male strength of his arm. Her touching him sent a fresh surge of desire coiling deep inside her.

"Jamie, your words make no sense to me. I am not so innocent that I do not understand how men and women mate."

"And who taught you all the delights to be found in a lover's arms?" he demanded in a harsh, rough voice.

"No one. I but listened to the serving maids, those who were married. They said it hurt at first, then eased. And to lie still was best."

He flung himself onto his back and threw one hand over his eyes. Damn himself for opening his mouth. He should have kept kissing her and losing himself right along with her. Now…now, he had best set this matter to right, and yet how was he to explain? He could not. He would show her.

He rolled to his side, braced his head on one hand and with the other stroked her from shoulder to the curve of her hip. He sought her lips, kissing her as his fingers trailed across her thigh, slipping up to the nest of bright copper curls on the petal-soft flesh that he sought.

She moaned softly, rocking slightly beneath his hand. His mouth traveled to her breasts, laving attention on both as he opened flanks that sought to defend themselves against his encroaching, searching fingers.

A light sheen of sweat covered his body when he found dewy warmth and welcoming heat. His lips trailed down the silken skin, over hip and belly until his lips touched the copper curls that her hand suddenly shielded from him.

Jamie knew he had shocked her from her passion-drenched madness, but he was not about to have his desire thwarted.

Against her faint resistance, he drew her hand aside and very slowly proceeded to claim the sweet satin pulse of her. She gave forth an odd cry, of shock and pleasure as she writhed helplessly against him, her frantic moves only furthering the caressing progress of his soft, heated mouth.

Gilliane closed her eyes tight against the intimacy of what he did to her. No serving maid, no married woman had ever spoken of this. She should fight him, but she was on fire from his restless, discovering fingers and the sear of his lips.

"Nay," she finally cried out, for the heat and the ache he caused were near unbearable.

It was a sweet but savage torture that she did not know how to halt or fight. Jamie had made her his creature, a woman who gloried in every quivering sensation he drew from her body, as the finest lute players brought life to every note they played.

"Temptress," Jamie murmured. "Yield all to me, lass. Yield and I'll give you more pleasure."

Gilliane could not find the breath to answer him. Her hands curled on the sheet beneath her. The tremors, at first faint, seemed to be building and building, spreading heat through her body, higher still, frightening and exciting until wild, sweet crescendos cascaded through her.

There were her breaths then, ragged, broken sounds that were all she heard for he did not stop, but drove her on, yet again bringing her to a height, quicker this time, hotter and deeper yet, and she cried out over and over, willingly lost to the enchanted ecstasy he brought her.

Jamie moved almost immediately to mount her. He held on to the last shred of his sanity, trying to remember his promise not to despoil her. But when she parted her thighs for him, she nearly made him forget all. He fought the raging need that swept over him to thrust his violently aroused flesh between her thighs, and instead pressed her legs closed with his own powerful ones. And she had so broken his control that in moments he was done.

Gilliane chose that moment to shift her hands and grip him, she knew not where. Passion's throes still grasped her tight and all she knew was that she desired to touch him.

Jamie could not stifle his groan as her fingers bit into his wound. The pain forced him up and off her, and he sat at the edge of the bed, trying to collect his wits and bury the throbbing pain that resulted.

"Sweet saints!" he muttered moments later.

"I hurt you! Let me see, Jamie. Let me see to you." She scrambled up on her knees and came around to his side. But as she reached out to touch him, he jerked away.

"Do not touch me. Minutes more and I would have broken my word. You'd be a maid no more."

She retreated a bit, but the long, silken length of her hair brushed his bare flesh, and that quickly he was aroused yet again. Arousal fought with the throbbing pain of his shoulder.

"Jamie, please, I hurt you. Look at me," she pleaded.

"'Tis all right. Be at peace, lass."

"I cannot," she whispered. "I do not know myself when you are near. You make me lost to all reason when you kiss me. And now this. I fear the passion you show me."

"Fear it? And you think I do not?" He had to look at her then, and found to his surprise that the candles were almost guttered. His breathing was returning to normal, but the heat of his blood had not cooled.

He was torn. He should leave her. The anticipation for the next night would be that much sweeter for waiting.

And a devil's torment, too.

"You say you fear this passion that burns between us, but you know little of it. 'Tis a gift, lass, truly a gift to have two so matched. And you have no cause to cry out. I did you no hurt. You are still a maid. I kept my sworn promise."

The tears that sprang to her eyes were not from fear. She did not yet understand the frustration that her body felt. He sounded content, but within her there still raged unquenched fires. At least withdrawing had served to return her to clearer thought.

As if to aid Jamie in his decision to go, his wound began a heavier throbbing, one he could no longer ignore. Just as well, he told himself. And he should go quickly, for Gilliane was an enticing sight, kneeling on the bed with copper lengths of hair spread about her, teasing and taunting his eyes by turns with bared flesh, rosy nipples and green eyes offering invitations she would deny.

"I'll go." But when he stood and bent to retrieve his clothing, she came from the bed to help him.

They both reached for his shirt at the same time, and again Jamie jerked away from her. "Can't you listen? Do not touch me, Gilliane. My will is strong, but my flesh grows weak with your touch."

"That was there between us from the first," she murmured, but backed away and allowed him to gather his clothes and dress. She watched him move toward the door, hurt that he said no other word of tender parting.

"Aye," he said, but did not turn. "You have the right of it. An' it'll be there at the last, too. Sleep well, my lady, for on the morrow I claim you as mine."

Jamie managed to get down the stairs, and then realized he would have to thread his way through the hall in the dark, for the fire in the great hearth had burned down to embers. He had indeed lost all sense of time with Gilliane. He looked over his shoulder and gave thought to returning to her to beg a candle to light his way, but he could not mount those stairs. He simply did not trust himself to go near her now.

Those few moments of indecision revealed that someone was crossing the hall. He could not make out who the man was, for he held a candle shielded with one hand. Jamie whispered for him to come and light his way.

"Jamie? 'Tis you?" Crisdean demanded with urgency in his voice. "Where were you hidden? None knew where to find you. I've been searching everywhere for you." Then Crisdean realized that this stair led to the ladies' chambers. He said no more as he approached.

"Well, now you have found me. Light the way to my chamber." Jamie pushed past him with an irritated grunt. He did not know why it should bother him that Crisdean had found him here and surmised where he had been.

They had shared enough women and wine between them. But Gilliane, a little voice reminded him, was not for sharing. She was his, heart, mind and soul.

It was not until they stood at the bottom of the stairs leading up to his own chamber that Jamie remembered what Crisdean had said. "Why have you been searching high and low for me?"

Crisdean held up the candle, and what he saw in Jamie's face told him that he was still in thrall to his likely thwarted body. It could be nothing else that brought such a black look to his eyes. Having grown to manhood with the three brothers, Crisdean knew the look too well, but held his tongue. Understanding came quickly that Jamie would not be pleased to be asked about the maid.

"Well, have you forgotten why you looked for me?"

"Nay, Jamie. Did you not set the task of finding where that pack of thieving Keiths crossed our lands?"

"Aye," Jamie snarled, for the reminder of how he'd gotten his wound seemed to set it to throbbing again.

"They found a hidden camp across the loch, Jamie. The two that escaped you were not there, but it was news worth telling you, was it not?"

A string of heartfelt obscenities trickled slowly from Jamie as he hurriedly mounted the stairs, with Crisdean following close behind. Jamie had not only lost time with his fiery-haired temptress, she had chased thoughts of the danger from the Keiths from his mind.

"Did I hear you right?" Jamie asked as Crisdean went hurrying about the chamber, lighting candles and then stoking the fire with kindling. "Did you say they found a hidden camp, but not the two who escaped my sword?"

Whatever Crisdean answered was lost to Jamie. He was so angry with himself that he had to stop and swallow the rage that flowed through him. And yet he could lay no fault on Gilliane. He had gone to her.

But these were the duties that should have demanded his attention—to keep his clan and their lands safe from all enemies. He rubbed his forehead as if to scrub away the sensual web that still clouded his mind.

"How long were they camped upon our lands?" he asked Crisdean.

"Two days and no more, Simon claimed. And well hidden that camp was. None saw sign of them until they attacked you today. But before you ask, I took all to task for not being alert. There is some good news. We found no damage done to any of the nearby crofts. Naught was stolen. I'd say they came to spy upon us."

Crisdean looked up, satisfied with the log and peat he'd set to burn, and saw that Jamie had turned away from him. "Are you taken ill, Jamie? Or is it something more that troubles you?"

"See if there is any wine left."

"Mayhap you've had enough. Water—"

"Do you think to play nurse to me now?"

Crisdean rose from where he knelt. "Jamie, what ails you? 'Tis no' like you to spit with temper. Micheil, aye, that's his way, but no' yours." And from their years of friendship and clan bonds, he spoke more boldly. "Well, it weren't like you till you found that maid in the wood."

"Spare me more tales of witchery, Crisdean, and pour me some wine. I've pulled open my wound and it pains me something fierce."

He knew that Crisdean would accept his excuse for what it was. Right now, Jamie could not offer him another reason for his temper.

He took the offered cup and drank deeply. He disliked shutting out his friend. Crisdean would provide the same sympathetic ear as he had in the past if Jamie wished to talk, but the matter of Gilliane, of his proposal of marriage, or handfasting— Abruptly, Jamie arrested his move to finish the wine. She had never answered him which it was to be! Och, she sent him mad! Insanity was where Gilliane would drive him!

"All is set to leave in two days' time," Crisdean said when Jamie's silence continued. He had to try and draw out whatever troubled him or all would suffer his temper on the morrow.

"Aye, it had better be," Jamie answered curtly. He started to remove his belt, wincing as he again pulled on the wound. Too little sleep, too much wine and the unfulfilled desire that Gilliane raised in him clamored through his body, weakening him. He knew his humor was foul. He stripped off the shirt, tossing it toward the chest.

"You have indeed torn it open. There's fresh blood on that bandage. Let me fetch—"

"No, Crisdean. You do it."

"My hands are clumsy…all right, sit then. It wants better tending before it festers." He noted the reddened marks on Jamie's shoulders and knew them for what they were. The maid had not drawn blood, but had he despoiled her? Crisdean was not about to ask.

"Hurry. I've much to think about."

"You'd best seek your rest for whatever is left of this night."

"Enough, Crisdean. Ouch! Have a care for my skin."

"But Jamie, you wanted me to do this," he protested.

Jamie cast his fierce gaze upon his friend, and whatever Crisdean saw within those dark brown depths, it held him silent as he washed, salved and then set about rebandaging the wound.

"A favor before you leave me," Jamie said in a much calmer voice. "Open the shutters. 'Tis too warm in here."

Crisdean did as he was bid, and opened the wooden shutters.

"Jamie! Jamie, they're burning our crofts!"

Chapter Eighteen

Jamie snapped from his brooding state and fired orders while he recovered his shirt and snatched up his sword. Crisdean was already down below, rousing the men and getting the horses saddled, when he reached the stair.

There was no need for Jamie to think about warning any in the castle, for the place was already stirring as he reached the great hall.

"Fire!"

'Twas feared and dreaded as no other threat.

Sparks and flames could not reach from one crofter's dwelling to another, but torches carried by raiders could, and oft did. Fire was the beast that could not be fought.

Jamie's rage returned, and he ran through the bailey to the stables, snatching Killen's reins and vaulting to his back without waiting for him to be saddled. Other men followed suit, and soon they thundered from the castle to catch their enemies.

Before word spread of the fire, Gilliane, alone in her bed, lay awake. While her state could not be compared to Jamie's brooding one, she fought to stop the remembered warmth of his mouth and the desire he had awakened with the sure touch of his hands.

Despite the strong passion between them, how could she believe that he wished to wed her? And why did the doubts come now that she was alone and could not have answers from him—answers she needed?

So distracted was she by her musings, it took a long time before she felt a sudden searing jealousy that he had learned such seductive ways with other women.

"Fool," she whispered. "'Tis the way of things."

Far from soothing her, her thoughts turned to all Jamie had said. He'd spoken of wanting to protect her, had shown her the desire that flared so easily between them.

But marriage? 'Twas far, far more than bedding together.

Here in her bed, where none could see, she blushed deeply to think again of the intimacy she'd allowed him. Once more she tried to turn her thoughts away from the heat that still shivered through her.

He knew nothing about her. Nor had he asked.

She was a fine needlewoman, praised for the delicate stitchery of *orfrois* that she had mastered and learned from the women of Flanders who worked that French art.

Did Jamie know she faithfully attended her herb garden and had a stillroom that was the envy of many?

He knew naught of her careful management of all the household duties, and of the coin so necessary to fulfill them.

Had he questioned her about the manor house or farms? She could not remember. But if he had, surely he had never asked her who sat in justice over the serfs and villeins. Her father could not be taken from his work to decide what fine was merited when a chicken was stolen, or what recompense a villein's cow trampling a serf's garden deserved.

And Seana was the lady here at Halberry Castle. All turned to her for their orders within the keep and without.

What place would Gilliane have?

Restlessly, she turned over, then pulled aside the bed hanging.

Freed now of the treacherous passion that bemused her and all her senses, Gilliane gave clear thought to what the future would hold. She had not lied to Jamie about her talk with Sister Ellen of retreating to the abbey.

What she had left out was that it was never meant to be the permanent end she sought. She knew she had no true desire to take the veil. At least she had admitted to that lie, and it was no longer between them.

Gilliane was not sure when the sounds penetrated her bemused state. But suddenly there were voices calling up the stair, and a great stirring both within and without the castle.

She rose and donned the shift Jamie had removed, then slipped on the bed robe.

Once she opened her door, she heard the voices clearly, talking with great anger and excitement about a fire and the men who had ridden out to catch the reivers.

Jamie! She knew he had gone. She turned back into her room, this time to dress. She would be needed to help with wounded, or whatever other chore Seana would set for her.

Gilliane hurried to find her and make her offer.

Jamie hurried, too, driving his great stallion through the dark toward the far north corner where crofts were reported burning. The wind sent the flames soaring. He knew they would be too late to save anything.

Gabhan rode close and handed over Jamie's shield. "At least take this! You've no armor."

"The better to ride faster. They must have been lying

in wait. Laughing to see that we fell for their cunning plan. All were looking for the two that escaped my sword—the damn misbegotten bastards!'' Those were the last words any heard Jamie speak as they galloped through the night.

After an hour's hard riding they came to the narrow path that led to the burning crofts. The stench was such that none could draw a free breath.

Jamie sat on his horse, staring down at the bodies fallen where they had been slashed with ax and sword.

''Jamie? Jamie, they killed the animals. Slaughtered all.''

''Find them. Not one man is to return to me without a bloodied sword.''

He stared at the wicked little flames that licked out for fresh fuel, but there was none to be had. All had blackened; all was burned.

Jamie was inured to hard labor. He knew how to spend days in the saddle, topped by days of fighting, and then ride hard again. He knew how to do without much sleep for long periods.

But sights like this sapped his strength. These were simple folk, content to farm, raise their livestock and come feast at the castle grounds when there was cause to celebrate or, far too often, cause to mourn.

They did not deserve to die a horrible death. His soul cried out for the peace he knew his brother Micheil desired above all things.

''Crisdean, detail two men to stay and bury them.''

''Where do you go?'' his friend asked, seeing Jamie turn his stallion away.

''I ride for Keith lands and Keith blood.''

Crisdean followed him through the night as they headed north. Across burns and over moors, through thickly forested patches, past other crofts where all slept behind barred doors, they rode in silence and they rode hard.

Black were the towering rocks as they followed along a path only Jamie could see, never stopping, never speaking, riding on until the ground leveled off and the going was easier for beast and man.

The sky was paling to the light before dawn when they had to slow their pace among tall trees. The moss-covered ground helped to silence the horses' hooves.

From ahead came the sound of swiftly moving water and the whinny of a horse.

Jamie drew rein, and Crisdean halted beside him. As he leaned closer to speak to his clansman, another noise caught his attention, this time from behind him.

Caught!

Jamie tightened his hand on his naked sword and saw that Crisdean, too, was alert to the danger. But he had sworn to spill Keith blood for the lives lost this night, and very slowly he turned.

There, arrayed behind him, were a dozen Gunn clansmen. Some were fully dressed, and others, like Jamie, wore their long shirts and breeks and little else. But in each hand was either pike or claymore or ax.

With hand motions he dispersed his men in a half circle toward the stream, where they were sure Keiths were watering their horses. The light grew brighter with dawn, and all heard the birdsong suddenly stop in midtrill.

Then, with the earth trembling beneath their horses' thundering hooves, the Gunns attacked.

Sunlight played into the small glen where the Keiths sought rest and shelter. Sunlight that glinted on bared blades and axes that whistled before they fell.

Six, eight or ten—Jamie knew no one had thought to count their enemies before they set upon them. The air rang with the clash of steel, with shouts and insults traded back and forth. With the wild neighing of the horses, rearing and plunging as they were battle trained to do—stunning and maiming friend and foe alike, for the space was small.

The devils of hell had broken loose, and would not leave until they'd slain every Keith present for the deaths carried out this night.

Jamie's arm rose and fell as if apart from himself. He lifted his shield as needed to ward off blows. He had a care for Killen, for the easiest blow a man on foot could deliver was to broach his stallion, hoping the rider would be crushed as the animal fell.

Eventually there came to that place of carnage a sudden silence, into which one of the Gunn men called out, "We are done. There are no more to fight."

Jamie looked around at those who had fallen, and the sight brought a prayer for the dead to his lips. He was not alone as labored breaths filled the air and weapons were lowered. Like his men, he looked around to see comrades safe.

"Tend to our wounded first," Jamie ordered. "Take all but one horse, and strip the Keiths of everything. Dugal, choose one body to be tied to a horse and sent back as a warning to those who reive and kill on Gunn lands. Leave the rest for the crows."

And then, sickened by the fact that he still held on to his bloodied sword, for he had come away with no saddle to hold a scabbard, Jamie used the point to lift a piece of cloth from the rapidly growing pile forming as his men did his bidding. He wiped his blade clean, thinking he wanted nothing more than to ride from this place of death. 'Twas a waste of all manhood, enemy or no. Yet he had to abide until his men were finished carrying out his orders.

"Jamie?" Crisdean said, drawing his horse close beside him. "We've two sore wounded that with care and prayer should recover. But Dermott won't last another night."

"Dermott?" Jamie repeated, then remembered the man. "His wife carries their first bairn." His face darkened with anger. "Take out my share of the booty to go to her. 'Tis small recompense for losing her man and her babe's father."

Crisdean did not answer. What could he say? This was the way they lived.

Another clansman came up to them. "The men are near done."

"Then let us start for home," Crisdean urged.

"Aye, 'tis a sorry night's work that we leave behind us," Dugal added.

Jamie nodded, and they all turned for home, taking the weapons and horses, and leaving behind a smoldering pile of clothing that would soon flame and turn to ashes. The Keiths would find their dead, and another wave of raids and killing would begin. Without end, Jamie silently mouthed to himself. Without end.

On this same morn, there came three men on half-dead horses, begging admittance to the Keith stronghold at Ackergill. It was one of the clan's smaller keeps, built at the time when the Bruce forbade the construction of large castles, which, if taken, afforded secure strongholds to the invaders. So those who built constructed the Norman-style keep of stone, only large enough to protect the laird's family and retainers from sudden attack. There was a three-storied tower, and it was from the topmost chamber that warning had come of the approaching riders.

By chance, they found the man they sought here, for George, chief of Clan Keith, had broken his journey to inspect and arm his keeps, and had stayed the night.

The Keiths had been engaged for years in conflict with the clan Gunn, with only relatively short periods of truce between them.

George, roused from the near drunken stupor into which he had fallen—too often of late, many thought— bade his man allow the visitors to enter the keep and offer them all that was custom: baths, food and a place to rest. But he would not see anyone at this time.

Befuddled by drink, his mind locked into the past, George had become a bitter and vicious man. And he blamed Micheil of Clan Gunn for most of his sorrows.

He had loved Bridget, the prize of Clan Gunn, and wanted her for his own. But her brothers had stood against him. Then his bonnie Bridget, with the hot passion that was hers, fell in love with Liam of Clan MacKay—sometime Keith allies—and would have no other man to wed.

George had had his revenge on the MacKays and the Gunns and stoked high the fire of vengeance, which led to a feud where the fire and sword had been carried across the northern Highlands.

He'd won his place as chief because he'd had a secret ally in Niall of Clan Gunn. George had known when the Gunns were out and away, and so planned his raids with little loss of Keith life.

But Niall was dead now, and no matter the schemes he had contrived over the years, the Gunns managed to circumvent his plans and live on.

He drained his cup, and spilled wine on the table when he refilled it.

"Failure," he muttered. "All has come to failure."

The ambush he'd set up in the guise of peace talks, the

raids to lure them…naught had brought about one Gunn brother's death.

And then came the pain of despair. His son, his bonnie heir and the only thing of worth he had from his puling wife, had been taken hostage by the Gunns and died.

Somewhere in the madness of his mind, George knew it was an accident that had killed the boy. But his hatred for the Gunns was so deep that he laid the boy's death upon their heads.

The drink-muddled train of thought had brought George back to the vow he had sworn when his son's body was placed beneath the stones of the chapel. He had pledged on the sainted relics within the altar stone that he would see the three Gunn brothers' heads hung from his own walls.

And that had yet to come about.

He had to find some success somewhere or his clan would turn on him and oust him as chief, if someone did not stick a dirk in his back first.

What? Where could he find them vulnerable?

While George's mind swayed between past and present, his visitor, having dismissed his two men-at-arms to mingle with those of the Keiths, had bathed and eaten lightly of the meat pie, cheese and bread brought to him. He quaffed the ale, and then demanded to see the chief, saying his news was of such import that delay would bring disaster.

It was not until further probing by the Keith man, Graeme, that Radnor mentioned the Gunns. Graeme left him immediately to seek audience with George.

The mention of Clan Gunn roused the laird, and he bade Graeme bring forth the man Radnor.

Now Radnor had a secret jealous spite for Louis Marche, and envied the place he held with their lord, de

Orbrec. All the hard riding Radnor had done to reach the Keith chief had allowed him to form what he would say to ensure the complete success of his lord's plan, and thus, he would win a great reward for himself. Radnor wanted the manor houses belonging to the de Verrill maid, and the two rich farms that went with it. He knew that his lord would be most generous; now all he had to do was to make sure that this Highland chief acted his part.

When he was ushered into George's presence, Radnor bent his knee to the man and spoke before either George or Graeme could.

"My lord, I have come with news that will fulfill your vow against the Gunns. My lord Guy de Orbrec holds at his keep at Castres the Gunn woman—the abbess of Deer Abbey. There is a ransom to be paid for her return, but my lord wishes to deal with you first."

At the mention of a Gunn woman, George's heart had soared, for he'd thought they held Seana, Micheil's wife. Killing her would be true revenge. But the aunt—for it had to be Lady Ailis, sister to Ingram, the old chief who had denied his marriage to Bridget—would do as well.

"Tell me all," George ordered. "Wait. Graeme, do bring another chair for our guest. And wine. Such talk is thirsty work." He turned again to his guest. "Is it not?"

"As you say, my lord. As you say."

And when they were alone, Radnor told the tale of how the abbess had fallen into Lord de Orbrec's hands, with great embellishment of his own part in her capture. He went on to explain exactly what his lord wished from the chief of Clan Keith.

"So you see, my lord, with you following close behind as they bring the ransom to us, we will have them caught like the blacksmith's pincers."

George leaned back and closed his eyes, mulling over

every word. He wanted to gloat, but too many times in the past he had counted on another's actions to destroy his enemies, and failure was the cup he'd been forced to drink.

He thought of the paltry ransom demanded for the Gunn woman, and knew he would wring more, much more from that clan. If he could succeed, his own standing would rise again.

Radnor grew impatient. He did not fidget, nor make a sound to call attention to himself, but inwardly he fumed. His lord's plan was sound. There was little danger to the Keiths. What could the man be thinking of to take so long in agreeing.

George, well aware that an immediate answer was not only expected, but necessary for the plan to work, nevertheless continued with his own thoughts.

He wanted more than this Norman's lord offered him. How best to get it required more than a few minutes of pondering.

He shifted and opened his eyes, leaning toward Radnor. "It was not lost upon me that you arrived in great haste. Go seek your rest. I will have an answer for you as soon as I gather others of my clan."

"But my lord—"

"I bid you go. To make your rest easy, I assure you that my answer will please your lord."

With that Radnor had to be content. But there was an avid gleam in the Keith chief's eyes that boded ill for him, and for his lord's plans.

Chapter Nineteen

For those who war, time is taken up by action and flees swiftly. But for those who must wait, there comes a belly-gripping tension that finds no release until loved ones return safely.

Micheil, cursing his injury, prowled the walls with a silent Davey beside him. As dawn's light spread to sun's glow, their joined gazes combed their lands, noting the thin ribbons of streams, the dark forests and the moors, but no sign of returning riders. Had each spoken to the other, the same thought would be shared, for it was not the clan tanist they worried about, but their own brother.

Down below there was a stirring as Janet and Mary, along with those who had traveled with them, made ready for their journeys. Carts and horses were brought forth, with most clansmen turning their faces from the vinegar-soaked shrouds of the betrayers' bodies as they were loaded into the respective carts.

Seana briefly oversaw this leave-taking, but another role demanded her attention—a role every woman of keep and castle, croft or meanest serf's hut knew when men made war. Salves and bandages, wine for strengthening, hot water for washing, silken thread and her best needles for the sewing of wounds—all were made ready under her direction to aid those who returned.

"My lady, I beg a moment."

Seana had politely bade both Mary and Janet a safe journey and naught more, for she could not forget the part the sister of one and the son of the other had played in almost taking her own son's life. She turned now to see the Welsh woman before her.

"Meredith, is it not?"

"Aye. I beg you to believe what I tell you. Do not allow Davey to accompany his brother Jamie. He will be wounded nigh unto death if he goes."

"Have you thc sight, then?" Seana asked, stepping closer. She wanted to see the woman's eyes, but the fall of her hood prevented that. Seana not only believed in second sight, she knew there were other bonds like the one she shared with Micheil, where dreaming of the other was so real it was like touching flesh. She knew, too, that Davey had the sight, but for him it was an agony to be borne, for it struck without warning.

"Did you tell Davcy of this warning?" Seana asked.

"I cannot. Do not ask more of me. You warn him. My life is at risk to say more."

Seana stretched out her hand, unsure if she would comfort or detain the young woman, Meredith turned and fled from the hall. Seana thought it very strange that the warning should come for Davey when it was Jamie who intended combat with the Norman.

That reminded her that, despite concern over the men who had ridden out in the night, there were still preparations to be made for the journey to rescue Ailis. Thought of her brought a silent prayer for her safety, for Seana had made her own peace with the abbess who had held her for almost ten years of her life on the orders of Micheil's father.

Thoughts of the journey brought her to look for Gilliane. Seana was not unaware of the attraction between the maid and Jamie. Although younger than Gilliane, she had lived through many losses, and having ended with the joy of her husband and son, she wished for the same love for Gilliane.

And for Jamie, too, for he loved with a fierce, deep passion. Seana's hand touched her neck. She would never forget the feel of Jamie's dirk held at her throat while he and Davey goaded Micheil into admitting that he loved her beyond all else.

No, she told herself, that was a memory best left in the past.

She wanted so much to seek out Micheil and have him hold her against the sudden fierce chill that beset her, but she knew he would be up on the walls, watching and waiting for his brother's return. And with the cold of these borrowing days, as the spring cold spell was named, she did not relish the thought of the icy wind coming off the sea to add to the inner cold she felt.

Peigi's voice was raised in the back of the hall, but Seana paid her no mind. Peigi would have maids and cooks harried, producing enough to feed those who waited, and setting aside the choicest bits for those to come.

What Seana did not see was the slender figure of Gilliane. She was not among those at the table, or near the great hearth, with its huge blazing logs. Seana wondered if she, too, prowled the walls above, or watched the sea lashing into great breakers on the rocks below. Sister Ellen had gone earlier to the chapel and must be there still, for Seana did not see her, either.

The noise and bustle of the great hall became too much for her. Seana thought of her son, and the comfort of his small body held in her arms. She had seen that all was made ready; now there was only the waiting. Leaving word where she could be found, she left the hall.

To her surprise she found Gilliane with her son. She sat beside the bedecked cradle watching the child sleep.

"He is a beautiful babe," Gilliane whispered. "And he has the look of his father."

"Aye. That black fuzz will be as thick as Micheil's, and if his eyes stay blue, the two will be as alike as peas in a pod."

Sleeping or not, Seana had a need to hold him, and she lifted him gently from the cradle. She buried her face in the soft fold of his neck, cradling his small body against her. Unexpected tears shimmered in her eyes when she looked at Gilliane.

"'Tis foolish, I know, to shed a tear, but having come so close to losing him, I need to hold him often and thank the Virgin that my little one is safe."

"It must bring you great joy, too, Seana, to know that you have a child of love to guide into manhood."

There was sadness in Gilliane's lovely green eyes and Seana responded to that. She lay her bairn down, covered him and motioned Gilliane to the other side of the room, where their whispers would not disturb his sleep.

"I have the joy of my son, but it will not be for long. Betwixt his father and uncles and others of the clan, they will see more to his raising than I. And it is a hard thing to give your love to men like Micheil and Jamie and Davey, for above all else they love their honor."

"'Tis no bad thing to seek in a man."

"Do you look for such, Gilliane?"

A flush tinted her cheeks and she glanced away from

Seana's gray gaze. "Did you know that Jamie intended to ask me to wed?"

"Wed!" Seana exclaimed.

"You did not know? I wondered if any did. You cannot be more shocked or surprised than I. He pressed me for an answer, and I know not what to tell him."

Seana caught hold of Gilliane's hand and felt a faint tremble, along with a decided coldness. "Do you want him?"

Gilliane was torn over answering her with honesty. "I find him attractive. He is firm of purpose."

"Is that enough for you? What of love? And do not say that it comes with time, for there are those who look upon one they desire and at once know that person to be their heart's choice. No other will do."

Gilliane studied their hands, glad that she had told Seana, for she needed to talk with someone who would truly understand. And she felt a warmth toward this woman whose words proved Gilliane right.

"This is no time for meekness, Gilliane. You must know your own heart. If it is too soon to decide, tell him so. But if you wish him for your husband, then do not hesitate, for there are many who would take him and think they had a great prize."

"I thought more about his reason to wed than my own. I told him the advantage was all mine. He claimed it was for my own safety that he offered, as I am without family to turn to."

"Look at me!" Seana ordered. "I know you are over-old for marriage, and perhaps you think me to too young to give advice—"

"Nay! 'Tis not true. It is why I hoped to speak with you."

Seana saw there was no guile in her eyes, and this time

she did not look away. "You have little time before you leave here. I say again, if you wish to wait, then do so. I know there are few who can marry for love, but I speak as one who did. To be half of someone's soul brings a joy like no other. Jamie has not fixed his attentions on any woman where the thought of his wedding came into play. For him to ask you means that he wants you and no other. I will add this. If Jamie is like my Micheil, and I believe that he and Davey are, they give their hearts once and it is forever."

"You speak of hearts given, of love. I heard only words of passion."

"That is no bad thing," Seana said, then softly laughed. She sobered at the darker flush staining Gilliane's cheeks. "He did not—"

"'Twas a near thing. But I am still a maid."

"Thank the Virgin for that. But listen to me. You need time, and I will talk to Jamie—"

"Nay! I would not have him know."

"'Tis foolish, but I will abide by your wish in this. None will look for you here. Sit then, in the quiet, sort through your own needs and desires. If you wish to speak to me again I will come."

"Thank you, Seana. I've not had another woman to talk to for a long time. It gladdens my heart."

"If you marry Jamie, we will be sisters. You'll not be alone, Gilliane. In that, Jamie spoke true. You will have brothers and me and my son Heth and the clan. Oh, and my brother Liam. You will plead for a quiet place if you stay to live with us."

Seana rose and smiled. "Do not fret too much. Jamie is a strong warrior. He will come safe among us soon."

She had to leave Gilliane and find Micheil. Had he known what Jamie intended? And if so, why had he not told her? She was not sure now that she had given Gilliane good advice. If Jamie's passion was anything like her husband's, she knew that he would do everything to have Gilliane to wife. Seana faltered in her step. Was there more to this? Could Jamie have another reason...? She hurried to find her cloak and join Micheil on the wall.

Gilliane had moved to watch the deep, even breaths of Heth. The peace of the child lent little to her as she thought over all that Seana had said. Night had turned to day without her mind settling on what to do. Seana's statement that love made the marriage served to remind Gilliane that Jamie had not spoken of love, only of the strong desire between them. And was that a thing to last?

She could see him in her mind's eye and knew he was not a man to be forgotten.

What did she want? She wanted to speak of her love and hear the same from him.

Then she heard a cry that the men were returning.

Gilliane hurried across the room, just as the child's nurse returned.

"Go, my lady, go. I will be here."

Gilliane needed no urging to fly down the stairs. He had come and, praise the Lord, he was unhurt.

Jamie dismounted and tossed his reins to one of the grooms who had run forward. He searched those who crowded the courtyard until he found the one he looked for, then neither saw nor heard any others.

As if it were the most natural thing in the world, Gilliane came down the steps and rushed into the arms that opened to receive her.

"You are whole and safe," she cried to Jamie.

Seana, following with her husband, turned to him. "Are you sure of this, Micheil? It appears a sudden thing for

Jamie to want to wed her. He scarcely knows Gilliane. I barely contained my surprise when she spoke of it to me.''

''Look at them, love. He sees no one else. I'm the first to admit that men will lie to themselves and likely others when they want a woman.'' He slipped his arm around his wife's now slender waist and drew her closer to him. ''When a man is held in passion's web he forgets that the loveliest of roses have the sharpest thorns.''

''You did not mind them.'' She looked up and smiled at her husband, then turned serious. ''But, Micheil, I saw little if any thorns from Gilliane. She seems more confused than a woman in love.''

Micheil, unwilling to explain his brother's feelings, merely remarked, ''Perhaps that is why Jamie wants her. A gentle woman is more to his taste.''

Far from satisfied, Seana let it be. She freed herself from Micheil to order the wounded men seen to, then went herself to comfort Dermott's young wife when she saw that his chance of surviving was small.

Jamie, holding Gilliane tightly and feeling rewarded by the way she clung to him, ignored the stir they caused. He saw none of the glances cast his way. Her greeting cast aside his doubts that he meant nothing to her.

''Gilliane, Gilliane,'' he whispered at last, ''does this sweet greeting mean your answer is yes?''

The strength of his arms, knowing he was not newly wounded, and the husky, intimate note in his voice were almost enough to dismiss every vestige of uncertainty. Almost.

''I've scarce had time to think. It is no light decision to make.''

Disappointed, Jamie held her a moment more. Her words stung him. He had been so sure he would have the answer he wanted.

"I bow to your wisdom. Clearly the timing is inopportune. Free me, Gilliane. My clothes are stained with my enemies' blood."

Gilliane stepped back. She looked only at his face, noting the tiredness.

"Will you allow me to tend you, Jamie?"

"It would please me. Go make all ready and I'll see to my men."

Jamie turned, unable to watch her go. He blamed himself for his carelessness in pushing her. He tried to separate his desire for Gilliane from all else, but it was impossible when she was near. His loins tightened and heated every time he laid eyes on her, which had not happened with other women. He was suffering too many of the symptoms that were celebrated or bemoaned in songs and stories. He knew himself to be considered a worthy catch for any Highland lass. Why then did she keep him dangling?

Micheil had heard what he wanted from Crisdean, so when Jamie finally came forward to tell of their success, his brother waved him off.

"See to yourself. I will deal with all else. I need you rested for the journey to rescue our aunt."

The words were both a welcome and a curse. Jamie wanted to be with Gilliane, but also wished for more time to cool his blood before he joined her.

By the time he reached his chamber, Jamie had made a decision. The tub was already in place and the menservants were filling it from the leather buckets they carried. Gilliane stood near the chest, a tray of salves and herbs and bandages holding her attention.

"Please do not take this amiss, Gilliane. Let me bathe, and then come tend me. Although, truth to tell, I do not believe you will find any new wounds."

"If that is what you wish."

"If you said yes to me, there would be no need for you to go. I'm not in a state fit for you to see," he countered with barely held anger.

"Then I will return when you send for me. I need to talk to you, Jamie, and the time is short."

Oddly, his anger disappeared at hearing this. He was filled with a sense of well-being, of pleasant anticipation. He stripped quickly, and chased everyone out, more than able to bathe himself.

There was nothing coquettish in Gilliane's manner. Perhaps when they spoke she would tell him what concerned her. He felt again that strong, nearly overwhelming surge of protectiveness for her. He had presented his proposal in the wrong way; he could now admit that. After all, it was most unusual to make a direct offer of marriage with a woman. It was with the father or other male protector that such things were discussed and agreed to. Fool! Jamie chided himself. Who could Gilliane go to here? She knew less of his clan and family than she did of him.

Anxious now, he hurried to scrub the signs of battle from him and settle with Gilliane to both their satisfaction.

Gilliane returned to the hall and sought out Peigi, to arrange for a tray of food to be sent to Jamie. When Peigi teased Micheil that he had no true Scots blood within him if he would not eat his brose, Gilliane laughed along with others for it was no secret that Micheil hated the porridge that filled a wooden bowl near every place.

With Janet and Mary gone the underlying hate of their relatives' betrayals went with them leaving a lighter mood but no less tense for those men who had chased the Keiths and were now answering Micheil's questions.

Gilliane returned to her chamber. While she had been

gone from there, someone had laid out a choice of garments for her.

Over her own linen shift, which had been washed and mended, she chose a yellow wool kirtle, the shade of which she was sure came from Saint-John's-wort. The simple chain girdled her hips, but there was one addition to her dress; she wore her own eating knife. She replaited her two braids, thinking enough time had passed for Jamie to finish his bath. She wanted to go to him. She had a moment's pang when, crossing the great hall, she felt that all eyes were upon her. But no one tried to engage her in talk or stop her in any way.

Gilliane arrived at Jamie's door a trifle breathless from her swift climb, only to discover it open. She grew flustered to find Davey in the room with Jamie.

Since her gaze went to Jamie and stayed there, Davey saw that his presence was unwanted. But out of sheer mischief, he bowed and greeted her.

"Have you come to break fast with Jamie, too?"

Jamie's eyes flicked toward his brother, and if looks could kill, Davey would have dropped where he stood. But Jamie looked again at Gilliane hesitating in the doorway.

"Come in. Davey was just leaving. Weren't you, Brother?" he asked sharply.

"But I came to see to your wound. Micheil was concerned. We all were."

Jamie sighed with resigned exasperation. "Gilliane has come to do the same. And frankly, Davey, I'd rather have her gentle touch than your heavy hand."

Still Gilliane looked from one brother to the other and made no move to enter. Jamie wore breeks and one of his thigh-length linen shirts. The tray she had brought up earlier to treat his wound remained untouched. Closer to Jamie's chair another small table was set with the food tray.

"Jamie, far be it for me to teach you the way, but should you not greet the lady with a compliment on her loveliness? 'Tis the way to court a maid, I've been told. By you, in fact."

"Gilliane knows she is beautiful," Jamie said.

"She would be a bletherin' fool if she did not," Davey agreed. "But I still say that women like to be told that they are most pleasing to the eye."

Jamie's hands tightened on his chair's arms. "Davey, brother or not, I'll do murder if you do not go away. Let me manage this affair in my own way."

Davey backed off, his hands held high, but at the door he stopped to whisper to Gilliane. She smiled and nodded, stepping aside for him to leave, then entered the room.

"Your younger brother is charming, Jamie."

"My brother Davey is an interferin' fool. I'll not need him to remind me that I should tell you I find you lovely. And I beg forgiveness for my temper. I was anxious to see you come."

"And I anxious to have our talk," she answered with the same honesty he showed her. "Let me first tend your wound. Can you lift off your shirt without help?"

Instead of answering, Jamie bent forward and pulled the shirt over his head. He held the cloth balled in one hand, his eyes watching every graceful move that she made.

He leaned forward so she could reach his lower left side.

"It is not very deep," she remarked. "And the wound is clean."

"Seana put the stillroom in order when she came here. She learned much of healing salves at the abbey."

"I, too, have a stillroom that is greatly envied," Gillian said in a soft voice, happy to have this opening to discuss what she wished. She took her time smoothing the salve, enjoying not only this wifely chore, but the clean scent of his body. There were long healed scars attesting to his life of fighting, and she found herself touching each.

"Gilliane, have a care. I'm no saint. And I already told you what your touch does to me."

He could not see her smile, but she hurried now to wrap the clean linen around him and tie it off. While she stood and set the tray aside, he slipped on his shirt. He was going to try and keep his word to hear what she had to say.

With his bare foot he pushed out the footstool. "Come sit here beside me. I promise to listen, but I want to look upon you."

Gilliane, well aware of the strong, sensual pleasure that flowed through her at touching Jamie's body both last night and now, was very careful to keep from touching him as she took her seat.

She began without coyness to express the doubts she had raised to herself about how they were suited. Jamie listened with every bit of attention she could have wished for.

"So you see, Jamie, my concerns are valid ones. Where would we live? 'Tis no small matter to think of two women in one keep, not even a castle the size of Halberry."

"Gilliane, there you present me with a grave problem. I am tanist of my clan. I must be close by my chief. For me that means living here. I can take the tower that once belonged to my sister for our own. I have another small keep at Dirlot in the far north. And you would keep your manor house and farms."

Jamie drew on his store of patience, for he believed that her mind was made up and her answer yes. Why she needed to have all this sorted now he could not understand, but was willing to allow Gilliane her way in this.

"Do you know, I feel strange in talking to you about this, Jamie. I wish my father had settled me with someone long ago and none of this would have arisen."

"There I disagree with you, Gilliane. I would be heart-sore not to have you for my own."

"Do you like children, Jamie? You've never said."

"The more the merrier, and before you think to ask me, there are no bastards with my blood. At least," he quickly amended, "none that have been claimed and brought to my attention."

Gilliane looked up and saw his gaze upon her. There came that treacherous heat, that most insistent need to cuddle in Jamie's strong arms and to taste again passion from his mouth that smiled down at her.

Jamie reached out and took one of Gilliane's hands in his. He felt the faint quiver that passed through her and heard her quickened breath. His own picked up apace, for Davey had been right to say that she was beautiful. Caught as she was in a shaft of sunlight from the unshuttered window she appeared gilded. Her delicate features framed with the braids that hung on her shoulders.

"Gilliane, I know all these doubts are serious to you. But not once have you spoken of what is in your heart. Can you have me?"

She gripped his hand. "Do not be angry, Jamie, but I am truly afraid."

"And I told you there is naught to fear from me. I would never raise a hand to you."

"Yet it would be your right."

"Then never give me cause. Gilliane, do you not see,

we can go around and around, like a mad dog chasing its tail, and I will soothe where I can, and you will again raise another question.''

''But marriage is most serious, Jamie.''

''Then handfast with me. A year and a day. Give me that time to drive away your fears and doubts and answer all your questions.''

''A year and a day?'' She pulled her hand free, unwilling to have his touch distract her. She was not surprised that he renewed this offer. In truth, she admitted to herself that she had expected their talk to come to this. And would it be so bad a thing to steal a year from Jamie? Provided he lived through this combat he was so set upon having with de Orbrec…

As if he sensed her wavering, Jamie said, ''How can I give you surety of the months and years to come? Am I not aware that I could die in a sudden way? Did I not tell you that a lucky stroke by this Norman bastard could end my life? And so, Gilliane, I snatch at what life has brought, and pray that tomorrow will bring a renewal of whatever joy there is.''

Her eyes, wide and green, targeted his face. Her teeth cut off the cry that came. And Jamie cursed himself for the reminder of death when he wished all else from her.

But he could not look into those eyes and lie to her.

''Gilliane, you know me for a fool for mentioning it, but I cannot deny I think about it. And you must also. If you recall, I first asked you to wed to give you all the protection that is mine to give. I will not see you fall into the Norman's hands no matter the cost.''

She bit harder on her lower lip. Here again was the hero of dreams, a man for her to love, and she had to give him something. Then it came to her.

"Jamie, I will agree to handfast with you, but I will not share your bed. Nay! Listen, please."

"I'll not be cheated—"

Gilliane jumped up. "You dare talk to me of being cheated! How will I cheat you? I will be wife to you in all ways but this. You said that at the end of the time I could be free. And what of you, Jamie? If you leave me what will I have? Naught to bring to another!"

Even as she spoke the words, Gilliane rejected them. She did not want another. But she did want love. And still, no matter how she probed or led him, Jamie did not speak of love.

She renewed her plea. "Jamie, I said I would be wife to you in all else. I need time to know you and your ways. It is well and fine for you to say you will not beat me if I quarrel with you. Can you truly have a care for me and not understand that I need the surety of seeing this proved to me? I have no one else to speak to you thus. If you cannot accept this term when you win all else you claim to want, then I will not hold you to your offer."

He came up from his chair with all the lethal grace of a hunter and followed as she backed away from him.

"'Tis custom to give the kiss of peace when a bargain is made, Gilliane. Give your mouth to me, and let me taste the truth of your words."

"You will accept my term?"

The wanting he had for her almost robbed him of speech.

"It will be as you will. But know this, Gilliane," he whispered as with battle-trained swiftness he caught her and drew her tight to his body, "I will have you, and what's more, you will come to me."

He gave her no chance to answer. His mouth claimed hers, and this was no kiss of peace that he offered.

Despite his words, Gilliane was taken by surprise. She truly expected a kiss of peace, and found instead that Jamie offered a swirling passion that swept her up in its turbulent tide.

She pressed closer to him when it seemed he would withdraw. She was truly caught in a net of her own making. How had she forgotten for a moment the potent fire he set?

He drew her against his lower body. His hands were on her hips and slowly moving her from side to side, teasing and tormenting them both by turns.

His dark Gaelic whispers required no explanation, for their passionate intent was as clear as the kisses he pressed to her throat and lips. There was a danger here that her own body would betray her will, and Gillianc managed to turn aside from his next kiss.

"Jamie, I beg you. I trust you."

Jamie struggled to collect himself. Gilliane laid her head on his chest, a trusting move, while her words replayed in his mind. He shuddered to think how close he had come to taking her where they stood. He pressed his lips to her hair, knowing he had nearly been out of control. But he claimed her as his, and he loved her. Should he speak of what was in his heart? Nay, he warned himself. He could not. For his battle with de Orbrec still waited.

"Jamie, do not take this amiss," she whispered against his chest. "I feel I have no right to happiness now. It is all tainted with your aunt paying the price for my freedom. I want you, Jamie. I...I do desire you, but denying myself and you makes...oh, Jamie, try to understand?"

"I do. All too well. Go, Gilliane. Go, before I forget my word of honor that it shall be as you want."

She fled, wondering if her honesty was a terrible mistake.

Jamie watched her flee. He thought to himself that she was right. Bitter as it was to admit, his aunt's capture had brought about Gilliane's freedom. Time and patience, and his warrior's skill, would bring him all he wanted.

His smile was rueful. Meek, sweet-natured, lovely Gilliane proved to have a strong will. If matters were not so serious, he would enjoy pitting his own will against hers.

Time…damnable time.

Chapter Twenty

Micheil, having been informed by Jamie of the exact terms of the handfasting, went to his wife and told her. He had a care for Gilliane, not only as his brother's choice of wife but for her courage, so similar to his wife's, in not meekly accepting her lot. He also needed his brother's attention on plans of patrols and such while Jamie was gone.

Thus it was Seana who took Gilliane in hand and kept her busy overseeing the provisions necessary for the journey. Far from the discomfort of her trip north, Gilliane understood they would travel with plenty.

In the large, cool storeroom by the kitchens she found the air rich with the scent of spices kept in large jars and smoked hams and bacon hanging from large iron hooks set into the ceiling beams. There were barrels of dried fish and sacks of flour, beans, meal and dried fruits to be had.

Gilliane had only to point out what they would need and tell one of the servants assigned to help her how much to set aside. Micheil was sending outriders to range ahead of their party, to ensure their safe arrival with the ransom. Seana made her swear not to tell Jamie. But she admitted to Gilliane that she had grave doubts any coin would find its way into the Norman's coffers.

They went into the buttery, where the cloying sweet odor of the rich, fresh milk made Gilliane hurry to take the cheeses from the smaller, darker storeroom set in the back. The walls were of a double stone thickness, and the floor was covered with straw. She shivered in the cold of the room, for there were no windows. One of the maids held the candle for her to see the great wheels of cheese kept on ledges hollowed out in the walls. Gilliane had to duck her head to avoid those cheeses, smaller and rounder, that were hung in rope nets from the ceiling.

There would be no cart. All they took had to be loaded on dray horses. There were sleeping tents to choose from, but Seana sent word to Gilliane to take one only, for herself and Sister Ellen. Small casks of wine and ale were selected, and then off she went to the stillroom for salves and herbs and lengths of cloth.

There were many stops and starts for Gilliane, for Seana was constantly at her side explaining that most of the comforts ordered for the journey were for her and Sister Ellen, and later, of course, for Ailis.

The thought of what Ailis might be suffering at the hands of de Orbrec spurred Gilliane to complete her tasks with fervor.

In Castres Keep, Ailis was helped from the prison pit by Louis. She blinked in the flaring torchlight.

"My lord has set aside a chamber for you where you may bathe and eat and take your rest. It was his temper, now cooled, that left you too long below. Come, if you can walk. If not I will carry you."

"Go slowly," Ailis said. "There was little room below to walk and my legs are unsteady."

She accepted his explanation as reasonable. The mere thought of being where there was daylight, or where she might see the stars, was temptation enough. The mention of a bath after however long she had been in that pit rivaled her pious thoughts of heaven.

It was not as far as she thought to go, only one turning of the winding stair and there stood a guard near a door.

Louis opened it and stood aside for Ailis to enter.

"You will find all that you need, and if not, send the girl to me."

Had Ailis come as a guest to this keep she would have protested this mean chamber, but after what she had experienced since that pit opened, she welcomed it.

The fire had not been burning long, for the room held the chill dampness of an unused place. There was a tub of steaming water, and on her knees beside it, a young girl waited. One thick candle burned—of the poorest tallow, for it smoked. Ailis stepped closer, desiring that bath, and saw the girl's face.

Shadings of blue, purple, and older bruises of yellow marred whatever claim to beauty the young one had. Her eyes darted from Ailis's, nor did she move as Ailis forced unused limbs to rid herself of her nun's robe and shift. It was harder still to sit and untie the leather that held her shoes, for it had grown stiff with her sweat.

"Come help me, child," Ailis ordered in a soft voice. "None will do you harm while you serve me."

Instead of rising and walking to Ailis, the girl crawled to her.

"What are you called, child?"

Ailis barely hid her recoil when the girl opened her mouth to point at the place where her tongue should have been.

"Did that monster de Orbrec do this to you?"

The wild shaking of her head covered with matted hair made Ailis forbear from asking any other questions.

With the girl's help, she bathed, and understood enough of the girl's motions to know she was to don the clothes laid on the pallet. When she protested that she could not wear any but her robe, the girl motioned that she would wash it. She smiled to encourage Ailis.

Knowing only that the girl would likely be beaten if she did not do as asked, Ailis complied. But it felt strange to her to wear such rich, heavily embroidered clothing suited to a younger woman.

Ailis thought of what Gilliane told her of the other wives de Orbrec had taken. Whoever's clothing this had been, she was of a size with Ailis. The girl rubbed her cheek against the rich cloth, her eyes and smile showing her approval.

Ailis grew more uncomfortable. She was not afraid of being assaulted, for any man who touched a nun or novice would be drawn and quartered.

The girl gathered up the wet drying cloths and Ailis's clothes, and before Ailis could stop her, she fled from the room.

A quick search revealed nothing but the candle and stool that could be used as weapons. Ailis did not think her soul would be imperiled because she thought of violence. The Norman's imprisonment denied her completing her duties as abbess, as nun and as guide to those under her care.

She went to open the door and found that it was either latched or barred from the other side. And likely the guard had remained. There was nothing more she could do but pray and wait.

But it was not so very long before there came a knock, and when Ailis called out ''Enter,'' Louis came in followed by the same bruised girl who had served her. Behind her, menservants entered carrying a small table, two low-backed chairs and a large tray, the aromas from which made Ailis swallow against sudden hunger.

Louis stood aside until all was in place, then held a chair for Ailis to sit before the fire.

"I told you my lord wished to make up for your earlier mistreatment and hopes this small repast will satisfy you."

It was not until he spoke that Ailis realized there was but one gold plate and goblet on the tray. She could find no reason to be uneasy, yet she was. But food enticed her, and she silently begged pardon for a hurried grace before she allowed Louis to serve her. Thin slices of roast venison, sweet roasted onions, a fine-grained bread and cheeses of a variety she had not tasted soon filled her plate. There was even a sweet dried-fruit tart and wine.

As she ate, Louis spoke about the wines his lord imported from Aquitaine that he hoped pleased her.

Ailis, trying hard not to greedily stuff herself, complimented him on the rich vintage's taste. When he attempted to fill her goblet for the third time, she had to stop him. Being near starvation, having had only water to drink, she found the wine took on a potency that left her dizzy. She could not make out Louis's features as clearly as when she had first sat down, nor did she see the girl any longer.

"What have you..." She said no more, feeling herself fall forward, unable to stop herself.

But Louis placed his hands upon her shoulders and pushed her back against the chair. "Take the tray," he ordered, and saw the girl creep from the dark corner to obey him.

He made short work of binding Ailis's ankles and

wrists and covered her over with one of his own long cloaks. Then he motioned his two men-at-arms to carry her out.

None spoke of the body the men carried through the hall. Most had sought their pallets for the night and knew better than to query whatever Louis did.

Outside in the bailey, horses were already saddled. Louis mounted, and while it annoyed him that he should have to set Ailis's limp body before him, he could not trust any other but himself to see to her.

Out into the night they rode, to follow de Orbrec's orders, and Louis hoped that Radnor had made all arrangements according to their lord, or hell would be a pleasant place for them all.

Far, far to the north of Scotland, Radnor buried his impatience as the night passed and he still had no word if the Keith chief would agree to de Orbrec's proposal.

Radnor had chaffed at the rest he was ordered to take, and was uncomfortable when asked to join Keith clansmen in the hall for supper.

He had no liking for the foods set before him. He enjoyed the spiced and herbed dishes of Normandy, and not the bland roasts and tasteless bannocks he was served.

One thing he could not fault was their ale. It was rich, with a pleasant taste, and stronger, much stronger than others he had tried.

When he asked what it was, he was told it was heather ale, and there were smiles all around as Keiths watched him drink. That alone warned him to keep his wits. He could not fail due to his own drunkenness.

There was yet another undercurrent that he began to sense between the chief and his clansmen. They encouraged his gluttony, and proposed toasts, one after the other, so that his golden goblet was constantly refilled.

One man across the table said to Radnor, *"Na h-uile là gu math duit, a charaid, sguab as e!"* and lifted his cup to drain it. Radnor had no choice, for he did not wish to anger any of the Keiths, so he, too, emptied his cup.

"Did you know what you drank to?" the man to his left asked.

"It sounded friendly enough," Radnor replied, but lowered his hand to his long knife at his belt.

"Aye. 'Tis a friendly toast. 'May all your days be good, my friend, take it down!'"

And he heard it yet again, the Keith voices raised in the Gaelic toast, and roars came when George, their chief, stood and drained his cup in what appeared to be one long swallow.

Radnor tried to make himself as small as possible as he sat for another miserable hour, sure that he would never have the answer he sought, sure all the great plans were done for.

As he sank into this morass, musing about all that had gone wrong, a whisper in his ear told him that he was to come to the high table where their chief wished to speak to him.

There were smiles and nods as he approached the chief and Radnor told himself to take heart. All might be well. He heard the words he had waited for, and silently cursed that now it was too late for him to set out. Well, the company was merry, perhaps would be merrier still when they heard what was planned, and Radnor had no choice. He had to wait until morning to return to his lord.

When morning arrived, Radnor found that all did not go quite as he had planned, for the chief ordered that four

Keith clansmen ride along with him and the two men he had brought.

It was for his own safety, he was informed when he protested. And with that, Radnor had to be content.

Chapter Twenty-One

Even after three days on the road, Gilliane still could not accustom herself to the sight of Jamie armed and mailed. She had had very little trouble in keeping her vow not to couple with him, for Sister Ellen accompanied them and slept in the tent with her each night. There was very little chance to be private with him. Gilliane could not even talk as they rode, for he set a hard, but not unbearable pace. She had also discovered last eve that Jamie was well aware that his brother Micheil had sent men ahead to watch and warn of any danger.

Davey, who against both his brothers' wishes had come with them, rode close beside Jamie, so Gilliane had no opportunity to ask him about his brother.

She and Sister Ellen rode in the middle of the party, with Crisdean directly behind, guarding the ransom sacks. To the rear three more clansmen rode, armed with war axes, claymores and pikes.

Gilliane knew it was a small force for what they carried, but Jamie had shouted down all arguments to bring more men. He had claimed, and was proved right, that they would attract almost no attention in a small group.

She turned to Sister Ellen, but saw that the nun held

beads and reins and that her mouth moved silently over her prayers. Gilliane reached down to pat the brown mare that Jamie had chosen for her. Her gait, as he had promised, was smooth, but she had a good spirit, too.

As the afternoon wore on, Gilliane sensed an uneasiness within their group. Both she and Sister Ellen had taken to looking over their shoulders, and one time she caught one of Jamie's men looking behind as well.

She saw no dust rising behind them that would indicate others rode the same way, but then there were no true roads to follow. Jamie led them through mostly level country with few streams to cross, and twice took a ferry across rivers. Often in the distance she saw shepherds with their flocks of sheep, but even when their party rode near a croft no one came out.

Gilliane had been so deep in thought that she had not realized they slowed, or that a horseman approached Jamie, who rode forward to speak with him.

Jamie turned his horse as the rider rode back the way he had come. Crisdean had pulled ahead of Gilliane and Sister Ellen.

"Crisdean, take the packhorses and women up that track we passed. There's a large party of Sutherlands up ahead. Much as I hate to sneak and hide, it will serve us best."

Crisdean led the way, with Gilliane and the nun behind the extra horses. The three clansmen close behind them and Jamie and Davey brought up the rear.

Gilliane shivered within the thick, fur-lined cloak that Seana had given her. She dug her heels into the mare's sides to follow as quickly as she could, unwilling to bring any danger to their party by tarrying behind.

Up the track there was a dark wood, and into this place Crisdean led them.

Sister Ellen pulled alongside Gilliane and saw how anxiously she watched for Jamie and Davey to join them.

"Gilliane, have a care for hiding your worry. It would not do to distract Jamie when he must think of all our safety. I remember my mother telling me that men must fight and women must wait. It is the will of God and the times we live."

"I did not know I revealed myself. I will do better, Sister."

Jamie came with his brother, and drove them deeper into the forest.

No one spoke or made a sound for long minutes, although Jamie's expression clearly showed he found the need to hide galling—a sentiment echoed in his brothers' face and those of the other men.

Sister Ellen prayed, but like Gilliane she kept her eyes alert, looking around this sheltered place.

The minutes stretched, as did the tension. The cry of the curlew came, then came again and again. Jamie returned the cry in reverse—twice close together and then a single cry. There was barely any noise, but suddenly two more Gunn clansmen showed themselves and beckoned the party to come forth.

Gilliane knew them to be Gunns although they wore no Gunn badge. But to each horse's bridle a small bit of juniper was attached, which at first glance appeared only a twig of greenery caught by accident and lodged there.

Then another clansman came swiftly through the trees, but on foot. He sought Jamie and hurried to his side.

"There is another party of men behind—Keiths by the look of them."

"How many?"

"Seven, I counted. There is one whose armor appears different. But I stayed no longer lest they see me."

"We are beset, Jamie?" Davey asked.

"'Tis strange, you'll admit, to find Keiths this far south just at a time when we travel this way."

"Not so!" Gilliane protested as she drew her horse near. "Did you not capture three of their clan stealing your furs? Do you not hold them? Can it be that the Keiths have had no word of those men and only seek to find them?"

Jamie nodded his approval while he concealed his surprise that she'd remembered what he had forgotten. "Wisely said," he stated with a look at Gilliane.

He could not know that fear of him engaging a larger group brought the matter to her mind.

"What would you have us do, Jamie?"

"Och, Davey! I swear all this dodging and sculling, as if I were some thief, sets the gall to rise."

"I feel the same. But, Jamie, admit, there is no help for it. We must avoid them or…" Davey stopped and very quickly conceived a plan that he laid out before his brother.

"Nay!" Jamie rejected it out of hand, but as Davey persisted, he had to acknowledge that the plan had merit.

"If those Keiths arc scarching for us—and it is a wild guess that they follow, rather than, as Gilliane said, they only hunt their own men—I will bait them into coming after me. And you," he added, "can continue on your way without worry of what is behind you."

Jamie looked to his brother, far more slender than himself, but as canny a swordsman as he had ever seen.

Gilliane, still close enough to hear, paled and spoke without thought. "Nay! Let us not separate. If we abide here until they pass, none will be behind."

Jamie barely controlled his voice when he answered her. "If we allow them to ride ahead, who is to say they

will not set a trap for us? Davey is right. He will act as
bait and we will ride on.'' His voice was cold, his eyes
colder still.

Gilliane felt a need to protest the injustice of having
his warm approval turn to ice, leaving a forbidding
stranger staring at her. ''What have I said amiss?''

''All,'' he snapped. ''Keep to your woman's place and
leave matters of our safety in my hands.'' He gave her no
chance to speak, but jerked his horse's head to the side,
where he quietly conferred with his brother and clansmen.

Gilliane pulled her cloak closer around her, not looking
for sympathy from Sister Ellen, or for any more wise
words. She was hurt and searched for a reason, only could
not find one. It was all this tension of waiting, and now
having his plans foiled that made Jamie's temper sharp.
And if she were wife to him in all things, was it not her
place to allow him to vent his spleen upon her? Aye, it
was so. And she was contented.

Davey grabbed hold of his brother's arm when their
plans were set. ''Jamie, what ails you? One moment you
beam with pride at Gilliane and in the next you come near
to snapping—''

''Tis naught but the delay that strikes my temper.'' He
clasped his younger brother's shoulder. ''You'd best go.
Catch up when you can. And remember to keep your
shield high. You tend to raise your head above it when in
the thick of battle.''

''Aye, Da,'' Davey answered with a grin, for it was
oft-told advice from Jamie.

Jamie watched his brother and two men leave them.
But his thoughts were upon what Gilliane had first said
about the Keiths. He could not remember if Micheil had
sent word of the hostages they had. If he had not, then

Gilliane had spoken true. But if Micheil had sent word, then how did the Keiths know he had ridden out?

"Ware!" came the cry a small distance from where they sat their horses. Davey was already engaged. Jamie should order his party to flee, but something held him. He motioned for all to be silent as the faint clash of arms came to him.

Davey and his men were to have raced past, with a taunt or two to make sure the Keiths went after them. What had gone wrong? Three men were no match for seven. Jamie fingered the hilt of his sword, and without thought shifted his shield into place to fight.

"Do we join Davey?" Crisdean asked, his own hand hovering close to his sword hilt.

"It tears me to stay. But there's too much risk of losing the ransom and the maid. We go on." Jamie, who had removed his helmet for a few minutes to cool the sweat that formed, now pulled it on again, adjusting the strip of mail that offered a double shield for his neck over the mail hood. The prickle of unease stayed with him. He knew perfectly well that the situation was not good, but he had no choice.

They rode single file through the wood and around to the east, away from their earlier path. The sounds of fighting diminished, but for Jamie the unease increased until he felt the strain upon his shoulders from turning his head this way and that. He saw that he was not alone in his action, for the other men did as well, and to his surprise he saw that both Gilliane and the nun followed suit. It was well that all were alert, but worry for his brother and his men rode with him.

The sun slowly sank and still they went forward, but Jamie held hope that at any moment he would hear his brother hail him.

He pushed the pace harder, knowing he had his duty to see to, but it became too much for him. He motioned one of his men forward. "Go back. Find how my brother fares. If he is taken, ride hard back to me. If he comes, ride ahead so we may camp and await him."

Again he moved on, and those with him followed, but as dusk came, and with it the chill of night, all hoped that he would soon look for a place to camp. But an hour passed, then a good part of another, and Jamie offered no sign that he intended to stop.

Gilliane felt it was her duty and her right to move her mare up beside his horse and gain his attention.

"Jamie? Jamie, we need to make camp." When he merely turned and looked without seeming to hear her, she set out to provoke him. "Do you use me so poorly? My legs are numb. I cannot sit my saddle. I am no hardened warrior, Jamie, to ride through the night."

At the last her voice rose to a shrill note, for he showed no sign of slowing his horse and she had to make him understand that all were exhausted.

"Do you teach me how to lead now?"

"I merely call to your attention that you use us ill. Without rest, Jamie, none will be fit to ride on the morrow." She grasped her reins with one hand, and with the other reached out to him. "Please, can we not rest until word comes from Davey?"

"Aye, we await word from Davey. But I fear that word will not be from his mouth. There is a place up ahead where we will camp."

For Davey the choice had been clear. He had to prevent the Keiths, at all costs, from closing in on his brother's party. Thus he bade the two men with him to stay slightly back, one to the right, the other to the left, and instead of following the plan to lead the Keiths away, he attacked.

They rode out of the wood directly into the path of the oncoming warriors. Davey's sword was the first to blood. He wanted these enemies dead, unable to war with his clan anymore. With his great painted shield he thrust downward against the leg of a rider who pressed too near. His sword bit again into his opponent's arm, but Davey had to move forward before he could turn his horse and attack once more.

He saw that his two men were hard-pressed, fighting two each to their one. He himself had killed one and wounded one, but there was another—the one dressed more Norman than Scot, who edged his animal away from the fighting as if he would flee.

There were shouts and curses, and Davey saw one of his men go down, but he was intent on that single rider and went after him. He didn't notice that two Keiths had broken away from the fighting to close in behind him.

"Stand and fight, you cowardly dog!" Davey cried out, and had the satisfaction of seeing the man spur his horse around to meet him.

Radnor's blade met Davey's.

Radnor was no coward, but he did not know who challenged him. Why had three men attacked the larger party? He barely had time to draw down the visor of his helm before he was set upon. His was the heavier build. He landed a ringing strike on the other's shield.

Davey parried a thrust to his leg. He used his speed when fighting a stronger man. But he could not see behind him, where two swords were aimed at his back. Swords wielded by Keiths who were determined to see Gunn blood spilled.

Davey gasped. The point of a blade slipped under his

shield from the back. He turned his steed to land another blow at Radnor. A sword point gashed his ribs through cloth and mail. Two men he could fend off, but the third took him from his blind side and cut Davey's shoulder. Davey's shield dipped with the sudden pain. It left his side exposed for another cowardly thrust above the first wound.

He attempted to ward off the other sword strikes, but loss of blood had him swaying in the saddle. His only thought was to win free and get back to his brother.

Davey saw one foe fall from his horse. His pleasure was short-lived. His sword point caught. His difficulty in pulling it free showed how dangerously weakened he was.

Radnor chose that moment to thrust his sword into Davey's side. His experience as a fighter said this one was done for, so he turned away, calling to the three slightly wounded Keiths. They refused to leave until each had bloodied his sword with the two Gunn men they had killed.

Unnoticed, Davey freed his sword. He barely touched his spurs to his stallion. He felt the seep of his blood and knew he was done for. He had no way of telling Jamie that he was now alone.

The stallion, feeling no guidance in the loosely held reins, turned in panicked flight for home.

The man Jamie had sent back found the bodies of his clansmen by the light of the moon. He soon found their horses, but no sign of Davey. He quickly loaded up the bodies, thankful the Keiths had not lingered in this place to mutilate them. But he was torn, then, over what to do. By rights he should return to Jamie and tell him what had happened. On the other hand, he did not relish the thought of riding through the night with two dead, only to be told to return to the clan.

Lingering here over his indecision was not a choice.

He rode toward a stunted tree and there he tied the horses. He had to trust to the Lord's kindness that wolves would not attack the animals or carry off the bodies. Jamie had to be told. But how was he to tell him of his own brother's fate?

Hours later at Halberry Castle, Micheil smoothed the wealth of his wife's hair as she lay upon him. Passion spent, he cherished this time, for they were truly alone, with no demands but to each other.

Replete with the contentment brought by satisfied desire, Seana murmured against his chest, "Have you hired a new bard, Micheil, and not told me?"

"A bard? Nay. What—"

"I just remembered Davey's asking me of a maid whose voice was sheer music. Or so he claimed. He said he only heard it once, and that she fled before he could question her."

"He said naught to me of this. But there is none like that here."

"'Tis strange for me to think of this now, but that young woman who travelled with Janet had a lovely voice. She said a strange thing to me, too, before she left. She warned that Davey should not go with Jamie or he would be wounded nigh unto death."

"A woman of the sight? Seana, och, you should have told Davey. What a pair that would make. Could you tell if she meant—"

"Aye, she was serious enough. I did mean to tell Davey, but we were caught up in caring for the wounded, and I truly forgot."

"You tremble, wife of my heart?"

"A sudden chill, no more."

"My brothers are together. There is no reason to fear. One would easily give his life for the other and so both are overprotective of each other."

Seana rubbed her cheek against his chest. "Do not take this amiss, love, but what if she told true?"

"I'll send riders out in the morning. There is little I can do now. At this rate we will have men riding the whole northeast coast seeking out my brothers. Rest easy, naught has happened."

Far southward, as the small fire burned low, Gilliane repeated almost those same words to Jamie. He had drawn his camp stool close to hers when their meal was done, and sat staring at the fire for some time.

"You are worried still?" she murmured, boldly taking his hand and holding it with both of her own.

"They should have joined us by now or sent word."

"Jamie, we rode long and hard after he left us. With the dark, it may take them longer to find our camp."

"Every word you speak is true, but I cannot rid myself of this unease that sits like a cold lump in my belly. He was only to draw them away. He would not be so foolish as to engage with them. They were outnumbered. Davey knows tactics as well as I."

"He will come soon. You will see."

"Am I a babe to be comforted?"

"Jamie, I made a promise to be as a wife in all things but—"

"But one," he finished for her. He placed his arm around her shoulders and drew her closer. "Stay near. You do give me comfort. The trouble is upon us and we will see it through to the end. Besides, I count myself the lucky one to have come away with the greatest prize before I even fought for it."

"Had I not a care for you, Jamie, I would take insult from your words."

"Then I would kiss you into sweet compliance," he teased, and lowered his head as she lifted her face to him. "But alas, we are not private here, and I fear we won't be in the next few days." Then his husky voice became a whisper. "You are good for me, my lady."

Gilliane offered him a brilliant smile, though she would have liked his kisses. Yet holding his hand and sitting with him thus made her feel he valued her for more than the passion that sprang between them.

Jamie cradled her cheek, his thumb unable to resist brushing across the fullness of her lips. "You should seek your bed, Gilliane. As you reminded me, the ride was long and hard, and tomorrow it must be the same."

"Will you think me disobedient, and scold me if I would rather stay here by the fire with you? I do not think you will rest until you have some word of your brother. I want to wait with you."

"I did not expect you to be docile and obey. Stay then. But lean upon me, and I will wrap my cloak around you so that you will not be chilled."

This was the contentment she had sought—to share with Jamie his troubles and his worries. There was no need to speak, but a glow filled her when he pressed her head against his chest near his heart.

She turned slightly and pressed a kiss upon his fingers. She felt his unease and sought yet another way to pass the time. "Jamie, tell me about you and your brothers when you were young. I am an only child and never knew what it would be like to have sisters or brothers."

"We had merry times, the four of us."

"Another brother? But I thought there were only you three?"

"Bridget made our fourth."

"If it pains you, do not speak of her. I wanted to turn your thoughts from worry, not add unhappiness."

He spoke then, sharing only half his thoughts as he recounted a few merry tales he remembered from his childhood. But all too soon Jamie became aware that noises he heard were not those of small animals crawling about in the brush of the wood where they camped.

"Jamie! Jamie!" came a whisper from the edge of their camp. "Come quick. 'Tis Giles, returned with news of your brother."

Gilliane rose as he did.

"Stay. I will tell you soon enough."

The man had finished nearly a skin of wine, and Jamie had to wait until his thirst was satisfied before he began his tale. He heard him out in silence, the rage building and building until the man finished.

"No sign of Davey? No sign that he was taken?"

"None. I swear I searched, but even with the full moon, there was little enough to see. What would you have me do?"

Sister Ellen came from the tent at that moment and, wrapping her cloak tightly around her, stood close to Gilliane. "I see only one returned. The news is not good, I fear. I had hoped my prayers were not in vain."

"Never say that," Gilliane protested.

"Gilliane, you care for Jamie, so do not take what I say amiss. It is for you to be strong for him now. Remember, it is a woman's place to strengthen and not weaken a man."

Gilliane glanced down at her small-boned, white hands. If she could, she would take up a sword and slay de Orbrec for the pain he brought to all she was coming to hold most dear.

"And you must pray, Gilliane. The Lord will not abandon those who fight on the side of right."

Sister Ellen's words sent Gilliane thinking down another path—painful thoughts. If Jamie was suddenly lost to her, what would she have of him? Memories too brief, and only of passionate kisses?

Now, she thought, her reasons for delay did not matter. She looked up and across the fire to see his stricken face after he gave his order for Cador to take a fresh horse and fetch their dead clansmen home. She ran to him, and he welcomed her with open arms that closed tight around her while he slowly rocked their bodies.

"He couldna find my brother. Davey is lost," he whispered for her alone.

"Jamie, Jamie…think, love. He could have given chase."

"Nay, 'tis not so. He would've left sign for some to follow. Och, Gilliane, I didn't want him to come. He saw a sword, its blade red with blood, and feared for me."

Sheer terror encompassed her. She held her breath too long, letting it out in a rush, while her fingers dug into his back. Jamie was numb to it, and she forced herself to recover from the terrible image that sprang to mind.

Although he still held her, Jamie pulled his head back. Rage scored his words. "I will kill them all if he is harmed. With my sword and dirk I will take them apart. I swear it, and so it shall be."

His voice was loud enough for the other men to hear, and their growls and murmurs underscored his vow.

Jamie cupped her chin and lifted her face to him. In a very soft voice he said, "Stay with me, Gilliane. I need your warmth and your arms this night. I would not be alone with my thoughts."

And with those words of need the tiny seeds sown by

passion found a richer, sweet soil called love. For she knew he could not have more than he asked for. It was she, the woman, not just the body, that he wanted with him.

But this was not the time or place to speak of love. Still, she held out hope to him. "Jamie, think, love—he must be ahead. There was fighting. He must have been wounded. Surely we will find him on the morrow. But come and rest now or you will not be fit to fight."

"Beautiful and wise." He gave her a brief kiss.

And Gilliane was sweetly contented.

Chapter Twenty-Two

Before first light, Jamie ordered the breaking of camp. He had rested, if not truly slept, with Gilliane's words preying upon his mind. He spoke to Crisdean of what she had said about the Keiths getting ahead of them to set a trap.

"Aye," Crisdean agreed quickly. "It is a good thought. Surely they had wounded to tend. If we ride hard, Jamie, mayhap we'll catch up to them. There are anxious swords here to avenge our dead."

Dawn was but a thin gray line in the east when they set out. Jamie led, but not at so fast a pace as he had set yesterday. He wanted to find them encamped; he prayed for it to happen, and knew his men added their prayers for the same.

There was no way for them to know that the party they would fall upon would yield a richer find.

Louis had ridden hard through the night, with his burden and his two men-at-arms attending. He had agreed to do his lord's bidding in this, but as they found a place to camp, in a small wooded copse beside a stream, doubts crowded his mind.

He understood that much depended upon Radnor's success in getting the Keiths to agree to pay for the Gunn woman. And when the Gunns came to de Orbrec, they would pay in turn, only to learn that she was now a Keith hostage. With the double ransom thus paid, Louis was to be given a most generous share, along with the de Verrill manor house. But there was a sense of doom lying upon his shoulders.

He looked around and saw that his man had found a good place for them to hide through the day. He did not wish to ride with a drugged, bound woman for any to see and remark upon. Secrecy equaled success for all plans. He even supposed there were reasons enough to offer why a woman should be gagged and bound, but he wanted to avoid that at all costs.

He set one of the men to watch over Ailis and wake him if she stirred. He carried a wineskin just to keep her docile with drug and drink. The other was set to guard while he slept. Wrapped in his warm cloak, he thought no more.

Radnor had reason to rejoice that he had made much of his high standing with his lord to the Keiths, for it allowed him to stop those who were not wounded from riding after the sole surviving Gunn.

He pointed out that their own wounded required care, for lest they forgot, they would need every man to guard the hostage to be turned over to their chief.

None could offer any argument at his valid points, and so they had camped, if only they had known, not more than two miles west of Jamie's party.

With the coming of dawn, they were on the road to keep their meeting with Louis—to exchange ransom for hostage.

* * *

There was yet another on the road that morning, but his pace was very slow and he headed north. The Gunn man blessed the sun's rise, for he found tracks of a horse that wandered from place to place, grazing on the new spring growth. He had found a few drops of blood along the way, but he was worried at not finding the print of a boot anywhere. Leading his mournful burden, he continued along until he spied the stallion and knew it for Davey's. The horse shield as he dismounted and neared, but a soft croon, one that most of the Gunn horses were raised to obey, soon set the animal's fears aside.

Davey had had the presence of mind to know how badly he was wounded, and had tied his hands with the reins to keep his seat. His fingers were nearly frozen within the horse's mane.

Cador was young and knew little about wounds. What he saw of blood on Davey's body made him think at first that the young lord was dead. But as he stepped closer, he saw that Davey's mouth moved, although no sound came forth.

It was water he wanted, and Cador hurried to fetch his water skin and help him to drink.

"You are sore wounded," he whispered after Davey's thirst was quenched. He could feel the heat of fever come off his body.

"Home," Davey whispered.

"Aye, I'll find a way to get you there. And fret not. Jamie knows of the fighting." He bit his lip with indecision.

"I know not where to seek aid for you."

"Micheil…"

Cador could delay no longer. He mounted his horse

and, keeping Davey's stallion close by him, headed north again.

Davey was right to think of his brother, for Cador knew the chief would raise the clan over this. And at Halberry there would be the lady and others to see to wounds.

He felt steady of mind and heart as he continued his journey north. His fervently murmured prayers were heard by none, for the dead were at rest and Davey had passed into a world of red pain.

By midmorning Jamie's party had swelled with the addition of four more clansmen sent ahead by Micheil and himself. He had them ranging wide to see if they could discover the tracks of those who had fought with his brother and killed his men.

It was sometimes a small thing over which great plans ran afoul.

The clansman astride Cador's horse, which had had the heart nearly ridden out of it on the first jaunt north, then back with the discovery that Davey was lost, was thrown when the animal pulled up lame.

Casting about for a place to leave man and horse where they could wait for his return, Jamie spied a wooded place and headed toward it.

A horse's whinny brought the cry of "Ware! Arms!" to his lips, and he drew forth his sword, then swung his shield to his shoulder.

There was barely a need, for the drunkenness of sleep made Louis and his two men respond sluggishly to the danger, and with little fight, the Gunns had them beneath their swords.

It was not until Sister Ellen and Gilliane both cried out, identifying Louis Marche as de Orbrec's man, that the discovery of Lady Ailis's limp body was made.

Jamie almost used his sword as he came down off his horse.

"See to your aunt," Crisdean advised. "Soil not your blade with this Clootie."

"Aye, Jamie, leave the devil for us."

And yet another Gunn muttered, "'Tis more maukin than devil we've caught."

"Aye, a hare he looks, ready to shake himself loose."

Louis was no coward, but it was not only being outnumbered that stopped him from fighting. There was murder in the eyes of the one called Jamie—a look that pinned him in place. He set his sword down, lifted his long knife from his belt and dropped it in turn.

"I am unarmed. You can see for yourself that woman is not harmed."

"Not harmed!" Gilliane cried out from where she knelt at one side of Lady Ailis, with Sister Ellen on the other. "We cannot rouse her! What have you done to her?" she took her small dagger and used it to cut the bonds, while Sister Ellen offered a bit of water to the slack mouth.

Jamie stepped forward, knowing it would sicken him to torture this animal that had put hands on his aunt, but he knew that he needed whatever information the man had. It quickly made sense, when he remembered the Keiths, what the man was intending to do with his aunt.

Gilliane shared a look with Sister Ellen as both realized at the same time that Ailis's habit was gone. Even her prayer beads were missing. They bathed her hands and face with cold cloths dipped in the stream, while the men set up the tent. There was no question that they would not ride on until they roused Ailis and learned what had befallen her.

Jamie took Crisdean aside. "Take those three pieces of filth away from here and learn all you can of their plans.

And Crisdean, I give you fair warning. Do not kill them, but be not so gentle that they think they have fallen in with any but Gunns.''

Crisdean motioned to his men and, with their prisoners, walked a good distance from where camp was being set up. He quickly ordered them gagged, so their cries would not fall on anyone's ears. He chose one of the men-at-arms to begin with, and showed Louis how easily he reduced that man to little more than quivering jelly. When the gag was lifted, he had almost nothing to tell, which Crisdean knew. But seeing his man so cunningly cut that death would be a blessing loosened Louis's tongue.

And when he was done spilling all to Crisdean, he begged for his life.

''Aye, you shall have it, for as long as it takes to reach our clan. Likely you'll be drawn and quartered, or hanged. Micheil, our chief, is a man of great invention. And you've much to pay for, considering what you've done to one of our ladies.''

Crisdean then returned to Jamie and told him what he had learned.

''They were to meet where the Oykel and Carron come together outside of Invershin. 'Tis a small village no more than half a day's ride, Jamie. There'll be Keiths there awaiting our lady, to take her hostage. I swear I wrung from them what they know, but none could say how many come.''

''But we know that, Crisdean. There were seven in the party that followed. Surely they had some wounded. Davey and our men would make some account of themselves. Cador said the two who died had bloodied swords.''

''Jamie, give some thought to this being a trap.''

''The thought crossed my mind, but what choice do we

have? I should have listened to Micheil and taken more men. Those three of de Orbrec's belong in our clan's hands. I cannot leave my aunt, Gilliane and the good sister without guards. We will make haste to find this group that waits, and if it is a trap, mayhap we can spring it upon them.''

''Then set two to guard the women and the ransom sacks. We can ride hard and fast without them to slow us, Jamie. The day seven Gunns canna take a passel of Keiths is the day to lay down your sword.''

Jamie wanted to order the men to ride immediately; his blood was up to avenge the harm done and snag a few Keiths by their own trap. But he had proven worthy of the title of tanist, for his cool thinking of all aspects before he sent men to battle.

He glanced behind, to where Gilliane and Sister Ellen had disappeared with his aunt into the tent. Two of his men stood guard, one in front and one behind, with swords drawn. What Crisdean proposed tempted him, but the possibility of the women falling into either Keith hands or those of de Orbrec's men set a cold, cold knot to cool the heat of his warrior's blood.

''Jamie, the sun climbs high. What'll you have us do?''

Gilliane's call for Jamie to come saved him from answering.

''She is awake, Jamie, and asking for you.''

He ducked to enter the tent and saw this his aunt lay on the cot. Sister Ellen was arranging one of Gilliane's head veils to cover her shorn hair. Ailis saw him and beckoned him close. He went to his knees and kissed the hand she held out to him.

Ailis lay back and closed her eyes, holding tightly to his strong hand. The drug was still within her and she fought to clear her mind.

"Do not try to speak, Aunt," he whispered. "You are safe, and soon I'll have you back at the abbey, where more of your own good sisters will care for you."

"Jamie, do not speak, only listen to me. He stole my ring of office and my prayer beads. What he took from me was stolen from the abbess of Deer Abbey, and his fate is in God's hands for the sin he has done. But your aunt, Jamie lad, 'tis your Gunn aunt, sister to your father, who begs you to rid the world of this foul monster who preys on the weak. Make a promise to me, as I once did your father's bidding in all. Promise me you will take vengeance upon de Orbrec."

Jamie bowed his head over her hand and spoke the words she wanted to hear, then kissed each cheek and warned her to rest.

Gilliane bit her lip so as not to cry out in protest. She wanted to yell at Ailis that she was a woman of God and should not urge Jamie to fight a man who knew no honor.

But something about the way Sister Ellen looked on and nodded when Ailis spoke held her silent.

"Remember, Jamie, you are the steel of our clan. My prayers go with you. God goes with you."

Jamie left her then, unwilling to press for her details. But when Gilliane followed him outside, he turned to her.

"Did she tell you anything of what happened to her?"

"She said she was held in the pit prison and that Louis, who took her, also had the care of her. They gulled her by moving her and offering her all a guest could wish, including," Gilliane added with bitterness, "an apology from de Orbrec for her harsh treatment. She said the wine was drugged, and she recalls little else."

"Gilliane, come." He drew her far enough aside so that none would overhear what he had to ask her. "Did she say...was she harshly used?"

For a moment or two Gilliane frowned at him, uncertain of his meaning. The tight set of his mouth, the hard, fierce gleam of his dark eyes told her quickly enough what it was he wanted to know.

"Before the drugged wine, no. Afterward…she would not be aware. But I did not see any marks or bruises on her. Nay, Jamie!" She grabbed his arms. "Not even de Orbrec would dare dishonor a nun."

He held her against him, kissing her hair, her temple and her cheek. His gentle actions offered a silent apology for what he had needed to know but hated asking her. Gilliane took courage in hand and spoke her mind.

"What your aunt asked of you is wrong, Jamie."

"Aye. I know it well," he said with a grin. "But it fit my own plan for the Norman, so what use was there to argue with her? She is overset now, as any woman would be. In calmer times, she will regret asking it of me. But you need to recall that long before she took vows, she was born and raised in a warrior clan. Blood, they say, will tell. Truly, Gilliane, my aunt does have a gentle heart."

"Do I not know the truth of her nature? To help me, all this has come about."

"And you are not to take blame upon yourself, as I once told you. I would be without you, and that is a loss I could not bear."

"Oh, Jamie!" she cried softly, not caring who watched as she drew his head down to press her lips against his.

Gilliane put her heart and newly discovered love into that kiss. The desire between them ignited the flame of passion, which threatened to carry both away. Jamie pressed kisses to the corner of her lips, whispering of his need for her. To cool the heat that her most generous ardor brought to him, he separated himself from her.

"I ride with my men to find this meeting place where my aunt was to be given to the Keiths. Abide here under guard and wait for me. I swear to you, betwixt my men and myself it will be a short fight."

Nothing Gilliane could say would deter him, and she knew it. She tried to smile. "Then go with God, Jamie."

"How can I not?" he asked with a laugh, walking backward to keep her in sight. "Having two nuns and a most saintly woman praying for me, I dare not fail."

Chapter Twenty-Three

With Louis one of the Gunn clansmen rode pillon, keeping a dirk pressed to his side.

This small ruse allowed Jamie and his men to come close to the Keiths led by Radnor. The Gunns, having been forced to flee, now fell upon their enemies with a ferocity that stunned the Keiths. They rallied quickly, for much was at stake, but it was a matter of a little coming too late.

Those that were slightly wounded fought as well as they could, but were not successful in landing one serious cut with either sword or ax.

Louis had been quickly bound and tossed to the ground, so that his guard could take revenge for what had been done and for what was planned against his clan.

A short fight, Jamie had claimed, and in truth, it was. Within an hour the Keiths were done. Two lived. Radnor, not knowing that he fought the brother of the Gunn he had near mortally wounded, tried to protect himself from the two-handed blows that struck his leather shield with such force the embossed hide and frame were bent awry. He tripped over loose stones as he backed away, hoping to get some small space to breathe and rest his weary sword arm. But Jamie gave him no such chance. He leaped over the stones and renewed his attack, until with a cry he delivered a sideways cut that bit through Radnor's armor.

The man went down and was still.

Jamie turned away, for killing truly gave him no pleasure. He saw his men, a few tying crude bandages over minor wounds on their clansmen, and others already gathering weapons that had fallen beside the bodies.

"Jamie? Jamie?" Crisdean repeated several times before he saw the battle lust gone from his leader's eyes. "We await your orders."

"Leave them for the crows. But take that one," he said, pointing with his sword toward where Louis lay bound and bleeding from wounds taken during the fighting. "I've a use for him."

And then to his men, he called, "We ride for the Norman's keep. Who's with me?"

"A Gunn! A Gunn!" their voices chorused.

One of the younger clansman, Sim, seeing the need to bring a lighter mood to all, sang his own play on the childish rhyme other clans had made. "A Gunn, a Gunn. They come, they come. To steal the beasties, but never to run!"

There was a responding cheer as other voices picked up the rhyme, until they all chanted it as they mounted. Silence fell slowly as, one by one, hardened visages looked at the blood spilled, and then, to a man, they looked at Jamie, their war leader, who offered them a way to cool the hot blood raised by those who'd dared attack their clan.

"Who rides for Jamie?" Crisdean demanded.

"We do!" No one man's voice was silent.

Jamie, with a smile—albeit slightly bitter at how it had

come about—was pleased with their show of loyalty, and led them back to their camp.

It was near twilight when Gilliane's glad cry sang out as she caught sight of the returning party, leading horses loaded with weapons, but saddles empty of men. Her eyes went first to Jamie as she saw him dismount. Nothing could have held her back as she ran to him, uncaring that her heart was in her eyes.

"Stand away, Gilliane, you'll get blood—"

"I care not." She flung herself at him, and Jamie closed his arms around her.

"You're trembling."

She nodded, but could not speak.

"Surely this is not out of fear for me? You know this posed no danger. Have faith, woman. They were a cowardly lot."

Still she clung tightly to him. "You are sure you took no hurt?"

"Only a fool would be vain enough to lie about that." He pulled back slightly and could not resist a kiss to the tip of her nose. "None have called me a fool. Now, if you would welcome me, do so with well-watered wine, for I have an uncommon thirst."

Gilliane, despite his reassurances that he'd received no wound, placed her hand against the back of his neck, then to his forehead. "There's no fever."

"I told you so."

"Come with me, Jamie. The kettle has warm water for washing, and I'll fetch your wine."

Jamie hid the feeling of contentment that her care brought to him, but he was well pleased by the display of her seeing to his needs. He'd never had a woman of his own to do that for him. He had never taken a leman, for most of his years of manhood had been spent fighting.

More and more he was coming to believe that he would not fail. Soon he would be free to speak of the love in his heart for her.

And because she was dear to him, he said nothing of his plans for her.

But there was no avoiding telling Gilliane what he planned when they camped the next night. She sat near the fire with him, and he thought she listened to what he said, but for long minutes afterward she remained silent.

Finally she looked directly at him. "Let me be clear of your intent. You will send me with your aunt and Sister Ellen to the abbey under guard, where I am to await you?"

"I can travel faster—"

"Oh? I have delayed you?"

"Not you, Gilliane. But you must understand that I go into battle with this Norman. Where would I keep you safe while I fight him? Do I take men that I may need to hold off his, and set them to guard you? Be reasonable. Though I know the parting is hard, you know this is best."

"Have you thought what he will do if he does not see me there? He cannot know that his plans were foiled. He will think he has succeeded in gaining a double ransom and me. You have not forgotten that I was to be given to him in exchange for your aunt?"

"I have Louis."

"And you think he will pass for me?"

"Such a sharp tongue, when I only want your good! It is for you to obey me in this."

Seeing the fierce anger on his face, Gilliane bit her lip. She closed her eyes briefly, praying for wisdom and patience. He was right to think not only of her safety, but of the danger she would be to him. Yet how did a woman explain the terror of waiting for word of the outcome?

And while she thought, Jamie was having second thoughts about leaving her behind. He gazed at the play of firelight on her hair, turning it to a softer flame, at her flushed cheek and white throat, and her hands entwined and tightly held.

He could not deny that she made a valid point, one he had raised from the first—that none could pass for her with that hair. He would need to draw de Orbrec out of his keep, for he had not the men or machines to lay seige. Nor did he want to. Jamie longed for his own lands. He wanted no talk of war, or if it had to be—and he knew it would, because the Keiths would raise their clan over the recent deaths—then at least he would have Gilliane there.

But taking her with him made her a danger for herself and his men.

A true devil's dilemma.

Gilliane concluded that anger would serve her naught. She tried softening her voice when she turned fully on the stool to face him.

"Jamie, if you truly have a care for me, I beg you not to leave me to wait. There comes such a terror upon me that only the sight of you stills. I open my heart to you and promise all will be as you wish. I no more than you wish to be the cause of any man's death. If you bid me to stay in this place or that, I will. I swear I will. Only let me come with you. I do not want to add to your troubles."

"Och, lass, but you cozen me sweetly with reason."

"'Tis not my intent to cozen you at all."

"Nay, do not wear that flush of anger with me. I...I will give serious thought to what you have said. Now, leave me. If you do not, I will not be held accountable for what I may do.''

His hot gaze said what his lips did not utter. In this, Gilliane knew, he was constant. That look alone was enough to stir her passion, and she wished they could be alone.

She glanced behind her at the tent, where a much recovered Ailis waited for her to begin their evening prayers. With his aunt to observe that all proprieties were met, she bade him a good sleep and left him.

She had pleaded when she ought to have held her tongue. What was it about Jamie that made her act against her will? And what drove her that she had to be with him? Was this love?

A night's rest provided no answer, nor did Jamie inform her of his decision when they rode south for the abbey.

Once the joyous reunion with her nuns and novices was over Ailis took Gilliane into her room.

She had heard Gilliane's reasons for going with Jamie, and understood the need that the young woman could not express clearly. Gilliane confessed that she knew it was wrong to argue with Jamie or try to change the path he had chosen, but she had a dreadful vision of some dire fate happening to him if she were not there to protect him. She admitted the last made a foolish statement, for what could she as a woman do to prevent injury taken in battle or combat? And she knew that to argue or plead continuingly might make him distrust her and set him on guard, so she would never know where he went or what he did.

''Gilliane, speak plainly with me. You love him, do you not?'' the abbess asked.

''Aye. Though I admit that I did not want to.''

''But Jamie did not force this feeling from you. He could not. Your love is yours to give or withhold as you will. It is one of God's gifts to us, this choice. And so, if you love him, you must take what is good and cherish it, and what is not, you either learn to ignore, for peace between you, or go gently about changing it.''

''He gave in about my going with him, but he is not happy with the decision. I need to be there with him. I cannot say more.''

''Then I will pray for you both. And Gilliane, remember that a woman's love is no gentle thing. It is born of strength. Methinks that you would not love him as well if he were to abandon his honor.''

''Jamie would never do so, not for love nor for coin.''

''Then you do not wish him to be a coward?''

''Never say such. I promised I would plead no more to stop him. I will pray that he comes away with a whole body.''

Ailis leaned back in the tall chair behind the ornate table that served as her desk. She was glad to be among her own things, and with her sisters again.

''Let me remind you of one last thing before you must leave,'' she said to Gilliane's back, for the young woman paced the room. ''Jamie is a warrior. Live with it, or live without him.''

''A devil's choice, Reverend Mother.''

''Perhaps,'' she answered with a wry smile. ''But as God gives us choice, so the devil must give us temptation to subvert our will. Go, lass. He will grow impatient and then angry that you keep him waiting.'' She offered her hand as Gilliane knelt at her side, and the young woman pressed her lips to where Ailis's ring of office would have been.

And then she rose, made a quick sign of the cross to the murmured prayer Ailis gave, and left her.

Chapter Twenty-Four

The lands around Castres Keep were a mockery, for the fields this far south held a rich new growth that promised an abundant harvest, but the frightened, sullen serfs that either fled or cast themselves to the ground as Jamie's party rode past reflected ill on their master.

Two tense days had passed as the Gunns journeyed, for Jamie had had no word from Colin, the first clansman sent to spy on de Orbrec and learn what he could, nor were there signs or word left of what had become of Marcus, Gabhan or Edam, sent on ahead to gather Colin's information along with their own.

It appeared to Gilliane that everyone in the party avoided each other's eyes, and endeavored to squelch the foreboding by pretending there was good reason for the delay in contacting them.

They rode openly. Crisdean had unfurled the great Raven Banner of the old Orkney jarls who had been ancestors of the Gunns and the Keiths. The raven symbolized the spirit of the mighty Woden, from their common Viking past. He rode ahead of Jamie, proudly carrying their banner.

On another lord's lands, there would be serfs to run and

tell someone at the keep of the armed riders that approached. But de Orbrec had wrung every groat and so crushed the spirit of his people that not one sent word ahead to him.

Thus he was surprised and somewhat shocked to hear a summons for him to appear.

"Come out!" Jamie shouted, halting well beyond the reach of an arrow. "Come out, you little cockerel! Come away from your dung heap and do battle! Let us see if you can crow as loudly as a man as you do to defenseless women!"

"Be gone from here," a guard on the wall called down to Jamie, after he sent another to fetch his lord.

"Send out de Orbrec, the Norman slayer of women. Send him out, I say, or send who you will. I demand satisfaction upon that bastard's body for what he has done to me and mine!"

Guy de Orbrec stood at the open doors to his keep and heard every word. His eyes darted to this man and that, but Louis, his strong right arm, was not among them. Panic made him forget for the moment that he'd charged him to take and sell the Gunn woman to the Keiths. Radnor, too, was not to be found within the keep; he was a strong fighter to do battle with the Gunn clansman, who again hurled vile insults. Insults that no man calling himself one could bear. And de Orbrec saw in the eyes of all what they thought of his standing there.

He motioned to a man-at-arms. "Go among your kind and say I will richly reward any who will slay that crowing Highlander who dares think I will soil a Norman sword with his blood."

The man's eyes sidled away as he left to do his master's bidding. But none he approached would accept the Scot's challenge to fight.

"Are you cowards all?" de Orbrec shouted. "What will you have," he demanded of his men, "to rid me of this brute?"

And in clear ringing tones came Jamie's voice again. "Guy de Orbrec, I challenge you and no other to do mortal combat with me. Come forth! Else I shall not leave one stone of this keep, one stalk of straw or blade of grass, to stand and mark this place. And offer nothing but your sword and body, Norman scourge; neither gold nor blood will find you freedom. Only death can bring you that."

Guy hid his fear. "Tell him that I go to arm and will come forth." He knew there was no other choice. He could order his men to fall upon this barbarian once the gates were open. It was a great pity that Louis was not here to champion him. Guy went to arm himself after ordering his horse to be readied.

Jamie rubbed his unshaved chin. He heard the words he wanted, but he was also prepared for some form of treachery.

He glanced toward the riverbank where his men and Gilliane waited. Crisdean at least had had the sense to cease arguing with him over his coming forth alone to issue his challenge. Jamie was most thankful that his aunt was free of this place, for he knew not what he would have done or agreed to in his need to have her safe.

He studied the keep and thought that, if need be, it could easily be taken, but just then the great wooden gates were opened.

Instead of a single man on a horse, four men slipped through and ran toward him. Jamie drew his sword, set his shield and prepared to defend his life.

"Hold, Jamie! Hold!"

It was the welcome sound of Colin's voice, then Marcus, Gabhan and Edam cried out to him.

"What do you here, dressed like Norman dogs?" He addressed them in a harsh tone due to his own fear that treachery indeed had been planned.

"We set out to watch and wait as you ordered. Both de Orbrec's henchmen have left the place, and we could not follow. It was easy enough to gain a place here, but we were held close. There is no loyalty within," Gabhan explained.

"Aye," Marcus agreed. "The Norman offered rich reward to any who would fight you, and none would."

"Jamie!" Colin yelled to gain his attention. "Your aunt is no longer within. Every night I've searched for her. I think they took her away, but I know not where. I failed you in this."

"Nay! None have. She is safe. He planned to sell her to the Keiths and collect a double ransom. He'll spill his blood for his work." Jamie's head came up at a stirring by the gates. "Go down to the riverbank where Crisdean holds the men."

"Trust him not, Jamie. This is a man of evil."

"You wrong him to call him a man at all, Gabhan."

A rider came forward, but it was not, Jamie was sure, the Norman. All too soon he was proved right.

"My lord demands that you leave his lands as you found them. He will lodge protest with the king for your brazen attempt to seek his life. If you will not leave, then on your head rests the death of the Gunn woman he holds. What is your answer?"

"Send him forth. He holds naught of mine. Ask what I hold of his." Jamie drew his sword and waved it high.

Crisdean saw, and with a lead rein attached to Louis's horse, he brought forth the bound man, who bled from his untended wounds.

"See what I have here? He was to deliver my aunt to

my enemies and was foiled,'' Jamie declared. ''Tell your
Norman lord I will wait no more.''

And with those words Louis Marche died by Crisdean's
sword.

The man of de Orbrec stared in horror.

''Bring forth that coward,'' Jamie said, and watched as
Crisdean rode away.

The man turned and rode with haste to the gates, where
he related what had happened to Louis. Guy listened,
mounted, and with more of his normal arrogance, decided
he would teach this wild Highlander a lesson that would
end in his death.

He had seen for himself that he was more strongly built,
and his armor was the finest to be had. He checked the
loop of his mace over the saddlebow and slammed his
visor down before he set his shield on his arm.

Aye, he told himself, he would teach him well.

Guy looked toward the riverbank, where he saw a clus-
ter of men. And a woman. Gilliane de Verrill. None other
could have that flaming mass of hair. So the Gunn had
brought her to see this combat. Looking again at the Highlander, whose horse stood as still as the man, Guy suddenly felt himself grow cold, and even as experienced as
he was in brutality, he could not repress the shudder that
came over him. He knew naught of the Highlander as a
fighter, and noticed as he neared that the armor he wore,
like the large triangular shield he held, was well used.

Closer still he rode his brown stallion, which fretted
beneath his tightly held rein.

''So, you come to battle braying like an ass,'' de Orbrec
said, pulling to a stop almost ten feet in front of Jamie.
''For the death of my man, you give us your own life. I
will show no mercy to you and yours. And when I am

done with you, Scot, I will have the woman, but no longer to wife. For I take no man's leavings.''

Jamie refused to answer his insult about Gilliane, but a black fury built inside him that had him trembling with the need to bury his sword in this man's flesh.

''Perhaps my men will have a taste of her when I am done,'' de Orbrec stated with malice. ''You have erred. You are no match for a Norman trained to the ways of war.'' His tone was deliberately, insultingly contemptuous.

Jamie felt himself flush with rage. He knew de Orbrec baited him deliberately, and he barely held his control. But Killen felt his tension and danced in place, anxious as his rider to do battle.

''What? Does fear hold your tongue? Can it be you lost your taste to fight a man?''

Jamie's snarl came in answer. His hand clenched his sword hilt. ''Come, craven beast, cease your prattle. Let my blade still your tongue.'' He had one thing to be thankful for—de Orbrec had not come carrying a lance. Jamie had one with his men, but he was anxious—nay, bloody eager—to have done with the Norman.

There were no preliminaries. This was no formal contest with fine points to be judged. No rules. No commoners or nobles to watch and roar approval. There was no provision for yielding. It had not even been discussed. This was combat to the death, and the sun would shine its afternoon light on the victor.

Both he and de Orbrec backed up their horses a little way.

Jamie saw the glint of his sharpened sword tip and hoped the fine honing he had given it would prove to win him the day. He forced himself to ignore the thudding beat of his heart and the foul taste in his dry mouth.

He set his spurs to Killen's sides and went toward de Orbrec just as he, too, set spurs to his horse.

They came together and lashed each other's shield with great force.

Jamie licked his dry lips. He had no doubts about his own ability. But the Norman had landed two blows on the same point of his shield, and Jamie was forced to tighten his grip on the handhold, for the powerful blows nearly numbed his arm.

Jamie withheld the full force of his own blows. It was dangerous, but he needed to know how de Orbrec fought. The Norman pressed him harder and harder, increasing the force of his sword blows, and making Jamie bend and stretch to guard himself as he, too, increased the force he used.

Soon Jamie thought he had most of de Orbrec's offensive moves, and decided it was time to attack. He feinted viciously with his shield, and as de Orbrec countered the maneuver with his own shield held wide, Jamie aimed a blow at his sword hand. Orbrec caught himself in time, with a quick twist, and Jamie's sword whistled downward to strike against his horse's shoulder.

The stallion screamed in rage and pain, rearing up, hooves pawing the air.

Killen, challenged at last, reared also, his hooves coming down hard on the brown horse's wound.

Guy could not keep his seat. The horse went down and he barely managed to roll free.

To Jamie, honor was more than a word. Despite his hatred for the agony this man had brought to his family and clan, and even despite the deaths of his men and the unknown fate of his brother, Jamie pulled Killen back, and with a wary eye on the Norman, slid from the saddle.

He knew if he had been unhorsed, the Norman would show no honor at all. But Jamie had to live with himself.

He slapped his horse to send him away, and Killen obediently trotted off, but de Orbrec had already launched himself at Jamie. Dust from the dry ground rose and swirled under the furious play of quick moving feet. The dust choked Jamie, seeping his helm and visor to mix with the sweat that poured from him. There was nothing to do but bear it, for he engaged de Orbrec in a furious passage of arms.

Gilliane watched every blow to Jamie as if it were a dagger to her heart. The faint ring of sword to shield that reached where she waited was the start and stop of breath and heartbeat. She was so torn. She felt pride in Jamie's skill, and fear, and then came rage when she saw de Orbrec launch himself at Jamie.

She was barely aware of the advice the men of Clan Gunn muttered or called out as their avid eyes targeted the two combatants.

As the dust rose, she bit her lip until she tasted blood. *Give him strength,* she prayed. *Make him as strong as the Cid, let his sword carry all the magic of Arthur's, and let him be alive when done. Please, let him be alive.*

Her gaze fled to the walls, filled with de Orbrec's household and men-at-arms then returned to Jamie again. She cried out. The dust was so thick she could not see him!

Jamie launched a blow that should have cut into de Orbrec's side, but the Norman used his shield to deflect the sword. His powerful thrust made the shield continue its upward rise, catching Jamie on the side of his face. He felt the heat of blood seeping from the wound. He had to jump aside to avoid de Orbrec's counterstroke.

Jamie bled from two minor wounds, but had the satisfaction of seeing that de Orbrec's shoulder and thigh seeped far more blood. Jamie gasped for every breath of air.

He knew his strength, and he knew that he could not fight indefinitely. But he took heart, for he could see the fear in de Orbrec's eyes, and the blows the Norman landed no longer held the same powerful force as when he'd started.

Jamie wished for wine to wet his throat so he could taunt de Orbrec. Fear was what he needed to invoke. Fear could work as ten men at his back.

But he had as good when de Orbrec's next strike missed him.

The Norman pulled back a bit. His timing was off, and the Scot had proved that no matter where he'd learned his swordplay, he had fully mastered all the lessons. Guy had no more thoughts of arrogantly leaving this Highlander's body in the dust. He fought for his life. Never should he have given in to the insults. The Scot meant to kill him.

Twice Jamie's blades slipped under the shield to nick de Orbrec's thigh and hip. Guy lifted his sword over his shoulder with the intent of bringing it down hard to cleave arm or neck. Any hit would be worth it, to chase that knowing glitter from the Scot's eyes, to wipe from his lips that taunting smile. But he concentrated so hard on what he wanted done that Jamie twisted free, and the blow fell harmlessly to the earth. Not so Jamie's strike. His sword bit deep into the back of de Orbrec's shield arm. The Norman cried out, seeing before him what suffering he had offered to so many in his life.

But Guy had fought his way through many a battle and was not done. Spinning around, he swung his sword at Jamie's legs. Jamie jumped, dancing over the sword circle. Had de Orbrec known, none could match Jamie when it came to the dance of the swords, and his agile feet took him from danger.

Jamie decided then to end his toying with the Norman. He launched a flurry of blows that de Orbrec barely turned aside, beating the man back and back, giving him no time to rally or breathe.

Again de Orbrec backed away. He took Jamie's blow on his raised shield. The sword rebounded, but in Jamie's clever hands it was turned swiftly and brought round in a slashing sideswipe that bit deep into the Norman's thigh.

He fell to one knee, barely able to lift the shield as Jamie hammered blows at him. Guy had a sudden choking sensation of panic. Even when he thought he would die, he had not truly believed it. There was no more doubt, nor more time to lie to himself. Again he felt the bite of the Scot's mighty sword, and he toppled to the ground.

It was over. Jamie took a moment to strike the sword from de Orbrec's hand.

"You've won naught," de Orbrec cried. "If you fought to gain a maid, you're too late. I had her first. I had her on her knees like—"

Guy's face paled to near white, and Jamie drove home his sword through the mail that protected him.

Jamie looked up and his gaze went unerringly to where he had left Gilliane. Only she and his men were not there. He wrenched off his helm, turning slowly, and saw that one at least had come to catch up Killen's reins and hold the horse for him.

Jamie swiped at the sweat dripping into his eyes and beckoned his man forward.

Colin dismounted. "Are you bad hurt, Jamie? I canna tell with all the blood on you."

"Where..." Jamie swallowed a few times, trying to moisten his mouth to speak.

But Colin knew what it was that he wanted. "Crisdean led them into the keep. I swear, Jamie, if all such Normans in our land have men like these, we could have a string of keeps right to the English border. They offered no fight. Most, I think, have robbed whatever was worth taking, and while you fought, escaped through the postern gate that leads to the river."

"Help me to mount, Colin. I am sore all over." Jamie sheathed his sword without wiping it, and put his left foot into Colin's steady hands to be tossed up into the saddle.

There was admiration in Colin's young eyes, and Jamie turned away from it. He could never explain to anyone what the killing did to him.

"Tell me then, the keep is ours?" he asked.

"Crisdean leads our men to make sure there are none in hiding with a dirk ready for your heart. And your lady is seeing that all is ready to receive you."

"My lady," Jamie murmured to himself.

Once through the gates, Jamie remembered little more. The next few hours passed in a daze of tiredness and a blaze of pain as his armor was taken from him and his wounds tended.

It was Gilliane's face he saw most often, bending to wash and salve every cut and bruise, holding his head to let him sip wine, urging him to rest, then crying so hard it would be impossible to sleep.

"Come lie beside me, Gilliane. Nay. You will do me less hurt lying quiet then fussing about."

Gilliane, with Crisdean and his bared sword, had bullied everyone to make ready a wall chamber off the great hall for Jamie. She could not bring herself to have him taken to de Orbrec's chamber, using as an excuse his wounds and the need to tend them without going up and down the winding stair.

Her hand trembled as she brushed Jamie's hair from his forehead. Tears sparkled on her long lashes, and her lips were red and swollen from where she bit them.

To Jamie's eyes she had never looked more lovely, and his hand curled over the tip of her braid. Slowly, for to move did hurt him, he wrapped the braid around his hand until it appeared a bulky spindle of silken yarn.

Trapped by his hold on her hair, Gilliane sighed and gave in. She very carefully came to lie beside him. She tried to block out the images that formed and flashed of Jamie's fight with de Orbrec. That set her to trembling again.

"Love, if I move to hold you, I will undo all the good you have done."

"I'll be still. I will," she whispered, forcing her body to obey. Then she murmured, "Jamie, how soon can we go home?"

"Och, love, I hadn't thought of it. I had hoped to rest at least a day, Gilliane, and—"

"What did you say? Say it again."

"Say?" Jamie was vexed, for he was too tired to think at all. "I know not what you mean."

"Love," she whispered. "You called me love."

Jamie turned his head, but could not see more than her delicate profile. He grunted and groaned as he turned to his side and beheld her lovely countenance.

"So I did. Do you find that offensive, Gilliane?"

"Nay. 'Tis a word that is sweet from your lips."

"Then I will take note of your pleasure and use it often." There came a stirring of warmth within him as he saw her lips curve into a smile.

"Are we so easily settled, Jamie?"

"What is there to settle? You have given me your promise to live one year and a day with me. You will not break your word. I will not break mine. I mean to have you. Aye, for far longer than that.''

Gilliane sent her fear of the times to come, when he would go and do battle again, to a dark corner of her mind. Her hand found his and unwound her braid, so she could lift his hand and bring it to her lips.

''Gilliane,'' he said, softly so not to alarm her. ''Are you still afraid?''

''Aye. I will not lie to you. But I've come to terms with my fears. Jamie, you must know that my heart stopped when I thought you done for. I wanted to call you away. I wanted to slay him myself when he drew blood from you. I have come to cherish you—nay, that is less than the truth, and I have said I would not lie.'' She turned to her side as gently as she could. Her hand cradled his unshaved cheek. She gazed into his dark brown eyes and saw the gold flecks within them.

''I've a confession to make. Nay, let me speak, Jamie. I more than cherish you. I've come to love you,'' she said with fierce joy. ''I want more than a year and a day with you. I want you to be my beloved husband, and if we should be blessed with children, you are the father I want them to have.''

''Gilliane, Gilliane.'' He lifted himself high enough to kiss her gently, tenderly, leaving passion aside for now.

''I love you,'' he said, with such intensity that tears came again to her eyes.

He'd bent his head to take her lips once more when there came a scratching at the door. Jamie cursed silently, but knew that his men would want orders, and some things could not wait. He fell back against the pillow, about to tell Gilliane to stay, but she was up and fleeing to open the door before he could form a word.

Crisdean stood there, a black scowl upon his face as he looked past Gilliane to see if Jamie was awake.

"Come in, Crisdean. I know it must be important, for you could secure this place without orders from me."

"You look well enough," he said in place of a greeting. An' 'tis a matter of importance that brings me to disturb you. I found these," he said, beckoning out the open door, then standing aside as a raggedly dressed maid entered. She carried a babe of little more than a year in her arms. Another maid followed with a child slightly older, perhaps three, with a third child holding her filthy skirts and hiding as much of herself as she could.

Jamie, startled, forgot his wounds and jerked upright. "What the devil do you mean to bring these…this…what is in your daft mind, Crisdean?"

Gilliane, he saw, must be as daft, for she was bent over trying to coax the little one out from the skirts that hid her.

"These are de Orbrec's daughters, Jamie. And that is why I brought them to you. I'm no' daft, man. An' I refuse to deal with bairns," he added in a firm voice that made clear no orders, clan loyalty or debts would change his mind

"Sweet saints! What am I to do with them?"

"Keep them, Jamie," Gilliane calmly stated, having succeeded in her goal. She drew forth the eldest, no more than five, but dressed poorer than the meanest serf, and about as filthy, too.

"Keep them! Gilliane, you're not daft, you're a bletherin'—"

"Jamie, not in front of the little ones. You cannot refuse to care for them. There is no one else. Did I not tell you that each of his wives had no family? You cannot cast them aside. They need care, a home and a family."

Jamie took no offense at her scolding tone, but he quaked inwardly when he heard the last said. There was a decidedly stern look to his lovely Gilliane's face that as much as stated she would not be denied.

But Jamie was not of faint heart. "Love," he said, with the thought of softening his blow, "we are not yet wed. You canna seriously think I'd take—"

"They come with me, Jamie. Just think. We'll have three bonnie lasses to care for all the little ones to come."

Crisdean and the maids had stood silently by while this exchange occurred. But Crisdean was hard put to swallow his laugh when he saw Jamie's face. His eyes were wide, his mouth open, but no sound came forth.

"Come, come," Gilliane urged, ushering all outside the room, including Crisdean. "We must let Jamie have his rest. There are baths to be had first, then we must find something fitting for these lovely little ones to wear, and lots of good things to eat."

She started to say more, but the roar of Jamie's voice calling her sent her flying back to his side.

"Hush now! You'll do yourself more harm."

"You'll not leave me."

"Jamie, you need your rest," she chided in a gently reproving tone. She bent over to kiss his cheek and neatly dodged his attempt to capture her lips.

"I've needs, too. You were about to tend them before that daft Crisdean—"

"Now, now," she teased from the safety of the doorway. "Think, my brave warrior. If you rest until I come back, then you'll have the strength to tend your needs."

He caught the hot blush of her cheeks before she disappeared, and her name was uttered amidst his laughter.

Then he sobered quickly. Three little lasses? Three? Och, was ever a man so beset? He'd be roasted from croft to castle. He had set out to win a maid and avenge his clan, and would ride home with a family larger than Micheil's. But Gilliane had the right of it. He could not abandon the children. And despite their father's blood, Gilliane would have the raising of them.

But three?

Chapter Twenty-Five

There was hustle and bustle to set as much to rights as possible within the next two days. Hurry was spurred by Jamie's need to learn his brother Davey's fate. His Gilliane—and how he loved saying that—had not abandoned him. She had come to him, but only to hold him, as he kept a tight rein on passion. He had waited this long to claim her, and while she said naught to him of her desire, he felt that she wished to come a maid to their marriage bed.

And love made him unselfish, as love had made him give in about the three bonnie lasses he would soon claim for his own. They were frightened and shy, but scrubbed by Gilliane's hand, proved to be lovely. That his lady was in love with them without stealing a whit from his place in her heart boded well for their future.

At last all was ready, and Jamie gave a few last orders to the four he was leaving behind. Since Colin, Marcus, Gabhan and Edam were already familiar with the keep and the servants who had not fled, he ordered them to close the gates until he could send men and make some decision of what to do with the lands.

It warmed his heart to know that when Gilliane first

mentioned going home, she had meant returning to Halberry, for there was where she felt safest. Her lands, too, would require some thought and someone to oversee them.

Jamie had no regret at leaving. They had discovered de Orbrec's hidden place behind the stones, and found also a large, locked strongbox that none of the Norman's men had taken. The one prize that Jamie kept for his own was de Orbrec's finely made sword. That would hang with others in the great hall at Halberry. The plate and jewels and clothing belonging to the Norman were all gone, and he made no effort to hunt down those who had deserted their lord.

"Jamie, love, we are ready. We need only mount to be gone from here."

He smiled down at Gilliane; then looked beyond her to the cart piled with fresh straw and covered with thick blankets, to cushion the ride for the three little ones and the maids who attended them. He hardly recognized them now. Two had hair as dark as his own, one with black button eyes, the other with blue, and the babe had blond curls peering from her small hood and long lashes that veiled gray eyes. He had been as shocked as Gilliane to learn that de Orbrec had so hated these children of his blood for being girls that he'd refused to name them, refused to have them baptized. Gilliane had fussed and badgered Jamie in her gentle way until each lass had a name. The eldest he named for his mother, Onora, and he hoped that Micheil, who had the naming of the first boy, would take no offense at that liberty. The second Gilliane had named after her aunt Jeanne. And the third they agreed on instantly, with shared smiles and laughter, for what else could they name the babe but Ailis, for the aunt who had brought them together?

His Gilliane was a fierce tigress in her mothering, but with him, she came purring like a sweetly tamed cat. At least he could count such thoughts his own, for she showed a tendency to meekness while working her own wiles to have her way. But she meant only his good.

"Jamie, you linger? I would think you of all wished to go swiftly."

"We'll be hard put to do so, love, with two carts and loaded packhorses."

Her hand on his arm stopped him, and when he turned she lifted her hands to take his face and hold him still.

"Jamie. You try to hide your worry. Go ahead. You can ride harder and faster without us to care for. We are well guarded. Go, love."

He knew what it cost her to say those words, and what was more, meant them. He caught the shadow in her eyes when the fear took hold, and saw how she struggled to cast it aside. But how could he deny that she offered him his heart's desire now? Davey was more than his brother, and not knowing what had happened to him ate away at his happiness with Gilliane and the peace she brought to him.

"Gilliane, are you certain of this? I would not leave you."

"I would love you poorly, Jamie, if all was selfish taking. Go. And take my prayers that he is well with you."

He kissed her then, uncaring of who saw, knowing he needed this, as he needed all that meant life—the air, the water and this woman.

"I will leave you Crisdean, who will guard you with his life."

Jamie tore himself from her side and mounted quickly before he changed his mind.

For a little ways, he could look back and see the long

string of men and horses, and then they were gone from sight, but not his heart, as he set deep spurs to Killen's sides.

Without any to hamper him, Jamie rode like a madman, fording rivers where he could, swimming them when he could not. He had come away in such a hurry that he had to buy or beg a crust of bread, and ate it in the saddle, for he was unwilling to lose a moment's time if he could help it. Sleep was something to be snatched when Killen stumbled from weariness, but it was not restful. Jamie missed Gilliane, and he grew terrified to close his eyes, for the visions he saw in nightmares were of Davey's white face where no life moved.

Jamie was nearly asleep in the saddle when he was roused by the thunder of horses coming toward him. He jerked the reins to head for the cover of woods, but he moved too slowly and saw the large party of men just as they spied him.

Something about the gray lead stallion made Jamie rub his eyes. He knew that horse. Micheil had twin stallions that color. Could the Lord be so good as to have sent his brother to find him? About to go forward, he pulled up. Had Micheil come to tell him of Davey's death?

In minutes he was surrounded by his own Gunn Clansmen, but there was one whose gaze he held, and between him and Micheil there was no need for words. Yet after a few moments Micheil spoke.

"We have him home. But before you cease your prayers, know he lies wounded near to death. I came to fetch you home, Jamie. I need you there with me."

"Aye, I'll come." It was all Jamie could manage to say.

"But wait, Jamie, what do you here alone? Where are the men I sent with you? and Gilliane? Our aunt?"

"Slowly, Micheil, go slowly. I've been riding without rest for days to come home." Again Jamie rubbed his eyes, unaware that he swayed in the saddle.

"Make camp. We'll take a few hours' rest here."

Men hurried to obey Micheil's orders, and once seated before the fire, with a cup of wine in hand, the brothers talked.

Jamie told him all that had happened, thankful that his brother listened without interruption.

"So Gilliane follows with de Orbrec's children?"

"Micheil, you'll not hold the father's blood or actions against the little ones."

"Nay! What makes you missay me? I am thinking of how many to send on and help guard them while you and I ride for home."

"Speaking of riding, could Seana talk no sense into you and keep you home until that shoulder is healed?"

"You know she shares a special bond with Davey and has not left his side but for tending our little one. She begged me to hurry you back, and bring myself with you."

"Then we are agreed. You send men to Gilliane. And I will rest awhile."

Three days later Gilliane arrived at Halberry. Gone were the shouted greetings; all spoke in soft voices, with many a look toward the chamber where Davey lay.

Exhausted as she was, for she had pushed everyone to hurry once Micheil's men had joined them, she felt new strength flow into her when Jamie took her into his arms.

There was no need to ask how Davey was, for the dark circles beneath Jamie's shadowed eyes told the tale all too well.

But here was Peigi to take charge of the children and maids, so Gilliane was free to be with Jamie.

And within his chamber, she held him while he cried out that naught that had been done was helping his brother get well.

"Seana told me of the witch that said he would be wounded unto death if he went with me. We've sent men to fetch her here. If she values her life, she had best find a way to save my brother."

Gilliane managed to get him to lie on his bed, swearing she would not leave him. The maid, Nora, came up with a tray of food, but all Gilliane had was a cup of mulled wine. She sat with Jamie until he fell into a restful sleep, then she went to see Davey.

Seana sat in the dimly lit room, for only one thick candle burned along with the fire. She started to rise as Gilliane entered, but Gilliane pushed her gently back down.

The warmth between them was a firmer bond now that Seana knew Gilliane would be her sister by marriage. She shared with Gilliane all she had done for Davey, knowing that she, too, had skill with herbs.

"I refused to send for a leech," Seana whispered. "It makes no sense to me to bleed him after all the blood he's lost. But the fever will not abate. The wounds are healing, but it is beyond my ken to do more for him than pray."

They sat in silence for a little while, then it was time to bathe Davey with cool water. Gilliane helped her, but both were near exhaustion when Micheil came to fetch his wife.

"Go rest. I will sit with him," he stated. "And you, Gilliane, seek your bed."

Neither woman argued, leaving quickly, but Seana summoned the maid Cuìni and sent her to help Micheil.

Gilliane returned to Jamie's chamber, knowing there was no danger for her to rest with him. Her sleep was broken, as his was, with restless turnings and wakings, then each would sleep again in the other's arms. It was in the false dawn that both stirred, faint sounds drifting up to them.

But with Gilliane nestled by his side, Jamie fell into his first true sleep in weeks. Loath to disturb him, she lay quietly, even as the sounds of running feet came to her ears.

A little while later, Gilliane slipped from the bed. She still wore her travel-stained clothes, but thoughts of a bath and changing flew from her mind when there was a scratching at the door.

Nora had come to fetch Jamie, for all their prayers were answered. Davey's fever had broken and the laird wanted Jamie to know.

Gilliane thanked her and turned to the bed. Jamie was awake and had heard the good news.

He held out his hand to her, and she flew to his side, more than willing to be drawn down and held against him.

"The only thing that brings my happiness to overflowing is that you are here with me to share this. I missed you, Gilliane," he whispered, stroking her hair. "I never knew what emptiness was until my days were without sight of you. I needed you so. To see Davey so helpless in the grip of that fever, and Micheil worried and Seana worn to nothing—och, it was a pain made worse without you."

"I'm here now, Jamie. I'll never leave you again. Sleep now, love. Micheil and Davey will need your strength in the days to come. Sleep."

"Kiss me. Wait. When he is well enough, we'll have a *reiteach* for you. You've not had a true Scots *fáilte*."

He laughed at her frown over the Scots words he had used. And the laugh was joyous as he hugged her. "A welcoming feast, Gilliane. A great one, then we'll have our wedding."

The door burst open just as their lips met, and it was a glowering Micheil who stood there.

"Can ye not leave the lass alone, Jamie? Dinna you hear that Davey's fever's broken at last?"

"Aye. Mine's still rising. And Davey won't be knowing who's come and gone for a day or two. Leave us be, Brother. I'm explaining to my bride how we will feast her before the wedding." Then Jamie turned serious. "He's well out of danger now?"

"Aye! Would I come myself if it was not true?" He turned to the door, then turned back, and once more Jamie was thwarted from the kiss he desired. "You'd best hurry that wedding, Jamie lad. There's a nursery full already. I'll be thinking of the years to come and you trying to explain how you took a maid for wife with three bairns clinging to her skirts."

"Out! Out!" he cried with a mock snarl. "If you'd latch the door that willna be true."

"Jamie!"

He heard the door close, and looked to be sure it was before he grinned at Gilliane's rosy cheeks and shocked expression.

"Would it be so bad a thing, love?"

"Aye! You'd give me no rest, Jamie. Remember, I have three bairns to look after now."

"You have me," he whispered, setting his lips to her.

"Aye, I have you, love."

* * * * *

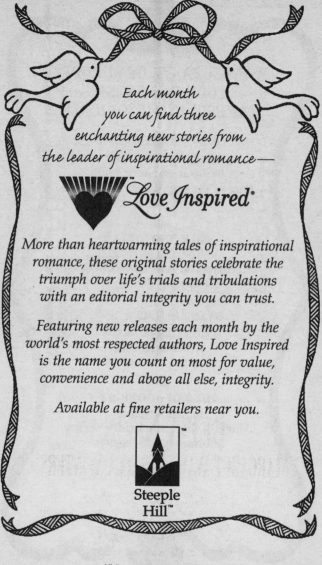

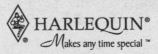

THERESA MICHAELS

is a multi-award-winning author who resides in Florida. Her joy as a writer comes when she can make a reader part of her fictional characters' world, so they cry, love and laugh, then rejoice with them. She believes in the healing power of love. When not writing or spending time in her office dreaming up the next adventure for her star-crossed lovers, she is researching the medieval world or that of America's Western past. She rescues stray cats, makes potpourri from the herbs and roses she grows and reads everything but horror. Readers can write to her c/o Author Mail Box, 2535 Polk Street, Hollywood, FL 33020-4317.

HHBIO536